# A BEGINNER'S GUIDE TO ELECTRICITY

P.S. Russell



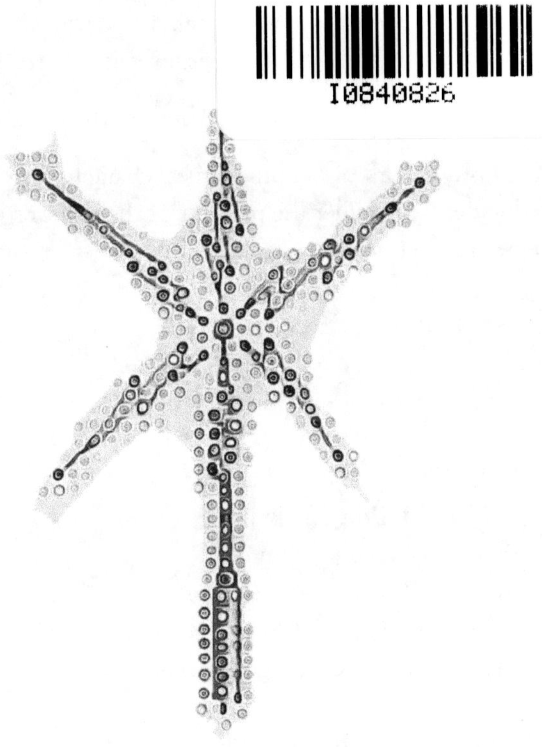

"I sing the body electric…"

-Walt Whitman

A Beginner's Guide to Electricity
Copyright 2024 by P.S. Russell



This is a work of fiction. Names, characters, places, and incidents are either the product of the author's imagination or are used fictitiously as backdrops.

ISBN 979-8-218-58558-7

Library of Congress Control Number: 2024927701

PS1-3576. American Literature
PS370-380. Prose fiction
PS430 - 439 Wit and humor.
MDS 813.087 Literature / American / Adventure
FIC066000 Fiction / Romance / Small Town & Rural
FICTION picaresque/counterculture/ animal magnetism

Published by **billectric** in January 2025

For Grace.

# A BEGINNER'S GUIDE TO ELECTRICITY

P.S. Russell

billectric

# TABLE OF CONTENTS

SECTION I


THE TROUBLE BEGAN


"When wireless is perfectly applied,
the whole Earth will be converted into a
huge brain, which in fact it is, all things
being particles of a real and rhythmic whole."
—Nikola Tesla

## CHAPTER 1

**RADKIN WROTE HIS BOOK JUST LIKE** he would build a fireplace, a sturdy structure in which he would conjure a flickering warmth to enchant a lady. He was sure that his story would be compelling when seen from the remove of some perfect distance, and that the gliding of his pen across the white paper, like sticks expertly rubbed together, would spark a tiny, precious curl of golden flame in her kindling heart- here his scrawl expanded from the tight timid salutation to unfurl in gradually unruly rhythms to mark the pitch of his declaration- which would move her to gather his book closer in her gentle grasp and feed the words into her flashing eyes like wood shavings into a whispering fire so durable that, even after thousands of nights, its warmth would sustain them through every humdrum scrimmage, and they would burn quietly together, through flat tires and electric bills and macaroni and cheese, even after the naughty ecstasies of their original collision receded, and their clear-eyed children would bind them together in an abiding love.

He hoped that his shapely mind would be visible and would dazzle her, as her eyes, or the idea of her eyes, dazzled him. And by hiding himself in the words, drawn from the deck of 26 letters that he shuffled and reshuffled, he was safe. After all, these letters were rich in phlogiston and free and available in unlimited supply and combinations, and might jump and shimmer and press-fit just as he directed, after long practice. He bent over the blank page with all the tender urgencies of any dreamer, cross-eyed in desperate foolishness.

Radkin began writing his book in a hammock near Chimney Pond, in Maine. The spiral-bound sketch pad and black gel pen cost $9.49. He knew that the rest of his scribblings before then had been just errands, dirty dishes, old magazines. In emails, private journals, letters and poems, his visions had been leaking in disarray, in safe, timid chicken scratch. No one would read his journals, numbered and dated, full of cryptic joy and loneliness, grocery lists, unsent letters, haiku, and bird tracks. Poetry was a dying format, a pensive cul-de-sac for scholastic melancholies. The modern poem was too dry for bread, too crooked for money. So, with two hundred and fifty pages of thick rag-paper and the hydraulic current of ink flowing through his fidgety hands, he resolved to follow his personal stream of alphabet soup, as urgency would dictate, confident that a pattern would emerge, visible only from far away, as of a river mapped from space. He set forth in earnest gravity-fed scribble.

He knew, of course, that he needed to construct a proper story, with tension to resolve and descriptions of faces and all the requisite stuff. He had studied the three basic plots, or the seven basic plots, all the plots and the twists, rags to riches, riches to rags, boy meets girl, boy loses girl, man in a hole, even the surprise nipple offered to the starving stranger in the straw. But he resisted the implication that he needed to spell everything out, insisting that he could learn from the lessons of birds, who sing once and softly, and better are heard. In this delusional romantic style, he generated page upon page of actual kindling, ironic kindling, that he fed into his campfire, which warmed no-one but himself.

## CHAPTER 2

**AT BIRTH, WALTER STRINGFELLOW JR.** had the mark, just as plain as day. As he came out of the hatch, his first move was to grab the hemostat from the obstetrician's hand before he could clamp Walter's umbilicus. This assumption of control, this reflex to touch the steely instruments of the world, was some type of brave sign. What ensued was a progression of freckles, skinned knees, and defiant demands, all topped by a head of red hair that flashed in the sun like copper wire. Contrariety ran in the family, especially in the long line of bony, stringy first born sons who knew better, and knew they knew better, and therefore had so much more to learn than the others who knew nothing, and knew it. Taunts of "string bean" led to a streak of ready aggression, and as his younger brother came along to nip at his heels, Walter - by then known to all as "Bean" - learned to tickle Wyatt into brotherly play every morning, and eventually, to destroy him every afternoon in whatever sport was in season, in an endless cycle familiar to parents of red-haired boys everywhere.

Walter's given name was unremarkable, although he developed some crackpot Möbius strip theory of time that led him to argue that he had always been named Radkin, even though he had also always been named Walter Stringfellow, Jr. His parents and his brother had stopped acknowledging his existence after they learned he had changed his name to Radkin. In so doing, they facilitated his utter re-invention of himself in a manner which, he argued to anyone who would listen, validated his idea that the power of thought, radiant spirit voltage, was the animating principle of the fancy mammal meat known as mankind. The power of radiokinesis had demonstrated itself to Walter Stringfellow, Jr. in the early morning hours of New Year's Day 1973. His family's eventual decision to disavow his lunacy was easily traced to this event. Radkin, of course, flashed all Old Testament telling the story of his illumination.

## CHAPTER 3

**THE TROUBLE BEGAN IN HIGH** school, where Bean mixed with the brains, artists, jocks and freaks alike, placing him in a unique segment of the Venn, a fringe member of each group. When he was first offered a joint by a ragged group of teammates gathered outside the varsity soccer party in the shadows in the bushes at a house up the hill, he asked why they were burning leaves. Embarrassed, he commenced a private course of study of Huxley's *The Doors of Perception*, Watts' *The Joyous Cosmology*, and Wolfe's *The Electric Kool-Aid Acid Test*, the apparently definitive texts at hand, along with William James' *The Varieties of Religious Experience*. An experiment with beer (two cold tallboy Millers in golden cans to be exact, at another school party) resulted in a mildly religious experience. As young Stringfellow lounged on a staircase and appointed himself musical director by flipping and flipping the double album, *Allman Brothers Band Live at Fillmore East*, he grew strong in the magical discovery that this music got better with each swallow of High Life. Some form of warm certainty filled his belly.

In this phase, a novitiate in beer-mediated levitation as enhanced by electric blues guitar weaving, Walter found himself with a few school mates experienced in smoking pot, in another house up the hill, a grand creaking Colonial which had been left unchaperoned while Allen's parents had taken their annual winter trip to Miami. At first, Walter declined to accept the pipe that they offered, but he changed his mind once he realized how "set and setting" had aligned in such a propitious manner. It was, after all, New Year's Eve, the house was secure and distant enough from home to ensure privacy, and on the stereo was a broadcast of a live concert by a San Francisco band famous for a mixture of bluegrass, Stockhausen, folk-inflected redneck jazz and psychedelic inventions that veered to chaos and back, on raggedy musical wings a mile long.

The pipe was made from a piece of antler, worn shiny by many hands and pockets, and when Walter agreed to partake, Allen packed the bowl with a big crumbled lump of fresh golden hashish that sizzled and melted as Stringfellow drew in a deep pull for the first time. It didn't take long for the music to bloom, vivid, beautiful, as a brand-new ancient spring spilled familiar surprises all through his mind. Words were quickly exposed as stick figures, ridiculous thumbnails, mere effigies, and Walter and his friends laughed like drunken monks who had fallen into a holy lake while trying to touch the moon. Time passed as Bean explored the many hidden chambers inside his mind, until the advancing new year required him to return home.

Allen's Firebird rumbled away into the darkness, leaving Stringfellow to walk the last half block in stealthy approach, to avoid any chance of being forced to explain his red eyes to his parents by the glare of the porch light. He opened the screen door and slipped onto the back porch. The moon was near full, and the moonlight slanted down through the trees that marked the edges of the playing field in the front yard onto which Bean lured his brother to his eventual destruction every possible day. There was no philosophical watershed in sight for Walter Stringfellow, Jr., no inkling of impending magic, just the need to extract the hidden house key from the owl-shaped ceramic candle holder that hung in the corner of the porch, and to slip upstairs to bed without being scrutinized by his parents, who were suspicious of these particular friends based on some infallible extrasensory parental instinct.  And when he reached up into the owl, and felt around, and felt nothing, he felt a sinking feeling that burned like shame, like the first stain of bad drug trouble.

This hiding place was rigid procedure in the Stringfellow house. The house key was always kept there. But that night it was not there, and it was not on the floor beneath the owl, and it was not in the alternate hiding place behind the pegboard in the garage, where the inside door was double locked. And after he rechecked the owl, the floor, and the backup pegboard nook, over and over, he began pinging his brother's bedroom window with pebbles, tiny ones at first, leading up to a loud bang with a marble sized rock, but there was no brother Wyatt to the rescue, no flicker of light. Bean reviewed his options and wondered if this was how drugs worked. Ringing the doorbell was out of the question. The porchlight would blaze, and an examination was unthinkable. He checked for the key again, everywhere, and plinked his brother's empty bedroom window again in despair. It was now past 2 a.m., he guessed.

Bean decided at last to curl up and try to sleep on the screened porch and await the dawn, when he could try to slip into the house without being detected. In his strange new way of thinking, this was his best decision, to defer the interrogation. In what would prove to be his final official act as the original version of Walter Stringfellow, Jr., he lay down under the locked porch door, pulled up his jacket collar, rolled the doormat up to keep his head off the concrete, and he closed his eyes, stoned, for the first time in ten thousand years.

Stringfellow was not prepared for the cartoons, the velvet kaleidoscope that began to blossom on his eyelids the instant he closed his eyes. In this brief interval, or what history recorded as brief owing to the speed of the white-hot and purple-cool and moss-green shapes that swarmed his brain, the nascent prophet of radiokinesis began to suspect the existence of a natural power to use the electric mind to convert the world into a favorable shape. Because when he opened his eyes to investigate the magnesium vapor lamps that seemed to be illuminating the inside of the eyeballs of his brain, a key was lying inches from his nose, unmistakable, agleam in the metallic moonlight. The person formerly known as Walter Stringfellow, Jr. quickly closed his eyes and summoned his old sensible mind. This was not possible. The key was never put under the mat, the most obvious, most common, most unsafe, and most discoverable place. The key had never ever been there, and yet when he reopened his eyes, it was still there, and it was cold in his fingers as he quietly unlocked the door and found his way to his brand-new bed.

The complete conversion from Bean to Radkin actually took a few years, because Radkin couldn't see this allegory when he was close to it. But over time, as he began to explore this magical new land by learning how to unlock a series of physical and metaphysical doors, he was gradually able to recognize the psychokinetic device, the nature of this coincidental means by which he had been admitted to his own home, to his own bed, with the same skeleton key that had unlocked his own new radiant mind.

# SECTION II

## RADIO TRANSMISSION

"Music is some kind of electricity that
makes a radio out of a man and the dial is in his
head and he just sings according to how he's a-
feeling."
— Woody Guthrie

## CHAPTER 4

**AFTER HE FOUND THE PORCH KEY**, Walter was tempted to get fancy as he studied the machinery of luck. He began by considering the I Ching, TM©, prayer, chanting, the Heisenberg Principle, solipsism, the Ouija Board, poltergeists, séances, martial artists breaking boards, gamblers rolling dice and picking cards and numbers, sunset drum circles with grim, dirtyfoot gurus, every stripe of carnival quackery, the Magic Eight Ball, Tarot, speaking in tongues, fortune telling, and more. He spent time in the public library comparing the role of electricity in the brain (EEG) and the heart (EKG), and the mechanics of other newfangled devices like defibrillators and TENS units, to refine his personal theory of electrical spirit meat science, based on the ferromagnetic radiance of the nervous system. For someone raised with the Tom A. Swift Electric Rifle in mind, Walter had a ready understanding of the TASER. His research was not purely theoretical. One day, he watched as a squirrel darted into traffic, under the wheels of a car, or nearly so. When he examined the motionless squirrel, it was unharmed, perfectly intact even when he turned it over with the toe of his shoe and waited. Here was empirical evidence of how the spirit might flee. It was dead, apparently, from fear.

Reasoning, according to thermodynamics, that the same carbon had forever recirculated from dust to dust, and energy was neither created or destroyed, and stones and leaves and gleaming eyes were all stirred and mixed together by the wind and rain and the hands of the blender clock, Bean eventually followed Einstein into pure energy theory, in which waves of energy assume the shapes of things. He began to consider the name Radkin, short for radiokinesis. A human being, he reflected, is very much like a candle. Like the wax and wick, the meat and bone part is easily mistaken for the living thing itself. But Radkin knew that it was actually the combustible flicker in the eyes that animated electric meat, just as it was the tingling lick of flame that lit the candle. It was the current, not the wire, that was alive. Frankenstein had been jump started by electricity, he knew.  A living human was just complicated electrical meat, and a flat lined human was no longer electric, the spirit having fled somewhere into the flux. The spirit was electric. Radiokinesis would be his superpower, as he would precisely calibrate his personal frequency, over time. And he set about to prove this power to himself, never imagining how the electric world would toy with him.

Bean had always been mystified when his grandfather had cued up music for him, pressing buttons to turn little wheels inside small tape cartridges or dropping needles onto spinning vinyl platters or threading large reels of tape through scientific scopes, wired to thumpy speakers the size of dog houses. Stravinsky, Mingus, Paganini, Shankar and Khan played, and their instruments spoke in deep tongues, a tribal language that was left after the words scattered, like gulls scattered. His grandfather would point at the speakers to alert him just before the sounds would veer, and change vectors.  And after he found the key, Stringfellow then knew that his grandfather knew things, that his pallor and crepe were mystic and noble,

16

not failures. Walter understood that he would follow him down, in time.

Grandfather told him a story about Art Tatum, the blind jazz pianist, who had stalked an obscure musician in New Orleans who only played one chorus of blues in C, just one chorus, over and over in endless conjugation. Tatum was, he explained, a prodigy who could play every standard, and could reharmonize any set of changes in every key, but the singular blues of this unknown man had tantalized him. Tatum hardly ever wrote a song, and though he was a genius interpreting the songs of others, that stranger's signature theme had never fit perfectly under his fingers once.

Walter schemed to turn his own primitive convictions to his advantage, in the same way that Tatum's bluesman had embraced his crooked gift. Had Demosthenes gargled pebbles at the seashore, just to recite the alphabet? Young Stringfellow spread the pages of his first blank book like a new lover's legs, with intrepid ardor. Loneliness had driven him to the page, as surely as loneliness had written the blues in C that fascinated Tatum. He planned to start his story with his hero making the bed, but things did not go according to plan.

CHAPTER 5

**YOUNG STRINGFELLOW WAS BOUND TO GO TO COLLEGE AT ADELPHI**, where his parents and grandparents had matriculated, and mated, and where his mother's father had taught music.  After he settled into the cluster of ivy-covered sarcophagi haunted by his ancestors, Stringfellow was ready to change his name, to live in the jungle, to join the circus. Credit or blame, either way, was partly due to William Blake and Baudelaire and Nikola Tesla and all the other revolutionary thinkers that he had begun to study, as his own nervous system took shape, and his cognitive cake was baked. But his new sensibility did not come without new perils. Her name was Molly Rubato.

Stringfellow's first class on his first day at Adelphi was Creative Writing I, taught by a slim grey man named Geoff Rice, on the top floor of Munroe Hall, a granite edifice built in the 1800's, in a room with a ring of chairs around a central square of tables, and a view of the blue green mountains through huge windows in two of the four walls. After springing up the staircase, on which every slate stair had been scalloped smoothly by a century of students, Stringfellow burst into the room at the stroke of 9 a.m., just as Professor Rice was clearing his throat to begin the icebreaking process.

However, Stringfellow upstaged his professor by mistake. As Bean sidestepped behind a row of classmates towards an open seat, he tripped over a large metal trash can. The combination of the bong and clang that resulted, and Walter's graceful recovery, briefly wind-milling his arms like a trapeze artist, served to loosen the figurative woolen habit and cincture in which the solemn Molly Rubato confined her beating heart. In this moment, a double play of tragicomic scope ensued, an emotional relay from Tinker to Evers to Chance, flashed around the room. Professor Rice had a habit of conducting a desultory survey of the young women who took his classes each semester, with the purpose of entertaining himself in a casual and cruel amorous sport, as they handed in overwrought love poems extolling their "milky moon bodies" and other constellations of lust. Rice had been giving Rubato the side eye as a potential frontrunner, just before Stringfellow performed his feat of slapstick acrobatics.

As Stringfellow's eyes flashed apologetically to Professor Rice, and Rice's eyes assessed Rubato, Molly's eyes were fixed on Walter and his endearing pratfall. This moment marked another notable abracadabra in the lonely romantic pilgrimage of Stringfellow. Rice eventually seduced a groomable young lassie from Connecticut who wrote free verse and swam the butterfly, and Stringfellow…well, he continued to write his Encyclopedia of Longing.

At first, young Walter fell for Rubato's poetry. In particular, he admired a sestina that rhymed without strain, scanned like a cantering filly, and spoke ironic wisdom beyond her peach-cheeked years, about how something you want might not actually be nice to have. He seriously considered the possibility that she had plagiarized some obscure Romantic poet. He told himself that she wasn't really his type, resembling Venus on the Half Shell, by Botticelli. But, eventually he was caught in the web of her hair, which cascaded like amber waves of grain, or some other wavy golden farmland.

After his infatuation had advanced to a septic, systemic weakness, he looked Rubato up in the freshman directory, and hiked bravely across campus to find her room in the stone dormitory named after some long gone alumnus, Cockburn Hall. When Stringfellow emerged from the echoing stairwell, and turned down the dim hallway, he knew he was entirely out of his depth. The metal fire door slammed behind him, and a line of startled faces turned to him as one. These faces belonged to young women who sat along the wall outside her door, acolytes lined up to enter the Holy Hushed Temple of Molly Rubato, complete with incense. As he approached, still hoping there was some mistake, perhaps a line for the pay phone or an art history study group about to convene, a tittering began, and one of the girls rushed into Molly's room. After she and another girl rushed out, the whole group dispersed in a whispery flock. Stringfellow knocked as he entered the chamber where Rubato awaited, a clove cigarette burning between her fingers, seated cross-legged on her bed by the window. Walter pulled the door almost closed. Facing the bed, there was a pair of chairs draped with madras tapestries, with a candle and ashtray on a low table between them. He was invited to sit.

The substance and duration of his first session in Cockburn 525 was never recorded in Stringfellow's notebooks, and despite his persistent attempts to access whatever neural traces may have been stored on the hard drive between his ears, he could not even piece together a suitable re-enactment. They sat, he knew, and they spoke in the subjunctive mode, and their eyes darted to and fro like green and grey tetras, of this much he was certain. For many years the smell of cloves would trigger a warm fugue state in which Stringfellow would luxuriate, an achy confusion. When his time was over, there was no embrace and the hallway was deserted.

Within weeks of their meeting, the spirits of Walter and Molly fit together, easy and fast, like two hydrogen atoms fit an atom of oxygen, but their bodies were held apart, as if by the force of like magnetism. Molly could have passed for Rapunzel in a turret atop a tower, and in her eyes he found the reflection of himself in a suit of shining armor, or Walter may have resembled a questing pilgrim, and Molly, the oracle of the granite temple. Either way, he was hypnotized by the way her hands cradled a teacup, two perfect birds of prey, feather light and claw sharp. No ring was brighter than the loop of silver she wore on her middle finger. Molly claimed that she liked his poetry, for some reason she never explained. But they stayed apart, at a safe distance from what seemed to each of them to be a person-shaped package of fearful kryptonite. They hardly ever touched. In the end, he blamed her boyfriend back home, who seemed entitled to a purchase on her heart that Stringfellow couldn't presume to claim, especially since Walter knew his poetry was thin as tissue paper, spoon, moon, spittoon.

## CHAPTER 6

**MR. AND MRS. STRINGFELLOW HAD** always assumed that even the most recalcitrant red-haired boys would eventually become men. They believed that college was the crucible for this alchemical process, in which Walter Jr. was expected to learn to do laundry, operate an alarm clock, buy underwear, manage a checking account and budget, turn in assignments, and eat sensible potatoes and green beans and meatloaf. They failed to account for psilocybin cubensis, a species of psychedelic mushroom which sprang up whenever warm rain sprinkled the cow pastures west of the campus. The Stringfellows were utterly unprepared for the phone call they received near the end of Bean's freshman year. On the night of a full moon, Radkin's new tribe of friends had a ceremony which led to Walter using the pay phone in the hallway of his dormitory to call home and tell his parents how much he loved them. He conveyed no request for money, no question about how to find a dentist or get a coffee stain out of a white shirt, he sought none of the regular housekeeping or coming-of-age lessons that would pave his way to a corner office or happy home. He might have mentioned how their Ultimate Frisbee team played every day at 4:00 p.m., but mainly he had called to impress upon them that he really loved them, an urgent revelation he felt suddenly compelled to share with them at 9:30 p.m. EST on a Saturday night. He was very insistent.

Naturally, their response was to ask what was wrong, and their concerns only grew when he explained that everything was perfect, better than ever, in fact, and he wanted to tell them that he loved them more than ever. This sort of declaration was unheard of in the Methodist culture of the Stringfellow family, and by noon the next day Mr. and Mrs. Stringfellow pulled up to his dorm in the family station wagon. They were braced to look into his still-dilated pupils, ready to pack their son up and take him home, convinced that poorly disciplined miscreants had furnished their oldest son with powerful and dangerous drugs which would distract and derange him with delusions like peace and love, and other impediments to emotional maturity and vocational competence. What was this Ultimate Frisbee? What had happened to their alma mater?

Except Walter didn't make it home because he refused to go. When they explained that he had no choice but to get in the car, because they were getting his tuition refunded, he reassured them that he loved them anyway, and as they packed his clothes, he disappeared three steps at a time down the concrete stairwell with a backpack and his guitar.

At the beginning of the semester, Stringfellow had signed up for a part-time job as a DJ at the college radio station, spinning records from Sunday midnight to 6 am Monday morning. After he ditched his parents, Walter took refuge in the music library to consider his options and collect the music to play on his show. His parents didn't know about his job, and any BOLO was unlikely to result in the detective work necessary to track him to the radio station, so he figured he might as well do his last program. With an enormous climate-controlled alphabetical collection of records at his disposal, on the top floor of the massive granite library building that overlooked the valley and the Adirondack ridge to the west, from his very first shift he felt like an air-traffic controller atop a control tower bristling with antennae, sitting in a cone of light by the window, turning knobs and pushing buttons to send inscrutable music through the headphones clamped to his tender mind, and through the electric audio radiance into the minds of listeners in the town below. It was the night that he ran away, as he monitored his transmission, and contemplated the span of his broadcast, that he accepted radiokinesis as his new superpower.

He headed into the control room before midnight to get the hand-off from the 9-12 p.m. DJ, an exchange student from Mali named Zeyna Nomoko. Zeyna was a senior, taller than Walter, with an astounding smile featuring a single gold tooth in a bright white array. She played an eclectic blend of folk music from Africa, Egypt, Cuba, Japan, and Brazil, during the program that she had named "Storytime with Zeyna." Her on-air voice was velvety and deep, and Walter slumped in the chair beside her as he arranged his playlist, and listened to her introduce his show, which he had named "Smoke Signals." As she signed off and muted her mic, Stringfellow dropped the needle onto his favorite record, the Love Scene soundtrack recording from "Zabriskie Point," an obscure Antonioni movie. Zeyna bowed and touched her dhuku, a bright turban, and then gathered up her box of records and left. Before the elevator closed behind her, Walter had locked the studio door and dimmed the lights, all except the swing-arm desk lamp that hung over the desk where the turntables and mixer were located. He settled in, playing a Miles Davis concert next, eighty minutes of electric funk from 1970, called "Black Beauty." In a flawless display of logic, considering the faint possibility that Adelphi police would track him down as a runaway, Walter popped the remaining golden mushroom caps and blue-gray stems into his mouth, leftovers from Saturday night's ceremony. Safety first! He expected that his solitary overnight shift would permit him to get some thinking done. He was hoping to understand how an innocent expression of love could result in his parents' decision to stage such a misguided rescue mission.

In this setting, contemplating his froward choice to plunge into the Unknown by eluding his frightened parents, Walter bathed in a stream of audible delirium, a dark jungle of sound in which Miles turned him on a spit above a sparkling pit, while clashing tribes blew darts across the stereo field, snakes slithered from the bells of horns, cymbals clattered, falling trees thumped, boiling ant piles hissed, war drums throbbed, and a tiger trumpet flashed through the brush, tail on fire, dragging a train of echo. Some time passed. Out the window, in the dark valley below, there were rolling balls of lightning, and forked tongues of electricity spoke to Walter. His silver face reflected in the thick glass of the window, faintly illuminated by the VU meters on the console, just as a series of lightning bolts lent him a crown, a glowing nimbus. As he prepared to fade from "Black Beauty" to "Bitches Brew," and contemplated the waves of electromagnetic radiation transmitted by the metal antenna bolted to the roof above his head, Walter Stringfellow Jr. decided that he would change his legal name to Radkin as soon as possible. Before he cross-faded into the next record, Walter brought up the level of his microphone on the board, and he spoke his first words since ducking down the staircase at his dorm. Addressing the night sky, veined with flickering bolts, he growled, "Behold, the ghost of electricity!" He knew then that he would never return home. As the last album played out, Radkin built a nest in the back corner of the music library. A little while later, listeners heard only the recurring click of an abandoned platter of vinyl, side one of "Blonde on Blonde," until the Monday morning DJ unlocked the door just before 6 a.m.

## CHAPTER 7

**WALTER SPENT THE NEXT FEW** days considering his new situation. At 9 a.m. on Monday morning, he went downtown and withdrew all the money from his bank account, $155.25, a small fortune in rice and bean money. He returned to the back corner of the music library, where the only visitor was a conscientious but somnolent janitor, Mr. Sessums, whose cart clanked loudly as he rolled it off the elevator to make his daily rounds. The granite library building was climate controlled, carpeted, and featured vending machines, pay phones, and, for the use of the DJ's, the top floor housed a large and immaculate bathroom, complete with a shower and a pile of fresh folded towels. The Adelphi library had never closed, ever, even when the ice storm of 1967 had frozen the steel wheels of the Erie – Lackawanna train to the steel rails of the Main Street crossing for a week, shutting off all traffic in and out of the center of town. In his hiding place, high above the campus, barricaded behind cartons of unfiled record albums, outdated municipal codes and annotated statutes and other dusty jurisprudential books, Walter initially went undiscovered by the authorities, who, of course, had been alerted (and threatened) by his parents. He was free to play his guitar, pore over the maps he pulled off the shelves, and plan his next move, now that his time at

Adelphi was being cut short. He read up on lightning, its various manifestations, and its role in the legends of Prometheus and Frankenstein. He schemed to change his name, and to get out of town. It didn't take long.

Walter continued to try to write his book, but just as quickly as he filled page upon page (paper liberated from the tray in the copier in the library) with passionate drivel, he filled the exact same sort of industrial wastebasket that had tripped him up in Professor Rice's class. He began writing lyrics for songs as a change of pace, hoping that the miniature scale would build up his design skills. This approach actually filled the wastebasket even more quickly. Because the radio station library was so remote and empty, Mr. Sessums wondered, each time he dumped out a big nest of crumpled balls of paper, petrified eggs of the great inky literature bird, but he never wondered enough to uncrumple and inspect a single page. He whistled while he tipped the basket upside down over the black garbage bag suspended in his cart, and all the unborn songs and stories spilled into oblivion, and all his spray bottles of Windex and disinfectant swung back and forth where they hung by their nozzles. If Mr. Sessums had been curious, because there was usually no trash to collect way up there, and if he had selected a particular ball to smooth out on a table, he would have read something like this:

DOLLARSONG

I bought these letters on sale at the store
I mixed 'em up good, then I mixed 'em up more
then I set 'em in motion

like waves to the shore
they fit my mouth better,
like I sung 'em before

it's a dream I had in the fever night
a bad scene gone glad,
if you squint at it right
an alphabet square dance,
a wonderful sight
to see in the dark, so turn out the light

when I wrote this song, I filled it with words
built it real strong, then hitched it to birds
this song is simple, this song is small
it'll fit in your pocket, it'll come when you call

so gimme a dollar when I give you this song
you can't break it or lose it, you can't play it wrong
it'll glow in the dark, and float in the flood,
like any plain song that was written with blood

## CHAPTER 8

**WALTER NEEDED MORE PRIVACY THAN** the library stacks permitted. He was forced to relocate immediately one day, after a campus security guy peered into his nook on the top floor while whispering into a walkie-talkie.

Gathering his backpack and guitar, Walter took the fire escape stairs all the way down to the basement, where there were three cinder block rooms with thick soundproof "blast" doors, each room housing a gleaming grand piano. Only a few music majors even knew about these practice rooms, and Radkin built himself a bunker under the piano in the last room, with blankets and couch cushions scavenged from a store room. To pass the time, Walter searched the technical section of the library, and found several guides to the construction and maintenance of fine pianos. He spent a few days studying the machinery of the Yamaha he now treated as home, all the hammers and wires and pedals and levers, since he was flat on his back beneath it for much of his time. By carefully disassembling and reassembling various component parts, using his Swiss Army knife that bristled with tiny tools, Walter began to develop an understanding of the piano that would serve him well. In order to keep other students at bay, when he heard their faint footfalls descending the metal staircase, Walter played his finest originals loudly enough to be heard in the hall.

On such an occasion, having heard a clopping sound suggestive of wooden clogs on the staircase, Walter jumped up and launched into his favorite meditation in the key of D minor, complete with an improvised and extended detour through the adjacent lands of F, C, and A minor. So thoroughly did he submit himself to this musical journey that, upon arrival at his final destination, back in D minor where he started, the last chord having passed fully into the ether, he needed some air right away. As he pushed the door open and burst into the hall, he fell into the arms of a woman, seated on the floor in the dark.

Over his life, many fortuitous falls had occurred on the planet. Round white cowhide fastballs had arisen and fallen and been caught by round brown cowhide mitts. Clutches of round turtle eggs had tumbled into round nests dug in the sand above high water. Dancing ping pong balls marked with lucky numbers had risen and fallen on jets of thermals in Plexiglas lottery domes. Babies tossed from burning buildings had been cradled by sure handed firemen. Buzzers and bells had ring-a-dinged when pinballs settled into the tip top slot, and showers of silver had littered casino floors when three round cherries had fallen into a line. Walter had almost fallen, in Munroe Hall, while Molly watched.

Had Walter and Molly viewed their collision from space, with the detached perspective of such a distance, they would have seen a bony young man splayed in the delta of Venus among amber waves of splendor, and our story could have ended here, amidst the slippery merging of the glorious flesh and the glorious bones of electric love. But, no. Neither Molly nor Walter felt worthy of touching the other, so high were the pedestals on which they had placed one another.

"What was…where have…but I thought…" she sputtered as Walter rolled to his knees. "My friend told me I had to hear this."

"I know, I know, I've been practicing."

She was speechless so he continued. "My parents freaked when I called to tell them that I loved them, so I had to hide to think."

She gaped some more. This was the second time he had fallen, or had almost fallen, and amazed her.

"What was that music? I had no idea. Where have you been? Why did they freak?" She smelled like clove cigarettes, and even in the dim light of the EXIT sign in the basement, her hair was a cornfield running west towards the sunset. But then there was a thump of the door at the top of the stairs and Walter quickly tugged her to her feet, and into his modest piano-based residence, quietly closing the door. He began to play his Symphony in C, to keep the intruder away and to fill the awkward space between him and Molly. Having begun, and intent on melting her heart with music, rather than scuffling to explain how he had been withdrawn from school after his parents had been frightened by psilocybin-mediated love, he played on. Since there was nowhere to sit except the piano bench, Molly sat to Stringfellow's right and listened.

After a few minutes, a faint sound of scales being played on the piano in the next room signaled that the crisis of being discovered was past. Walter flicked the light switch off, and the room went inky black.  He paused and took her left hand, and placed one of her fingers gently on the keyboard, sounding a single random note that launched one thousand goose bumps across the surface of the Rubato ocean. In the screenplay that he eventually shredded, Walter had this scene tracked in utter darkness, with a piano dialogue between Keith Jarrett and Joni Mitchell that traversed the unutterable tenderness of love so new that it can't be spoken. They selected notes in the dark and spoke the tentative foreign language of piano, back and forth. They finished at the end, an octave apart, where else?  It had taken a while to get there.

If Molly had taken him to her room right then, she would have dismissed the line of waiting girls with a nod. What followed, soft and dim as any fading memory, would have been blanketed in the hush of dusk. Walter would have recalled later exactly how the last light came in at the window and slipped across the bed, and all the exact details of their slow and tender collision, the creamy hydraulics and glazed aftermath, her silhouette as she tilted her head back, and the way her eyes closed.

But they were both afraid, too dainty, out of phase, and they parted awkwardly, agreeing to get together again. His cover blown, after almost a full week of peanut butter crackers and water beneath the piano, Walter tucked his wizardly red ponytail into his hat and grabbed his guitar and backpack from beneath the piano, and hunched into the gloaming, headed downtown in search of real food and a new plan.

## CHAPTER 9

**THE RUMBLE SEAT WAS A** townie bar at the edge of Adelphi, built like an old timey saloon on the top two floors of an old stone mill by the river. It had wraparound balconies above the barroom, both inside and out, wood floors, brick columns and walls, and Guinness and Bass on tap at the long dark bar along one side. As Walter slipped inside, a scruffy group was gathered on the bandstand, performing tuning rituals, and arranging their tangled wires and mic stands and blinking pedals amidst the thonk and splash of the drum set, and the faint buzz of the amplifiers. Their gleaming jewel lights were blue. According to the sign on the bass drum they called themselves "The Funnybones," but they were actually a solemn bunch, touring college towns in a rusty van and living hand to mouth. Rather than engaging in any cheerful patter with the indifferent patrons, once the band had grumbled through their set up, they went out back to smoke and argue about their set list, and how their bar tab would be split up.

A local IPA called Hopalong Calamity was a popular offering at The Rumble Seat, prized for its delivery of a blast of hoppy grapefruit to the mouth, and a warm bath of calamity to the brain. Walter pulled his hat low as he ordered one, and he studied the small stage, which was crowded with a gloriously beat up blackface amp on a folding chair, a battered electric guitar leaning at a precarious angle, a fiddle case, a flat-top guitar, a set of mismatched drums, an ornate accordion, a big Ampeg bass amp, a red Guild bass, and a Hammond B3 organ, with a bird's nest of loose wires dangling underneath.

Eventually, the Funnybones wandered back inside, scratching and yet splendiferous in their finest Goodwill garb. They proceeded to hunker down on their instruments, re-tuning and conspiring before beginning their set, so quietly and gradually that no one but Walter noticed, at first. Slowly, they fired up a primitive musical steam engine of sorts, rubbing fingers on strings and bows on fiddles and letting the dynamics huff and puff, wheeze and shudder, each song teetering on the brink of some disaster at first, barely holding together, sort of in tune. Then, they grimaced and bore down, as this tiny lady squeezed the accordion on one song and scraped the fiddle on another, and then scratched the washboard with sharpened spoons on a few, and strummed an old Martin as she closed her eyes and launched into these original Appalachian zydeco songs. This Snuffy Smith guy wore a grey conductor cap and never even looked at his electric guitar, just closed his eyes and tilted his head back with a series of quasi-epileptic twitches, while his left hand wandered the maple neck of his guitar in a Jackson Pollock approach merging rhythm and lead, and it clucked and clanged and sprangled and jangled like only a Fender guitar plugged straight into a Fender amp can, as the crooked drummer pounded the pivot pulse on the snare with insistence, stirring an iron cauldron, the eye of newt and purple fungus, boom-FLAM-a-boom-boom-BAM.

Walter eventually tipped his hat back and unbuttoned his coat. He liked how, as the Funnybones got to drawing out these propulsive numbers, they'd let the bottom drop out and leave only a bonesimple whisper of the song, the mere wisp of the idea of the song, then slowly pump and bob and they'd look up as the song lifted, the snare lifted and the rhythm lifted with sweet-simple changes and rich refrains that came over the room like a fine mixture of fever and the light that leaks from stained glass windows, and all of a sudden the dynamics lifted and the plain drummer quit beating the snare and rolled onto the tom-toms, and the plain Cajun fiddling lifted, and the plain swirling B3 Leslie lifted up, and the bass thrummed, and the regular old Fender guitar clanged and popped and climbed into a levitating din that lasted quite a while, long enough to forget some things and remember some others, then they landed it, sorta crash landed it, to the growing amusement of the audience. And like nothing happened, they would wet their whistles, and lean together and roll up their sleeves and start another song. Each song wheezed and huffed and clanged, but like rubbing two sticks together, no fancyass stuff, just rubbing good simple sticks together (the band and the audience, the music tumbling all together like the agitator in full wash cycle) this thing happened where a spark met the kindling and all were warmed by the fire. When they took a break, Walter saw his chance and approached the Snuffy Smith guy, who was named Diego, and the tiny girl named Tinker. He began to work his way into the Funnybones like a snake works into a woodpile.

SECTION III

GAS STATION HOT DOG

"Man is least himself when he talks
in his own person. Give him a mask
and he will tell you the truth."
— Oscar Wilde

## CHAPTER 10

**FOR THE NEXT SEVEN YEARS,** Stringfellow and the Funnybones crisscrossed the Eastern seaboard in their rattling Econoline van, eating gas station hot dogs, washing up in gas station sinks, and getting paid in beer stained cash at every establishment that would hire them, mostly bars, clubs, saloons, theaters, farmer's markets, and crafts festivals. Summers they went north, and winters drove them south to every joint they could find.

Diego was the Snuffy-styled guy who led the band, and he seemed to have no home other than the van and the road, and no family at all other than the tiny lady named Tinker. At first, Walter couldn't tell if they were husband and wife, or brother and sister. It was a toss-up until the day Diego pulled the van over in Camillus, New York, and gathered up an armful of sunflowers that he presented to her, to make up for something.

Diego taught Walter the road life by demonstration instead of explanation. Diego wielded the words "yes, sir" with graceful alacrity on the rare occasions that he was addressed by law enforcement, whether on the highway or on the gig, when closing time was being enforced or the music was too loud. He taught his green new understudy how to tip bartenders, and how to get paid by reluctant bar managers. Diego could change a broken string in 30 seconds, and knew every shortcut between Lancaster and Falmouth, and every room with good acoustics from Utica to Key West. He could change a tire in the rain, he played each and every request, and he built a padded compartment into his guitar case just big enough for a quart bottle of liquor, boxes of which, coincidentally, were often stored in the same backrooms where the Bones were usually expected to stash their cases, and warm up before they played. Diego had learned to read a room like a dog reads a fireplug, with an instinct for making his mark.

Walter was a fast learner, and he earned Diego's trust almost as fast as he learned that the tip jar belonged to Diego and Tinker alone, not to their sidemen. Stringfellow offered to take an occasional turn driving the van through the night every now and then, but Diego never gave up the wheel. "This van is our kingdom," he explained, "we put every single nickel into this ride." So Walter learned to fall asleep at will, in any contorted position. The van could sleep only four, on air mattresses spread atop the amps and cases and milk crates of wires in the back. Until he gained some seniority, Walter was reduced to sleeping on the roof of the van, or a hammock up in the trees beside whatever dark spot or parking lot Diego had selected.

Tinker displayed domestic longings, on occasion. Once when they were stranded by a bum tie rod near Asheville, beside a playground full of mothers and their toddlers, she cried hard enough that Diego decided to call his uncle about going back to landscaping, for a regular lifestyle. Unfortunately, his uncle had just trimmed off half his big toe with a chainsaw, so his business was on hold. He convinced Diego to call this fast-talking talent agent he had heard about, a guy who managed some regional bands. When Diego placed the call, Walter and Tinker loitered near the truckstop payphone and listened to Diego's pitch, describing hundreds of gigs and their repertoire, from jazz to polka, from weddings to Irish wakes. Diego held the phone out when Pinkerton asked if the band was legit, with insurance and an LLC with a tax ID number, then waited a few seconds as a truck downshifted into the parking lot.

"Sure, sure," Diego lied as he pointed to Walter, who circled his thumb and forefinger like a fixer. He would find a guy. Stanky Pilferton promised Diego five gigs per week, and bragged how he would hook them up with radio station interviews where they could plug their shows and sell their albums. Diego nodded sagely, finding it unnecessary to cast a pall over these promising negotiations by disclosing that they had not recorded a single original song during their many years of itinerancy. When their prospective new manager explained how he would provide them with a credit card for gasoline and emergencies, the deal was sealed.

Seeing his chance to move up in the Funnybone administration, Walter figured out how to file a "do it yourself" LLC in Delaware for $69, and he bought them an impressive looking insurance policy that would cover them if their PA speaker tipped over and flattened a square dancer, or their van caught fire. Diego was impressed that $129 would get them liability coverage of $50,000 per person, and $100,000 per incident, and up to $25,000 for their van and gear. The certificate of insurance had a Hogarth-style engraved image of a constable holding a magnifying glass up to his eye, either investigating a claim or studying the fine print full of exclusions, either way. Stringfellow appointed himself their risk manager and custodian of their official new documents.

Over the next few weeks they were booked steadily, but at a series of disappointing venues. The 4-H fair was attended mostly by screeching kids, along with cows, lambs and pigs, all of whom were indifferent to any musical artistry. The used car dealer opening featured a pack of salesmen who handed out cold drinks and corn dogs as they preyed on innocent passersby who were attracted by the live music. The Funnybones played their entire inventory of folk songs, reels and jigs at a renaissance fair where damsels, draped in linen gowns and twirling parasols, cheered from beneath the trees as tubby men in leather armor and cardboard helmets staggered and sweated profusely in a field of full sun while they took turns whacking each other with medieval broadswords- actually wiffle bats that they had sheathed in cardboard and wrapped in black tape. It was at a multi-level marketing and time-sharing event where the Funnybones were presented with their first "monthly invoice" that Mr. Pilferton had sent along with their meager paycheck. Tinker started to hyperventilate as they realized that the magical credit card balance was actually their own responsibility, and had been deducted from their earnings, along with Pilferton's "credit service" charge and his 25% fee. At this point, Walter convinced Diego to let him try to renegotiate their contract, but he found that Pilferton was insulated by an answering machine which only permitted Walter to record a five second message before beeping and cutting him off. Walter left a series of messages full of escalating desperation, pitiful bleating, and even some experimental profanity, but the quality of their gigs continued to erode. At last, when Diego went into the supply room at a pizzeria in Albany to get paid, the manager handed him a large bar tab, an envelope containing $20, a slip of paper with the date, time and location of their next gig, and a short message from Pilferton advising that they still owed him $327 on the gas card, which would be canceled unless the Funnybones paid at least $109 of the balance in cash at their next gig.

On the spot, Diego decided to fire their drummer, their fourth since Walter joined. It seemed the rigors of that evening of drumming had required the consumption of an entire bottle of Heaven Hill bourbon, and by the time Diego went to find him, drummer #4 had already disappeared with a waitress. The bar manager not only declined to accept the gas card as payment for the bar tab, he promptly snatched the $20 bill out of Diego's hand. The waitress, it turned out, was his youngest daughter.

On the bright side, the drum kit that #4 had left behind brought $250 at a pawn shop the next morning. The Funnybones logo, of course, had been easily peeled off the bass drum. Diego used the card to gas up the van and feed the rest of the band microwaved fruit pies on the way to the address that had been on the slip of paper. Three hundred and twenty-seven miles later, the drummer-less Funnybones pulled up to their final gig under the cruel management of Mr. Pilferton. The Liquid Gold Pumping Company was celebrating its fifth year of providing sanitary services to owners of septic tanks and RVs in and around scenic Paterson, N.J. The "stage" was beneath a pop-up tent that had been pitched inside the chain link fence that surrounded this dioxin-infused industrial office park, and a single extension cord was coiled on the gravel, in the shadow of a 980-gallon carbon steel portable restroom truck, equipped with a shiny vacuum tank fed by a coiled fluorescent orange hose. Golden helium balloons were tethered to the truck and bobbled gaily in the breeze.

The Funnybones played the party because they needed the money, but their gas card was declined the next time they tried to use it, and the next time, and they never heard from Mr. Pilferton again. As a token of his appreciation for Mr. Pilferton's services, Diego called three different pumping outfits from a payphone and asked each of them for emergency pump-out service at Pilferton's office address. Walter was given the job of booking gigs and collecting their money. He discovered that the craft beer explosion was creating a new market that the Funnybones could exploit by adding upright bass and banjo to their lineup, and wearing overalls and John Deere caps.

The first time he realized he had almost $600 in cash in his personal pocket, Walter arranged a stopover in Adelphi. In the morning, while the Funnybones slept, Walter Stringfellow Jr. dressed in his best clothes and paid the court clerk $250 to file a handwritten Petition for Change of Name, which he copied from a form book and signed, inscribing his last official version of his born name with a flourish.  He was fingerprinted and given a hearing date to appear a few days later, after his background check could be completed. Since he was 21 years old, and there was no evidence that his petition was intended to escape creditors or paternity or apprehension by law enforcement, the hearing was perfunctory.  Judge Pinkerton wearily signed the Order, and handed it to his judicial assistant so that conformed copies could be issued to the appropriate authorities. Pinkerton was nonplussed by this unusual petition, but found it less regrettable than those paisley petitions filed by starry-eyed Aquarians that sought to change names to Blossom, Sunshine, Starchild, and the like. The Judge studied this young man, formerly Walter Stringfellow Jr., as he shifted nervously from one foot to the other while the clerk stamped facsimiles of Judge Pinkerton's signature on each copy of the Order, and shook her head.  A spark of static jumped from his hand to hers as he received his stamped certified copy, and Radkin was official.

As the Funnybones played three or four sets each night, six or seven days a week, for several solid years, Radkin found his way around his instrument, and he found his way around the songs.  He learned to look at the audience and the dancers, and he began to learn how to play them. Radkin realized that, despite his efforts to sound like his favorite guitar players, each night he only came closer and closer to sounding like himself. Night after night, he snuck up on a competent form of testimony that served as something resembling church, despite the cigarette smoke and beer and the many small indignities of their touring life.

During this period, a geeky guy with a funny hat introduced himself to Diego and Radkin during a break. Stanley Wickersham Healy IV explained that the Funnybones needed to consider recording their music, both in order to improve their musicianship and also to cultivate a loyal following. And as he explained how he had mounted two expensive German microphones in a stereo X-Y configuration inside the brim of his hat, he handed them a cassette recording of what he believed was one of their best recent sets, and asked them to give him permission to record them on a regular basis if they liked his work. Diego was stand-offish, but Radkin alertly spotted a small sheet of blotters imprinted with crossbones inside the cassette case, and he put the tape in his pocket. Healy said that the audience recording was quite good, but that it was a challenge to stand still and avoid any swiveling head movements to capture the highest quality imaging. He proposed that he could make the best recordings if they would let him place his mics onstage, or give him access to the PA mixing board. In return he would never sell any recordings for money, only trading to his friends, and he would give the band copies of all the tapes, plus the masters from any nights that they thought might be worth releasing. Diego shrugged, and Radkin agreed, and the Funnybones began to listen to the recordings on their long night drives, plotting to improve their harmonies and arrangements. Because Healy couldn't be bothered labeling every tape, or listing the songs from each night, Radkin resorted to storing the tapes in shoe boxes, numbering each box, and each tape in each box as they were handed over. Healy was a fixture from then on, and engaged in some covert business with other members of the traveling audience to sustain himself. Diego and Tinker left Radkin to deal with this distraction.

There came a time that the band reliably blended into one big instrument, and on a good night, when Radkin bent a note, secret trapdoors in the Fillmore Auditorium swung open. He learned to map the vast blue expanse of the stretched string, the microtonal liminality between fretted notes, where the heart flip-flops every few cents. He would push to the sweet pitch, the full step bend, then, jaw set, eyes closed, head tilted back, he'd push the note sharp into new territory, where one wrong move can cause a hernia. He'd shake it, and jiggle it, and tilt back further, and then he'd release and re-bend the string, and repeat, until he could slip in and out of that blue note like, well, these were G-rated songs, but Radkin learned to squeeze that blue note until the juice ran down its little blue leg. Some nights, the guys at the pool tables would pause, chalking their cues, and they would wait for Radkin to land his flying machine back on the landing strip of the song, before lining up their next shot.

After flat tires in Carlisle, Troy and Memphis, a blown gasket in Albany, and a dead battery outside Provincetown, Radkin learned how to read Diego and Tinker's moods, when to speak to them, and when to let them be. The first dozen original songs he pitched to them were dead letters, held by Diego at arm's length briefly, before being stuffed into his pocket, never to be seen again. Finally, Diego raised his eyebrows at a new chart Radkin handed to him, and then he gave it to Tinker with a nod. After running through the song at a few sound checks, they played it at a gig. The Boneheads that had begun to turn out for the band learned the words quickly. When a radio station in Seaside Heights, along the Jersey shore, got ahold of one of Healy's better recordings and put it on the air, the Funnybones got some lift off. It wasn't long until Radkin sang "Joy Ride" every night, a stop and go twang-a-billy rocker to end their set.

JOY RIDE

if you blame love, 'cause it lost its sweetness
will ya blame your boots for the faults of your feet (yes)
you can wrestle the secondhand to beat the clock
but it'll shuffle your deck, it's a cheatin' pickpocket
if you blame love, 'cause it's lost its sweetness

love is a gambler wearing polyester pants
a conspicuous fool doin a boogaloo dance
so make no mistake, all our lovers are loans
you watch for your chance, and then roll your bones
love is a gambler wearing polyester pants

commit your love like a beautiful crime
steal it and run, run away from time
even when you begin, to believe that you've won
file the serial number off your happy warm gun

the hands of the clock are the blades of a blender
where every love letter is returned to sender
the shiny gets dull and the comfort grows cold
but you should get high before you get old
the hands of the clock are the blades on a blender

I hope you get high before you get old
take a joy ride babe, before your story gets told
you should gas it and goose it and never look back
but don't blame your tires if your roads are all black
I hope you get high before you get old

Life in the van was as cyclical as any song that the Funnybones learned to play - verse, chorus, verse, chorus, bridge, chorus. They replaced drummers every 40,000 miles or so, like tires, but since their steam engine music only called for the snare to be bashed on two and four, the groove remained relatively durable and consistent. Some nights, Diego let Radkin drive the van towards the next gig, and he would press on until his mind got quiet, cueing up their latest tapes or rolling the radio knob back and forth at random, tuning in to whatever scratchy station he could find, keeping the volume low enough to let the others sleep, and loud enough for him to hear it above the noise of the singing tires and washing wind. Radkin tuned in to the faint signals, with a weakness for mariachi music that seemed to have been recorded inside a car wash, and gospel channels where sacred hymns about the golden harp up yonder alternated with calls for prayer and donations. There was a network of low-powered college stations like the one he had DJ'd at Adelphi, and when he listened to those stations, Radkin sometimes drifted into melancholy as he remembered his parents and their mistrust of his epiphanous phone call. Rest stops and gas stations and bars and clubs flickered past, and Radkin learned to sling his hammock in overhead branches where he couldn't be seen, where he would piss in a bottle, and burrow inside a sleeping bag.

## CHAPTER 11

**RADKIN GREW BOLDER IN PRESENTING** new songs to Diego, and his next song was much better, an ode to life on the road recorded during a sound check. Within weeks, "Gas Station Hot Dog" was getting regular airplay on a few college stations through New England, and Radkin decided to branch out. He picked his best short story, a tale of star-crossed lovers doomed by a feud between their farming families, springing from a disagreement about their competing rights to use water from the river that separated their properties. The story did not include an account of anyone making a bed, either alone or as a couple, but there were enough waving crops, muddy waters, and Romeo and Juliet and Hatfield and McCoy allusions to qualify as an example of pastoral literature. He picked out "The Ithaca Review," hoping to make a big splash with the same prominent magazine that had first published Beckett and Nabokov. Radkin labored over his cover letter on a typewriter on display at a big box office supply store in Pawtucket, mixing a casual businesslike tone with an ingratiating politesse. He signed his brand new name with his favorite fountain pen, and gave, as his return address, the street address of the storage unit in Adelphi where the band stashed their shorted cables, blown speakers and spare tires. He picked a Walt Whitman stamp for luck, imagining the way some grey-bearded bohemian editor in a herringbone jacket with suede elbow patches, puffing on a briar pipe like

50

Hemingway, would sit up and recognize the authentic Taconic bandwidth of this unknown sage, with a story that stretched from Kennebunk to Walden to Appalachia.

Meanwhile, The Funnybones resumed their hunting and gathering. Since they booked their gigs in a haphazard ad hoc manner, their path was reminiscent of Pollock, zigging randomly from Albany to Newport to Rutland to Eastham to Scranton. By now, Radkin was doing more of the gassing up, repairing and loading of the van, as a way of making himself indispensable and thereby improving his standing with Diego. He also got more frequent chances to drive and to sleep inside the van, when lodgings were out of reach and rain looked likely. Hangovers proved to be an occupational hazard, and Stringfellow learned to drive with one eye closed.

Diego insisted on controlling the keys and the navigation. Then one night while Radkin was driving on a backroad, he nodded off and the van drifted off onto the shoulder while Diego was asleep. When the van bounced, Radkin woke and braked, and pulled over as if he was just pulling over to piss, but Diego was in the driver seat when he returned, and Diego shook his head and muttered for the next fifty miles. It would be awhile before Radkin drove again.

The next time Diego could arrange it, he backed the van into the parking space in front of the band's storage space in Adelphi to swap a blown monitor, and collect some longer cables to suit the bigger venues that "Gas Station Hot Dog" was helping them book. Radkin had forgotten about his submission to 'The Ithaca Review,' but as he bent down to lift the heavy roll up steel door and inhaled the hot rat bouquet of their cinder block headquarters, he was surprised by a bright white envelope on the floor beneath the mail slot. Ah, the return address was printed in a suitably ornate colonial font, a sort of literate pirate calligraphy. The postage was not a stamp, he noted with disappointment, but a generic printed sticker from one of those thermal label makers. While Diego grumbled, Radkin sat on a road case and, brimming with the promise of glory, slit the envelope with a key and unfolded the single sheet of cream-colored linen paper that was inside.

Like the envelope, the letterhead and the body of the letter were printed in the same savage American Scribe font, one that had probably originated with Jefferson or some powdered-wig scrivener, imported from a Dutch foundry in revolutionary times.

> "Dear Mr./Mrs. Radkin:
> Thank you for your submission to **The Ithaca Review.** We are fortunate to receive many unsolicited manuscripts and you can rest assured that we carefully consider each proffered work. Unfortunately, we cannot use your story at this time, but we thank you for your interest in our journal, and wish you much success in the future."

Beneath the body of the letter was the word "sincerely" and the name of the associate editor, Elizabeth Mansfield, both hand written in blue ballpoint ink. The "i" in "sincerely" was dotted with a smiley face. Some length of time passed before Radkin sighed and folded up the rejection letter and tucked it inside his shirt pocket. He would use this experience as a goad and inspiration in hope that, some happy day, he would personally offer up his story to his one and only, whose indelible sincerity would be punctuated with an actual smile. This blue smiley face burned in his brain.

Radkin would go on to tell this story dozens of times, when he was questioned by friends and nosy strangers about his intended use of the notebooks that he scribbled in at the café most days, with a steaming cup of coffee at his elbow. "Are you writing a book?" was the common inquiry, usually spoken by the sort of solitary idlers who would install themselves in cafés without any means of entertaining themselves, other than by observing or interrogating those unlucky souls within earshot. Mostly, Radkin would just nod and hold up a waggling finger and smile and then move his finger to his lips and pantomime a "shhhh." But on occasion, he recognized someone on his wavelength, usually someone reading a book, and he would be persuaded to explain.

Radkin liked to preface his explanation with reference to Chekhov's bottle, as an example of the sort of tiny detail, the glint of the broken glass that serves to bring the moon into focus. Having primed the pump thusly, Radkin would explain how the one and only time he had submitted his work to a literary publication, he had received a rejection letter that had been signed in round ball point curlicues by an associate editor who had seen fit, for some unutterably ironic reason, in some cruel allegorical twist, to dot the "i" in "sincerely" with a smiley face.

Radkin would then, often, go on to confound his interrogator with a crash course in chaos theory, and the "butterfly effect" which Lorenz had used to argue the inscrutable and oblique means by which a tornado in the scrublands of Texas could be produced by a distant butterfly flapping its wings in the Amazon, a mechanism previously limited to the Rube Goldberg school of meteorology. Radkin would end his story with a description intended to contrast the grand literary tradition of The Ithaca Review with a rejection delivered by the sort of dilettante associate editor who dots her "i" like that. The ballpoint smiley face would play the part of the Brazilian butterfly, and Radkin's fury was the distant storm. Radkin would be more likely to try to hammer a nail with a daffodil than submit another story to the scrutiny of such an editor.

The Funnybones got booked for two nights in June, at a waterside bar in Steinhatchee, southwest of Gainesville, on the Gulf coast of Florida. Flathead's was a cinder block rectangle with a flat metal roof, in the middle of a gravel parking lot at the edge of a creek beside a boat ramp. There was an antique Harley flathead motorcycle parked outside the front door, and pickup trucks were scattered at random around the place. Along the bulkhead, clouds of flies and seabirds rose and fell from the oil drum trash cans full of rotting fish heads. There was a small dock jutting into the creek, and a ladder draped with broken fishing line. This lowland tableau was presided over by a tall grey blue heron standing in profile on one leg, regarding Radkin with one golden eye, immobile except for a tell-tale of feathery white plumage quivering in the breeze on the back of its S-shaped neck. Across the creek were two other bars with the same layout, cinder blocks, pickup trucks, and docks on the creek with ladders extending down into the black water.

After he stepped inside and his eyes adjusted to the dim light and thick smoke, Radkin saw that, although it was not raining outside, water was dripping into an array of buckets. A bartender nodded at the ostensible bandstand, a dank corner where an extension cord dangled near the room's primary source of light, a neon sign that flickered 'Cypress Lager' at random intervals. Lined up along the bar there were fishermen in wet rubber boots, bikers in oily black boots, and farmers in dusty cowboy boots, and they all gave the same cracker side-eye to these scraggly strangers who began dragging their equipment through the back door and assembling their launching pad. A few locals played pool and drank Pabst Blue Ribbon tallboys as they lit cigarette after cigarette. The discarded butts hissed in the buckets. It was a typical cool reception that the Funnybones had come to accept, and eventually, to embrace as a workingman's challenge.

As usual, the Funnybones began their first set that night without fanfare, and they gradually worked up a series of feverish lathers, pausing only to wet their whistles and tune up, before embarking again. Their first night was well received by the locals, and the take was far enough in excess of the usual total that Mr. Flathead himself invited them to join him for dinner at the bar after closing, sharing buckets of shrimp and hushpuppies, and a pitcher of sweet tea to wash it down. He offered to help them catch up on their sleep in the overgrown Airstream across the street where he stored broken traps, torn cast nets, crooked chairs, and a few trunks of musty clothes that had been left behind by the sea captain who had sold him the trailer. Despite the frogs and mosquitoes and oppressive humidity, they were grateful for the shelter. They cranked open the windows and let the wind clear out the mildew smell, as the sound of Flathead's departing bike, a burbling din, sank into the noise of the swamp.

The same regulars stared at them again on Saturday night, but the place was filled up by an influx of tourists, most of whom were sunburned after a day of scalloping in the shallows of the Gulf of Mexico. Diego and Tinker had gradually accommodated more and more of Radkin's musical input, but not without some friction. They had given him some dire warnings not to indulge in the sort of extended excursions that would clear the dance floor in a hurry, but they had never imagined the steady growth of the Boneheads, a network sprung from fans of Radkin's original music like "Joy Ride," "Gas Station Hot Dog," and a new country-western weeper in G that Radkin had written as a follow-up, called "Mixtape Valentine." He had wisely suggested that Diego and Tinker sing it together, and when their fans began singing along and following them from town to town, Radkin was rewarded with more opportunities to depart from certain scripted passages and shoot for the moon. That Saturday, the sun-stroked scallopers were waltzing as Diego and Tinker alternated verses, and "Mixtape Valentine" cast its spell.

## MIXTAPE VALENTINE

I'll send a mixtape valentine
a set of songs from back when you were mine
I'll build a bridge to mend a broken heart
and the wheel that pulled our love apart
Joni Mitchell and the Rolling Stones
Counting Crows and even Funnybones
Steely Dan and maybe Rusted Root
slip 'em on like a broke-in boot

the trail of breadcrumbs in the woods
traces all our shoulds and coulds
scattered there, along the ground
are you scared to turn around?

I'll write a mixtape valentine
like all the songs you left behind
like all the records that we used to play
a box of pictures from that sunny day
J. J. Cale and the Grateful Dead
Lucinda's songs, like an unmade bed
and every crooked melody
sure to lead you back to me

the trail of breadcrumbs in the woods
traces all our shoulds and coulds
scattered there, along the ground
are you scared to turn around?

I never thought that love could fade away
I still believe in yesterday
in castles hidden in the sand
in songs that say the things we can't
I wrote a mixtape lullaby
so you can sleep, so you won't ever cry
murmured words and a melody
to help you dream of how it was with me

With the dance floor full of swaying couples, and the clock nearing closing time, Diego nodded to Radkin to give him his solo spot as the band played on. Radkin started with a single note that he fanned and milked like a Neapolitan mandolinist, before he slid down an agonizing chromatic heartstring like a fireman going down a pole, ten seconds of a descending microtonal Bedouin blues phrase that made both Boneheads and scallopers squirm and hold their breath. Next, he began to play an ascending figure, climbing a pentatonic ladder with a series of bright arpeggiated daisy chains, to lift the room gradually, and with proprietary pride. His eyes were closed, and he took his time, even as a bartender flicked the lights for last call.

As the dancers rose to meet the surging melody, Radkin realized how the Funnybones had evolved into a sturdy band of vagrant angels shot through with a personal relationship with the keys of G and C and D, with a sound that infused the Bakersfield Hymnal with his electrical power glide. His copper crown encircled by a faded bandanna, Radkin pulled a glass slide out of his pocket and, holding his mouth funny as a slide player must, held his breath as he slid the bottle neck along six highly amplified strings. After Radkin played the literal vocal melody with authority, with immaculate string-talk clarity and the inimitable CLANG of an electric guitar, he then iced that workingman's cake with slippery steel dog whistle sounds. As he landed the solo at the top of the chorus, Diego and Tinker stepped to the mic, and the words rang true in an instantly familiar style, and the oldsters in the room drew a bit closer to be warmed by this new fire, moving carefully so as not to trip over the half-full buckets. When Radkin finally lifted his head, he saw that a group of drunks from the bars across the creek had jumped in and swam across, and they stood dripping and howling at this blooming music that had echoed across the water. Even the bartender was persuaded, calling a second time for last call, and raking in wet money from the swimmers.

Instead of spending another sticky night in the trailer, Radkin convinced the others to help him load the van so they could stretch out and sleep in the back, while he drove through the dark pines towards their next job. Diego stared at Radkin. "If you run this van off the road again, it will be your last time." Radkin opened his mouth, but Diego just wagged his finger. "Your joy ride had better be straight ahead." Radkin nodded and reached into his pocket. He had collected the master tape of that night's last set from Healy. It turned out that tape five from box three contained lightning in a bottle, and any time Radkin was discouraged or unsure about his musical path, he played the tape. As he drove and listened, Radkin braced for the sour notes that never came, and Diego watched for deer, potholes, cops, or a deviation from the marked lanes of travel, but he tapped his foot. Eventually, in this retail manner, the band marked its arrival in the Little Big Time by working steadily enough, and selling enough beer with its brand of steam engine-styled music to invest in occasional motel room accommodations. This luxury eventually proved to be the undoing of the Funnybones.

## CHAPTER 12

**RADKIN LEARNED TO DRINK AS** he went down the road with the Funnybones, an unremarkable development for a bar-room troubadour. What was remarkable was the means by which he eventually learned not to drink. It was a painful process.

The Funnybones' van had been leaking oil for months when they lucked into a weeklong gig at The Nickel Bar, a biker and stripper bar on the outskirts of Mechanicsburg. Through a natural and incremental process, so gradual as to be imperceptible, Radkin had worn out Diego, and had assumed all responsibility for the van, driving it, fixing it, and loading it. So, after loading their gear into the Nickel Bar, Radkin drove back to their motel and he jacked the van up in the back of the parking lot, so he could try to find the source of the infernal leak. Over the next few days, Radkin would crawl under the front end every chance he had and tinker with a fitting, poke at a gasket, or bang his knuckles trying to tighten a different suspicious bolt. The leak persisted.

As promised by the owner of The Nickel Bar, The Flying Dutchman Motel had offered the band a discounted weekly rate. The motel was just a few miles away from the bar, and the gift shop sold brand name oil, along with an exquisite selection of beef jerky, birthday cards, adjustable wrenches, tampons, diet soda, kitty litter, The Farmers' Almanac, jumper cables, lighters, boxes of wooden matches, condoms, screwdrivers, umbrellas, decongestants, batteries, bandannas, flip-flops, padlocks, trucker hats, medicated ointments, keychains, postcards, spark plugs, a selection of laminated wallet-sized horoscope guides, one for each of the Astrological sun signs, rubber gloves, air fresheners that looked like pine cones, wiper blades, switchblades, shotgun shells, rain jackets, bumper stickers, sunglasses and every variety of sweet and salty snack. Also, other stuff. Plus, the rooms had cable TV and mini bars. The Funnybones had finally arrived.

From the start, the locals at the Nickel Bar, mostly bikers whose motorcycle club was called "The Mechanics-Burglars" were sufficiently pleased by their swerving music and their herd of hippie followers to tolerate The Funnybones, but by the end of the week they approved heartily enough to assemble an actual wang-dang-doodle to mark the last night of the band's residency. "The Burglars" invited several motorcycle clubs from adjacent counties, including "The Holy Ghosts" of Carlisle and "The Nightshades" from Scranton. The 'Bones outdid themselves that night, and the bikers raged while the Boneheads twirled. At closing time, just after 2 a.m., all five of the town's police cars were lined up outside the bar, keeping the peace by strobing the parking lot in prophylactic blue light. Radkin had put the van back in service that day so their equipment could be loaded out that night, to simplify the band's drive to their next gig in Ithaca in the morning. (Nobody had asked, but the van was still leaking.) While Radkin directed the Tetris-like job of packing all their amps and cases and stands and wires and drums and hardware and fans and lights, the police decided to hurry things along. The cops had a K-9 dog in one car and opened the rear hatch to take him for a walk and give him a sniff of the van. He was interested in the left rear tire, but just to piss. Suspicious of this provocation, Radkin locked the van with a big smile and ducked back inside the bar to enjoy the situation and to recruit a few of his unpleasant new biker friends in case of trouble.

The Funnybones had come off stage vibrating, and they had immediately begun to pour extra rum on the fire in their brains. They faced the full assortment of typical post-gig hazards, adrenaline, uninformed praise, vampires wearing lipstick, half beautiful strangers wearing patchouli, party favor salesmen, swerving drunks in search of a fight or a bathroom, either way, bikers juggling tire irons, grim strangers cutting lines on overturned shot glasses, ringing ears, spilled drinks, and other dubious residue of the temporary glory of the Funnybones' latest musical invention. The Nickel Bar staff made a half-hearted effort to clear the room at closing, but money was flowing and the police stayed outside, and the party continued. Tinker had corralled the rest of the band to catch a ride back to the Dutchman with some friends, but Radkin stayed behind to bring the van back to the motel after the parking lot cleared out. Blame it on Mount Gay, on the quivering escape velocity that had driven their music, or perhaps, Radkin later postulated, a dropperful of pharmaceutical confusion had been slipped into his glass by a sly prankster. At some undetermined juncture, Radkin fell into a vertiginous whirl that spun him into oblivion.

Sometime later, a painful sulfuric white light trickled into the front of Radkin's brain. He winced awake and attempted a primitive inventory. Furry tongue, frontal lobes stuffed with steel wool, beating tympani for temples. He found himself lying on a scratchy jute couch under a thin blanket at the Dutchman. After being shipwrecked, Gulliver had awakened beneath dozens of ropes, but nothing like Radkin's hangover had ever been known in Lilliput. Radkin burrowed back into darkness.

It wasn't long, however, before Diego shook him awake, gargling harsh imprecations and spitting ominous plosives. When Radkin peeled the skins from his onion eyes, he found that his legs were caked with a mixture of blood and mud. His arms were scratched, and his head spun. Diego shook the keys to the van in his face and observed that the van was not in the parking lot. Diego and Tinker hauled him outside to see this evidence. There was no van, no gear, nothing but an oil stain shaped like Florida where the Econoline had been parked for the week. They were demanding an explanation. Radkin had no answer. Why did he have the keys and no van? Why was he bloody and muddy? Curtains were pulled aside in a few of the nearby windows, as Diego grew more vociferous in his tantrum. Radkin threw up in the shrubbery, but Diego did not consider this a valid answer.

Diego fired Radkin without ceremony, and left him to his own devices. Radkin weakly attempted to speak in sentences, to explain how they were insured now, how the oil leak could be tracked, how the police would find the van quickly, and how he had no cash, having not yet been paid for the week. But Diego and Tinker were beyond any discussion, seeing as how everything they owned, their van and all their instruments and the PA equipment, had been "misplaced" by Radkin. So they took a cab to the nearest Greyhound terminal, where they missed the morning bus to Ithaca.

Radkin went back into the motel room to sleep it off, but the maid let herself in a few minutes later and announced it was check-out time, in broken Spanglish accompanied by vigorous hand gestures. She was surprisingly tender, but referred his pathetic pleas for mercy to the management. Radkin was driven to the Nickel Bar by the assistant desk clerk, and after agreeing to wash dishes and mop the place, he managed to borrow $300 to pay the motel tab. None of his temporary friends from the Nickel Bar could explain his predicament, claiming he had driven the van off around 3 a.m., just a bit more spun than usual, while the bar was still awash in blue lights.

Radkin reported the loss to the police, and immediately vowed to avoid rum, and all its treacherous cousins, especially tequila, vodka, bourbon and gin, henceforth. Even beer. Wine. Champagne. Amazingly, after a brief investigation, the insurance company paid Radkin for the van and all their lost gear, including Radkin's old guitar. He paid back the Nickel bar for his loan and recalibrated his plan.

SECTION IV


FLOTSAM


"I ain't often right, but I've never been wrong,
It seldom turns out the way it does in the song."
— Robert Hunter

## CHAPTER 13

**OBVIOUSLY, RADKIN NEEDED TO FIND** a healthy new line of work, so he volunteered at a turtle conservancy project he had heard about from an amiable Bonehead. In return for a plane ticket, room and board and a trifling stipend, he signed up to join a tribe of scientific eco-hippies who patrolled a 15-mile expanse of the north shore of Culebra, an island off the coast of Puerto Rico, at a place called L'Estacion des Tortugas. Year-round, volunteers spent every morning staking, numbering, charting and monitoring every new nest that the huge leatherback turtles dug and filled with eggs. The turtles were steady, leaving fresh nests above the seaweed line that marked high water, most nights from February to September. The staffers lived in a dormitory of sorts, a gaily painted single story concrete block square, topped by a wooden frame supporting slanting sheets of welded metal. The volunteers were assigned regular shifts, rising before dawn, and driving along the beach in antique Cushman golf carts loaded with shovels, hammers, wooden stakes, ribbons, Sharpies, etc.

At L'Estacion des Tortugas, there were bananas, conch, beans and rice, lentils, peppers, limes, lemons, sesame oil, Mahi, grouper, tuna, mangos, and all the fire pits and hammocks that the sales pitch had promised. Most of the patrol crew retired for siestas as the tropical heat descended at mid-day, right after their post-patrol meeting where they reviewed new nests, equipment and staff updates, pending tide and weather information, and reports of predators or spoiled nests due to erosion or other accidents. At dusk on clear nights, the crew socialized over dinner served al fresco on a sandy patio, usually fresh fish, vegetables, rice and local rum and fruit juices. Afterwards, a gaggle would drift out to the edge of the trees near the beach, where a stone fire pit was tucked inside a circle of stout clattering palms. Radkin would pass the house guitar around, or try to, but mostly he would play it and, eventually, the others would sing along. He did not falter in his determination to avoid alcohol, but Radkin discovered that every time it rained, psilocybe cubensis mushrooms sprouted in a nearby cow pasture. In due course, as he was tickled into daydreams by these old friends, he forgot about booze, and he remembered the way She would emerge from the waves. Not a mermaid, of course, but a wayward sailor, or a surfer, or a turtle monitor, any of these manifestations would serve. She would be his quicksilver twin, the chick to his boom, the Bonnie to his Clyde, and She would turn the pages of his story.

Radkin realized how, like so many wannabe writers and musicians before him, he had been seduced by strong drink, in thrall to the debonair derangement romanticized in centuries of ballads and blues. He blamed Sinatra and Morrison and Joplin. Obviously, he had been carried away. Losing his old Gibson haunted him, and he had been stung by the manner in which all his imagined Funnybone solidarity had vaporized in one night. As he watched the locals pour hot water on fire ant mounds, he remembered the way his mind had boiled when he had poured liquor into his brain. He was resolute in his abstinence. He began a new story.

Radkin's conviction that his story should begin with the domestic ritual of making a bed was shaken and rebuilt daily, like his bed itself. When he made his cot in the dorm, he felt briefly heroic, slipping the fitted sheet over the first corner of the mattress, so brave and sad. And the second corner was even sadder, whether he went north/south or east/west, no matter, because it led to the challenge of stretching the sheet over the third corner, which inevitably pulled off one of the other two corners. What a tragic hypotenuse. Was it slapstick that he was after?

He contrasted the symmetry and ease of a couple making their bed together, and how the east/west rhythms would be a grand pas de deux, preparing the allegorical garden of delight. He also considered the corollary (even braver!) in which the couple first wrecked the bed in lubricious urgency, and later, flushed and glazed, opened the window and pulled the sheets back into place, so the cats could resume their throne in the slanting stillness. At this point, he crumpled up the page and watched the dorm cats yawn at the paper ball coming to rest next to all the others.

Radkin draped a few shirts as a curtain around his cot in the back corner of the dorm, by a west-facing window. There was mosquito netting partitioning each bed, so he ran a length of thin line over the netting and through the armholes of the shirts to give him a little privacy in the evenings while he wrote and read, using the same battery powered headlight he had used on sleepless nights in the Funnybones' van. As he worked late one moonless night, he was startled by a hum that quickly grew louder, like a cranky compressor in the rusty kitchen refrigerator. But as the cycling up noise grew louder and turned into a high pitched shrieking, Radkin recognized the sound of a small plane tearing along the beach, skirting the treetops, and rattling the tin roof. He clapped his hand over his light, and peered out the window, but there was not a single running light, not even a glimmer, marking the shadowy Doppler. The hum dropped in pitch as it passed overhead, and it was gone in a minute, leaving the sound of the palm fronds clattering. He got used to these sporadic treetop flyers over time.

## CHAPTER 14

**SOME EGGHEAD SCIENTIST THEORIZED THAT** it took 10,000 hours to master a skill, but Radkin was suspicious of such an arbitrary and mechanical marker. Nonetheless, he wrote every day on Culebra, and every day he played a department store electric guitar made of Masonite that some prior staffer had left behind to rot in the tropical steam. He bought a used Fender amp at a pawn shop in San Juan, and fixed it up with tubes from a junked TV set.

For both his writing and his playing, Radkin's metric skewed to quality, not quantity, but he had second thoughts. He decided to conduct an experiment after he observed a small community of monkeys rummaging in the jungle surrounding the compost heap at the edge of the compound. In the golf cart garage, he found an Underwood typewriter, rusty but operable. After he worked it over with a toothbrush and some palm oil, and fitted it with a fresh ribbon and a sheet of paper, he put it on a stump in the shade beneath a clump of palm fronds in the palmetto scrub where the monkeys congregated. For a few days, Radkin made a conspicuous show of typing on the typewriter vigorously, in a rhythmic clatter, and then re-racking the carriage and ringing the bell. Locals claimed that the monkeys had originally been imported to Puerto Rico for medical research but were released after the laboratory went defunct. For this reason, Radkin liked to imagine that these monkeys recognized and appreciated his scientific vigor, as he demonstrated how to use the typewriter. Every few mornings, Radkin checked the paper for what he hoped would be inevitable snatches of Shakespeare or, who knows, a short story or haiku. He was discouraged when the monkeys' only engagement consisted of stealing the paper, and tearing it up into pieces, when it proved less than delicious. Nonetheless, he persisted for a few months. After finding only one solitary string of letters, "iklo-p," the result of an apparent right-handed punch, Radkin brought the rusting machine back into the dorm and cleaned it up again. He briefly tested its effectiveness in his quest to write his story, but then resumed his preferred scribbling mode.

In the course of his work, Radkin became acquainted with a grey-bearded fellow, a shift leader who had worked at L'Estacion des Tortugas for many years, since the very beginning. He went by the name of Green Gene, and he wore green overalls, and nothing else, no shirt, no hat, and no shoes. Gene had gradually turned a deep red mahogany color in the laser sun. One afternoon, Radkin leered nakedly at an ice cream cone-sized spliff protruding from Green Gene's bib pocket, so they took an extended walk down the beach together, and became friends.

Radkin volunteered to serve as an intern in the Green Gene Ganja Garden, a private organic, carbon-neutral, vegan, non-profit farm that Green Gene had quietly developed in his spare time, in which cannabis blended in beside sugar cane, corn, mangoes, avocados and coffee. Gene had grown expert in the use of cuttings, drip irrigation, how to sex seedlings and how to time trimming and harvesting. He had tested the relative merits of drying and curing the buds in mason jars as opposed to Rasta-style "sweat" curing. Radkin learned the low tech basics, using knives, clippers, five gallon buckets, soaker hoses, shovels, jars and burlap. He was, in fact, paid in buds and free master class training about the cultivation of cannabis, since Green Gene believed in a cashless local network based on produce and barter alone. At night as they listened to the swish and rattle of palms being thrashed by sea breezes, Green Gene would fulminate and fume about money, its corrosive influence, and its insidious role in shifting political power from labor to management. Radkin was deeply affected the first time Green Gene casually twisted a dollar bill into a tube and dipped it in the fire to light a joint, but despite Gene's subversive babblings about the evils of money and his measurable influence on Radkin, fate would challenge Radkin with a test that he would fail in spectacular fashion.

Most nights, around the fire pit Green Gene would riff like a combination of Marx and Ferlinghetti, while Radkin played artsy noise on the guitar to back him up. Gene claimed that, back in the '60s, he had been paid to participate in the CIA's MK Ultra experiment, as he was flunking out of MIT. The capsules that he took in a Cambridge hospital, under supervision by medical men in white coats holding clipboards, changed his mind dramatically, and he liked to hold forth about those days with antic flair. Gene fancied himself an Emersonian transcendentalist, but no one was generally welcome to debate his stream of didactic soliloquies on intuition, self-reliance, and simplicity. When Gene veered into outright quackery, for instance his theory that chemtrails of pharmaceutical barium salts were being streamed in the atmosphere by government satellite geo-engines in order to create a massive electromagnetic super weapon, Radkin finally felt compelled to question him, but Gene swept aside Radkin's tentative remarks like a plume of septic exhaust. Eventually Radkin steered their discussions to the topic of his personal superpower, radiokinesis, as often as he could, hoping for some re-amplified glory. Every time Gene would pause to reload his verbal vituperator, Radkin would summon all available gravitas, and transmit his personal variety of faith.

"All we have to do is tune in to the right frequency."

Gene snorted at this upstart initially, but stopped snorting after Radkin launched into a very cogent series of lectures of his own, cataloging the combined electrical systems that wire the nervous system. His presentation included a bastardized version of Cajal's law of dynamic polarization, which he relied on to conclude that the electric human functioned as a simple antenna, consisting of an isotonic battery of meat suffused with blood, tears, and sweat. Gene finally engaged, after Radkin had concluded with a flourish, explaining the electric nature of spirit, the animating spark of life.

"All right," Gene challenged, "so what happens to this electric energy when the host, the human battery, runs down and dies? Where does it go?"

This question was welcomed by Radkin, as an improvement over the derision that Gene had begun with. Gene regretted his question, as Radkin gathered his second wind, and leaned into his thesis.

"The First Law of Thermodynamics states that energy cannot be created or destroyed. When the electric spirit expires, it is converted to heat and migrates into the flux. And when a new electric baby is born, she is animated by a nimbus kindled by her mother's warm spark."

He continued in this manner unabated until, twenty minutes later, Gene rolled and lit a spliff, and muttered some vague terms of surrender based on his personal belief in a much more literal manner of passing the spark. However, Radkin was now deep into his theory, segueing from the Akashic Field to quantum physics, "as above, so below," and into the theosophical spark posited by Madame Kravatski, a famous Ukrainian spiritualist. Recognizing that he had grown pedantic and out of breath, Radkin accepted the dutchie and, as he savored it, Gene seized the opportunity to change the subject to the role of the Gulf Stream in regulating the growing seasons and turtle fertility. He never again mentioned chemtrails to Radkin, or any other human, and he begrudgingly regarded Radkin's occasional discourse with something resembling respect, thereafter.

## CHAPTER 15

**THE FIRE PIT WAS THE PLACE** Radkin came under the spell of a new volunteer named Calico. He inspected her hands and feet with a surreptitious side-eye when they met, but he had no inkling of the nature of the tutelage she would provide.

She said she had been named Calico because her mother had given birth to her at a desert commune in a ghost town called Calico, an old mining camp, somewhere near Barstow, California. She wore no jewelry, and her clothes looked homemade, without logos or belts or buttons, just a linen serape draped over a black and gold woven huipil blouse and black leggings, all suitably loose and dusty. Her hair was a sheaf of matted, golden dreads, streaked by sun and rain, and wrapped in a criss crossed black band.

She belted out "Me & Bobby McGee" with natural blues power on her first night, closing her eyes on the bridge and outro like it was her personal anthem. When Radkin introduced himself, he announced his single name with the same guarded inflection she had used in introducing herself to the group, the armored confession of the mononymous. He inventoried this new apparition, starting with her dark green eyes, and her sure hands, strong and clean, suited for both work and play. Her bare feet were honest too, and built to move. They did two more numbers together, both suggested by her, "Melissa" and "As Tears Go By." Radkin finished the Stones' ballad with a coda consisting only of harmonics, a melody that he had not played for a decade, but still remembered as a function of muscle memory. The easy intimacy of their music augured other impending forms of harmony.

Calico had declined to live in the dormitory, deciding instead to sling a double hammock in the breezy stand of yucca plum pines on a bank up above the grounds of the turtle station. Her nest was sheltered by mosquito netting and hanging mesh bags of necessaries, water and books and incense and matches and such. The night of their first meeting, after they wandered down the beach together and took a baptismal dunk in the moonlit shallows, Calico began to educate Radkin in the abstruse mystery of a woman's pleasure, a graduate course of study that he hoped would last for months, no for years, wait, for a lifetime. He had already begun to conduct his own research with the help of such lovelies who had passed inspection in his teenage years, but his progress had been limited by the tender years of his teachers. In Calico's hammock, rocking beneath the sighing pines and washed in the syncopated clash of flashing surf and dark tilted sand, Radkin resumed his schooling in the arc of womanly delight, the little death that might knit two souls together. Or three.

It was this last prospect, that of the creation of a third soul, that kept Radkin focused exclusively on the non-reproductive curriculum, and Calico adjusted accordingly, from the very start of their first scrimmage. Or so it seemed. Their hours of interview that night, after the fire pit had been deserted by the others, had flowed to and fro with natural ease, and enough earnest mutual rhythm to propel them to a tacit understanding that might be called by the most tender name in any culture, a prologue to trust and combustible friction. The ease with which Radkin and Calico collided was suggestive of a covalent bond of deep molecular origin, a two-part emotional epoxy. Either that, or Radkin was a helpless romantic for whom, like a bull in Madrid, waving red flags served as a tractor beam. He wrote this down, then threw it into the fire pit one night after Calico explained that bulls were colorblind.

Later in life, as Radkin reflected on his education by Calico, and as he refined his understanding of the tender cultivation of the woman's innermost floral arrangement, he employed many licentious metaphors in his manuscripts. He wrote of the prestidigital safe cracker, rolling the dial so slowly, so gingerly as to reveal the sound and feel of the hidden inner wheels and gates and fences falling into place, a manual pareidolia through which the treasure is spilled at last in a gasping puddle of jackpot. Radkin also reflected on his Boy Scout training, remembering how he had watched a park ranger start a campfire by spinning a dry stick that he had inserted into a small recess in a dry branch that he had packed with a pinch of dry kindling, dandelion fluff and bits of sawdust and resinous pine bark and fine dry grass, and how, beneath the spinning point of the stick, he had pushed more and more tinder carefully onto the glowing ember that resulted. When the ranger had pulled off his hat to gently fan the climbing flame, Radkin had decided that he was born to be a park ranger. He considered Aladdin's lamp, and how lifesaving fires often bloomed from such microscopic combinations of friction and pressure, and how the magical wisp of smoke, the djinn of pleasure, might rise up as the very genie of love to warm the soul. The attentive reader will foresee that Radkin eventually used these pages for kindling on the cool nights that followed the end of his scrimmage with Calico, after he concluded that his metaphors were overwrought and clumsy, and unsatisfying.

Calico was angular and athletic, and, if invited, she was happy to explain her devotion to lunar rhythms as the animating principle of her faith in the divine, supernatural and sacred power of the Natural and Stoked Vortex of Curly Surf, in which the tides, the salty waves, birds, winds, solitude, and the sunlight conferred transcendence upon the surfer. Because he was freckled and had learned to hide from the sun to avoid the hideous burns that had poisoned him many of his childhood summers, Radkin marveled at her even cocoa skin, set off by thin light lines that linked four lighter triangles where the panels of her bikini had been battened down to preserve her modesty.

It became evident that surfing was not a social activity for Calico. She did not try to convert others to take the holy waters. After the patrols had returned from their rounds and caucused at lunch to share the latest data, she would putter off on a moped alone, with her surfboard strapped onto a rack Green Gene had made by bolting two bent metal tubes onto the frame. Radkin tried asking a few tentative questions about how long it might take her to teach an adept beginner to catch a few of the big Tamarindo Beach waves she talked about so much, but she just changed the subject, without any suggestion of enthusiasm. When Gene carried on about Culebra's endless growing season, and how the seesaw of rainy season cloud cover and full sun winters required varying farming strategies, Calico warmed to the lunar-adjacent topic. She was animated as she explained how the October swell would be shaped by offshore winds to produce a glorious break near a certain reef. She added, with a glance at Radkin, that the danger presented by the reef was extremely gnarly. When she said this word, gnarly, a little tremor went through Radkin, like a cloud had covered the sun. It began to dawn on Radkin that he might not be exactly on her frequency, or vice versa. The word offended him.

As the crew gathered around the fire most nights, Calico listened with strategic forbearance to the contrasting sententious and scientific didacticisms of Gene and Radkin, great spumes of benevolent gasses that merged with the fire pit plume as they ascended. Their lofty discourse concerning the electric spirit, the principles of thermodynamics, the measurement of valence and frequency as explained by Radkin, and the diabolical Federal Reserve, the Bohemian Club's connection to the Illuminati, and similar Masters of the Universe as postulated by Green Gene, these musings passed Calico like smoke. Eventually, she was emboldened to hold forth on her own simpler theory, in which all aspects of the natural human condition were indexed to the moon. Astrology, the quirks of personality and fortune, the seasonal cycles of aridity and fertility, all these were tethered to waxing and waning gravitational forces, and the shifting phases and antipodal bulges of the tides, according to Calico. While Radkin admired the undeniable scientific basis of most of Calico's sermon, bathymetry and centrifugal force and the like, he completely misread the subtext of her speech. The subliminal thrust. The ulterior motive. The yearning.

One night, following a few weeks of progressively synchronized safe crackings, luscious jackpots, shiny lamps, etc., Calico began to lecture Radkin on the reliability of the moon, and the rhythm method of birth control relied on by many ancient cultures. As she did so, she passed a small cup of rum and lime juice to Radkin, along with a lingering glance that asked a question. Across the sparking fire, Gene couldn't help but notice.

In retrospect, Radkin realized how his clueless response, a lengthy account of the mysterious disappearance of The Funnybones' van and his consequent decision to abstain henceforth from any fermented and distilled spirits, marked the beginning of the end of his enrollment in the University of Calico. Had he been so inclined, an opportunist willing to engage in ovulatory roulette, he would have sipped the rum before discreetly spilling it, and he would have attentively studied the bracelet she had taken from around her wrist, a string of 29 wooden beads that he had never seen her wear before. She began to explain how she used the eleven red rosewood beads and the 18 black ebony beads to calculate her lunar cycle, with the same degree of certainty as permitted the precise calculation of the time of high and low tides. When he handed the cup back to Calico, and waved off the proffered bracelet, Radkin failed to foresee how the tide would turn against him.

Gene had always reserved the plumpest seedlings and sunniest location for his personal crop, but when Calico began getting preferential treatment, Radkin noticed. He came upon a whispery meeting around this time, in which Gene and Calico passed a shiny new device back and forth, through which they squinted at the buds, and then they mumbled about brix, some sort of sugar measurement that, he later learned, helped maximize yield by pinpointing the best time for harvest. When Radkin inquired, Gene waved him off with some comment about measuring the proper frequency of the trichromes with his new refractometer, and how Radkin's harvest was overdue, while Calico busied herself stripping leaves below the third node of each plant. Radkin blew off this imagined slight, and went about the business of checking on his own plants, and scribbling ill-fated odes to the glories of the celestial hammock.

About this time, Radkin received a message on the answering machine attached to the house phone. After being kicked out of The Funnybones, Radkin had given his new address and phone number at L'Estacion des Tortugas to his brother for this very reason. Wyatt's message was terse, just the date and place of their grandfather's funeral, and the sarcastic suggestion that Stringbean might try to make an appearance. All these calls were logged for reimbursement, because volunteer staff came and went, and some homesick people used the phone more than others, so Radkin put a check mark and his initials next to this entry on the phone log with the time, date and incoming number of this call, so his account could be charged. He scheduled his absence from the patrol for a few days, booked a round trip flight, and packed a bag.

The funeral was never chronicled in his journal, and he honestly couldn't recall much but the awkwardness of the gathering, and how his mother was coughing during the eulogy that was delivered by some vacuous stiff of a minister in a dress. Over the next few weeks after his return to Culebra, Calico gradually left Radkin in an excruciating limbo, as their assignations became increasingly intermittent. Of course, he tried not to panic, even as he searched her eyes, gauged her pulse, and maximized his Romeo at every opportunity. Afraid to smother her, given her ghost town birth and lunar tendencies, Radkin decided to play the introductory chords to "Me & Bobby McGee" as a test, every night that the wind was right, in hopes that he could remind her how feeling good might be good enough. Alas, not only did she decline the cue the first few tries, she seemed to project a certain weariness when, after finally giving in, she looked directly at Radkin as she sang to remind him, with some implicit prejudice, that "nothing ain't worth nothing, if it ain't free." He declined to take the hint, and in a rare spasm of vanity, began squeezing lemon juice into his hair every morning for a few weeks, until his red turned to gold. Whether it was pity or a subliminal effect of his new hair color, Calico led him back to her hammock one last moonless night, and submitted to his ministrations. He teased her cruelly, at great length, a process that was interrupted by another appearance of the treetop flier, who strafed them so closely that the palms fluttered and the hammock rocked in the prop wash. Radkin was awakened near dawn by the hammock tilting, as Calico quietly puked over the side, holding her bundle of hair back with one hand, before she settled back and pretended to sleep. This night marked his graduation from Calico's school of pleasure.

The next morning, fortune combined with the tides to test Radkin with two small blue packages on the beach, as he patrolled alone at dawn. Awash in foam on the tilted sand, these wayward bricks presented Radkin with a fascinating and perilous dilemma, a conjoined threat and opportunity of epic proportion. Festooned in seaweed, tightly wrapped in blue shrink-wrap and gray duct tape, and bearing cryptic Sharpie markings and stamped Disney logos of Pluto, Goofy and Dopey, this flotsam cast a strange shadow on Radkin's mind. He briefly considered ignoring them or returning them to the salty deep, to steer clear of the difficulties of possession and transport, exposure to the unsavory process of recruiting distribution help, and the risks of testing, or not testing, the nature and quality of the product. But there was also the temptation of money.

Radkin was sure no one else had had the chance to see this contraband. There were no fresh footprints or tire tracks on this stretch of beach several miles from the compound, and daylight was just barely creeping over the sea. Had this cargo been jetsam, jettisoned in an emergency or in response to an interdiction, he would have expected to have seen law enforcement patrolling by air and sea, scanning for a vessel in distress or a go-fast boat attempting to escape their scrutiny. He thought of the dark planes he had heard, buzzing the treetops on moonless nights. Radkin's knife blade came out dusted with unmistakably fresh cocaine. After patching the small puncture with several layers of tape, he quickly created turtle nest #51 among the dunes, burying the bricks deeper than any nest. He staked it with the mandatory sign reciting all the scary official warnings about the steep Federal penalties for interfering with the nests of the leatherback turtle. No one would dare disturb a turtle nest, and Radkin would have time to logisticate his dilemma. From first sight to the last touch (dragging a bucket up and down the slanting beach between two squiggly rows of "flipper tracks," one from the water to the nest, and one leading back to the surf, to recreate the track of the hypothetical turtle) this whole process took only five minutes, and Radkin carried on as casually as a man could, with a head full of felonious temptation.

## CHAPTER 16

**SEPTEMBER CAME, AND CALICO VANISHED** without any warning or trace. The small permanent staff at L'Estacion des Tortugas was accustomed to turnover, and observed a strict policy of declining to comment on departed volunteers, even when rumors of some intrigue were circulating, like homesickness, broken hearts, spider bites, sunstroke, bacterial diarrhea, or other tropical blessings. Gene offered no explanation, nor could he explain how Calico's hammocks, moped, and surfboard came to be concealed behind the concrete pump house that provided water to the camp, under an array of solar panels tilted towards the south.

The nightly fire pit gatherings were sadly diminished after Calico's disappearance. Radkin's regular performances of "Sitting on the Dock of the Bay" suddenly felt like suicide notes. Gene finally broke his silence when they were alone.

"She was transactional, man. You can't get hung up like this."

Now it was Radkin's turn to shrug.

"I mean, it's right there in all that moon business, those beads and fertility dances. Think about our plants, man, how we cull the males and how the female plants make the best buds as they drown in all those lovely trichromes."

"What's your point, Gene?" Radkin was ready to be convinced, but this analogy was leading him nowhere.

"They're backwards, man. The woman is not to be starved, not like our crop. They live to make babies, just like we live to make babies."

Radkin's eyes were slits, now, and mad filaments blinked 'danger' in his wizardly golden nimbus.

"What exactly are you talking about, Gene?"

But Gene was now lighting and pulling on a spliff, a symbolic olive branch, which he offered to Radkin instead of an answer. Radkin declined and stepped away from the fire just as a piece of green wood popped, and a shower of sparks arced out onto the sand. On his way back to the dorm, Radkin stopped by the house phone and ran his finger down the phone log. There was a 203 number that Calico had dialed every Sunday at noon and initialed "C," right up until the end of September. He wrote it down, and headed to bed early.

His grandfather had been buried in June. Radkin had been gone for three days. Calico had puked in August. She disappeared in late September. Radkin waited an icy few weeks after his exchange with Gene. On a Sunday at noon, Radkin called the number that Calico had been calling. The man who answered the phone seemed older, and when Radkin asked if Calico was there, he paused.

"You mean Calpurnia? Hold on."

Thirty seconds went by, and Radkin heard a door open and close, then Calico said hello, but as a question.

"Calico, is that you?"

She said nothing, but exhaled and waited.

"Are you expecting a boy or a girl?"

She exhaled again, and he could hear her cupping the mouthpiece as she whispered. "I'm sorry, but don't call me again." She hung up.

Radkin began planning a new story as he plotted to visit nest #51.

## CHAPTER 17

**THE BLACK TOLEX BAG THAT** held the spring reverb tank inside the 1973 silverface Fender Deluxe Reverb guitar amplifier could accommodate exactly 35 ounces of compressed cocaine, almost a kilo. Compacted in triple shrink wrap, painted with aromatic coffee sludge, and then vacuum sealed in more wrap, the contraband weighed just more than the original two-spring Accutronics reverb tank which Radkin removed and left amongst the piles of dead batteries in the golf cart garage. Radkin's amp was suspiciously overweight by the time he fitted the baffle board with a false front made of sturdy veneer salvaged from the remains of a bleached sailboat. This plywood sandwich concealed a compressed and wrapped sheet of the remainder of the dope.

In a visceral response to the final lesson meted out by Calpurnia, Radkin had fused his radiant powers, his expedient sense of Puritan economy which left nothing to waste, and the mercenary survival reflex of a scavenging beast. In keeping with his belief in the power of neuro-electric projection, Radkin checked his amp along with his duffle bag when he headed home to the States. As he arrived in Miami aboard a short Sunday afternoon flight full of tourists, Radkin stood out. He read from a Bible, and chanted sing-song hymns from memory, Onward Christian Soldiers and the like. He wore sandals made from tire tread fitted with loops of mismatched bits of rope, and his sun-bleached hair cascaded over his shoulders. When he claimed his duffle bag and his amplifier, the baggage handlers in Miami declined to lay a hand on Radkin or his ratty baggage, lest it crumble into bits. Radkin was ready to ask the TSA guy to pray with him, but the man just waved him and his cloud of patchouli through, and Radkin rolled his amp out of baggage claim on wobbling casters. After buying scissors in a store along the concourse, he found a handicapped stall in a restroom, where he cut his hair and changed his clothes. He discarded the smelly bandana and applied a splash of Aqua Velva. A shuttle took him to the Miami Amtrak Station, and the Silver Star deposited him at Penn Station late the next afternoon, after 32 hours of blurry racket. Radkin spent a night in the Hotel Chelsea, then took a bus to Brooklyn.

He knew it would take months to find a buyer for this amount of coke without getting busted. There could be no hurry in these outlaw matters. Radkin still had most of his Funnybones insurance money, and he had saved some money in Culebra, but it had to last for months, so he only stayed in a motel a few nights, as he scouted for a better place. He took the amp apart and packed the blow into three round Tupperware containers. He then buried the containers in a bucket of Aloha-scented kitty litter that he stashed, along with his reassembled amplifier, in a locker at the bus terminal. Every few days, he moved them to a different locker.

So it was that, underneath an overpass, wedged between two of the enormous steel girders that supported a span of the

Belt Parkway where it crossed over a tidal canal in Canarsie, Radkin constructed a rent-free palace. For the floor and back wall, he used 2x6's, pallets, and scraps of plywood boosted from the site of a convenience store under construction. Radkin lined his ad hoc structure with flattened cardboard TV boxes, Styrofoam blocks, and yards of bubble wrap. In the mornings, he swam in the Paerdegat Basin to clean up, before climbing into his nest to hide from daylight.

Underneath the Belt, Radkin was tolerably warm, dry, and safe. He slept through most of his days, like an emperor of vagrancy, lulled by the intermittent scree and thum of the overhead traffic. On cold nights he was warmed by a can of Sterno propped inside a short chimney made of stacked cinder blocks. A curving access road that fed merging traffic onto the bridge framed a round courtyard beneath him, chest high in weeds and blueberry bushes hung with festive trash ornaments, mostly Styrofoam cups, plastic bottles and aluminum cans, along with sodden box springs, shopping carts and tire treads.

In his journal, Radkin ruminated about the process by which ink and paper are joined in a noble quest in which the writer strives to convey precise meaning through pictograms, inky traces of the author's mind which are scratched onto a blank page, designed to be converted by the scanning reader's prismatic eyes, and projected onto the screen of radiant mind behind those eyes. He felt that writing in pencil was primitive, prone to smudging, the easiest to erase, best suited to crosswords. In the indelible marriage of ink and thirsty cellulose, Radkin found an alchemical process in which the reagent ink was consumed by the reactant paper. The romantic impulse in his mind guided the inky catalyst, and this reaction yielded the valentine glyph that was left behind. But his manuscripts still read like a dictionary of extinct alphabets.

Radkin continued to discard his manuscripts almost as quickly as he could scribble them. His fascination with the process of documenting his mind at play was genuine, but the literary product tended to spoil overnight. In the unforgiving morning light, his work was execrable, full of mixed metaphors, misaligned voices, tense tensions, and dangling modifiers. He considered the likelihood that his true aptitude was for the process of yearning, not for the humble sort of plot-oriented carpentry that would produce a sturdy story. He worried that his mind was not truly shapely, and that each story only served to map out a grotesque mixture of solipsism and conceit. Radkin experimented by forging his next draft in a single, continuous effort, through the use of caffeine and isolation, using a lengthy roll of butcher paper salvaged from the recycle bin outside the Wawa, which was now open for business. The resulting gibberish burned as well as all the rest had, providing a useful but more humble type of illumination than he had planned.

## CHAPTER 18

**AFTER ESCAPING FROM HIS PARENTS,** vagabonding with the Funnybones, and retreating into exile in Culebra, Radkin was determined to use his residency in Brooklyn to recalibrate his ambitions. An alarmingly emphatic declaration of his love for his parents, fueled by psilocybin mushrooms, had forced him to flee. The mysterious disappearance of the band van had left him forsaken. The magnetic moon had pulled Calico home, even as the very same tides had dangled a double-edged temptation under his sober nose. He concluded that some Biblical-level smiting had been afoot. The reconstruction plan that he plotted during his residency under the Belt Parkway, with perfect views of the Paerdegat Basin, would be different. He floated in Jamaica Bay in an inner tube and plucked blue irises growing in the median among the retreads and flattened beer cans. He was lulled to sleep by the boom and whoosh of the mighty trucks of commerce that streamed along the parkway overhead. He dreamed of money.

Using a time-honored code familiar to hustlers, freaks and dope fiends, Radkin sized up candidates to help him find a connection. He cultivated a nodding acquaintance with a drummer for a band that played every Friday night in the Gutterball, a local bowling alley/bar that was a popular gathering spot for the nervous punk, techno, hipster, stubbled, tatted, dreadlocked, vegan, multiracial tribe that had made Brooklyn the "New Frontier." The drummer called himself Diesel, and his band, Tyrone Thighbone and the Nocturnal Emissions, covered Sly Stone, Funkadelic, Steely Dan, and the Meters, as well as more off-center offerings by Eugene Chadbourne and the Yeti Trio. Diesel was stocky, dressed in a leather vest and blue jeans, and he shaved his head, all the better to show off the tribal tattoo that covered the top of his skull. His earrings were small Bosch glow-plugs that bounced as his head twitched to the beat. After a few casual exchanges spread over a couple weeks, Radkin ingratiated himself by mentioning the biodiesel he had been using to fuel the ancient Caterpillar generator in Culebra, where palm oil was cheap and plentiful, but clogged the valves. Diesel raised his eyebrows at this topical offering, and then belched and lit a cigarette. He changed the subject a little bit.

"'Diesel' is getting old; I might change it up."

Radkin would have belched if he could have, but he just waited for more information. Diesel continued.

"I'm considering a gig as head bouncer at a new club these guys are opening at another old bowling alley."

Radkin was patient.

"The place is gonna be called the Punchbowl, and they've offered me some decent money to handle the door on weekends when Tyrone doesn't have a gig."

"What's all that have to do with your name?"

Radkin was following the story line, and he tried not to wave his hand around after Diesel blew smoke in his face, before getting to the point. He was ready to introduce himself as Gene Green, but Diesel never bothered to ask.

"Whatta ya think of the name 'Propane'?" He took another big drag and exhaled in Radkin's face again.

"If I'm gonna have to stare down assholes and beat down the occasional punk, I was thinking that 'Propane' would be a warning sign, you see, that I am a professional fucking pain technician, you get it?"

The subject seemed to make him quite angry and he glared at Radkin, as he blew out another plume, clearly expecting an actual answer to this existential quandary. Radkin was trying not to cough, but coughing was better than laughing, so he coughed for safety's sake.

"You're really stuck on this fuel thing, man. I've gotta say, 'Diesel' is plenty cool with your glow plugs and everything, and I don't think the sort of dopes that consider messing with a guy like you are gonna get the whole pain theme of 'Propane.' I like 'Diesel' better. I'm just saying."

The cigarette was now between Diesel's teeth, and as he checked to see if his earrings were in proper trim, he squinted against the rising smoke.

"You might be right.  I might be overthinking it."

Radkin coughed again and turned away to go take a leak before he laughed out loud.

After telling Diesel about his time on the road with the Funnybones, Radkin got a little nostalgic, and decided to buy himself a good guitar. He wandered through a claustrophobic pawn shop, the busiest one in Canarsie, packed with glass cases of gold and silver baubles, hundreds of watches and cameras, black and gold and silver guns of all sizes, bicycles, generators, meat grinders, blenders, jack hammers, and every type of phone, VCR, boom box, and other obsolete gadgets. Almost hidden in the midst of a wall of guitars, hanging between a pointy neon Ibanez and a Chinese strat covered in skateboard stickers, he saw a Gibson gold top, with the unmistakable soap bars and a retrofitted stop-tail bridge. Radkin tried to act casual as he helped himself, but it was too much, and he sat down on the filthy floor heavily, his old guitar cradled to his chest, as he ran his fingers over the telltale clue, a nearly invisible factory neck splice behind the headstock. The pawnshop owner was a vigilant man named Sal, adorned with a single gold earring, a walrus mustache, and a large chrome Smith and Wesson pistol holstered on his hip. Good hippie training served, after Radkin regained his wits. First, he told Sal that this was his guitar, that it had been stolen or lost, and he explained the scarf joint clue.  Sal just stared. Then Radkin showed Sal a yellow newspaper clipping that he kept in his wallet, with a faded picture of the Funnybones on stage, with Radkin playing the guitar. After his story was met with a dubious sigh, Radkin offered the authoritative bit, explaining that, if he had a screwdriver handy, Sal would find the word Radkin etched into the back of the plate that covered the control cavity. This proof was more persuasive.

Sal wearily explained how he had acquired the guitar in a long term blind bulk salvage deal, a monthly truckload he purchased for a flat fee from the Pennsylvania Department of Transportation, full of abandoned furniture, appliances, boats, trailers, vehicles and other detritus recovered from the highway rights-of-way. Radkin described, and Sal confirmed, the nature of the gear that had been in the van, most of which Sal had already sold off. Then he pointed out the window to the parking lot out back, encircled by a chain link fence topped with razor wire. Again, Radkin had to sit, but this time he first found his way to a chair.

The van was faded, and the plates were gone, but it was easy to identify by the knotty piece of driftwood Radkin had found washed up on Nauset Beach, shaped like a lightning bolt and wedged between the dash and windshield. A gummy oil stain shaped like New Hampshire spread from under the front end. Turned out, the Funnybones' van had been located by a state survey crew in Mechanicsburg, deep inside a mass of dense bushes at the bottom of an embankment on the outside of a tight cloverleaf exit ramp, not far from the Nickel Bar. After playing his guitar for an hour or so, he agreed with Sal on the price and the amount of a deposit, and Sal agreed to install a reverb tank in Radkin's amp and ship it to him later. Radkin declined to report this development to his former bandmates or their insurance company, but his ironclad vow to never drink was once again renewed. He set about marketing his contraband with renewed urgency.

A few more weeks of passing joints on the patio during set breaks at the Gutterball had led to the sort of creeping conspiratorial familiarity with Diesel that made it natural for Radkin to make an offhand comment that he was looking for some blow. After sizing Radkin up more carefully, Diesel said that he knew a guy, of course, who knew a guy, of course. In due course, Radkin was introduced to a guy named Leo, a bow-legged guy in a beret, who started him off with a pearly gram, then another, and then an eight ball. Each time Radkin paid in cash, and each time Leo tucked the money away without counting it as he palmed a small packet into Radkin's hand. The count looked good, but each time Radkin dumped it into the bay without reservation.

The next time Radkin saw Leo, he handed him a small bindle of his flotsam.

"Hey, some things have changed for me. If your people like this rock, let me know. I've just gotten lucky and I'd rather work with you than against you."

Leo squinted at the little fold of paper, and squeezed it gently, before tucking it inside his hat. He then studied Radkin more closely, inspecting his hands and his shoes, and evaluating his level of grimy streetliness, his garlic breath, and his unblinking cool. "You serious?"

Radkin nodded and shrugged.

Leo was back the next night, and he wanted to talk business.

"What's the deal with that? How'd you get that kinda sneeze?" He had a wingman this time, a small but menacing goombah with his hands in his jacket pockets, and the pointiest shoes Radkin had ever seen, like a black leather pair of aces of spades.

Radkin explained, "It's a one time thing for me, and I need some professional backup. Long story."  Here he paused. "Leo, it's proper, no funny business."

"Why you botherin' with the stepped on shit you bought from me, if you got that?"

Radkin was ready. "How else would I find someone with the proper ways and means to take a few birds off my hands?"

Leo glared, then nodded. "Birds? Lemme check."

 He started to turn away, and then moved closer to Radkin to whisper. "You understand what you're into here?  My people don't play."

Radkin nodded, and Leo stared right through Radkin's eyes for an uncomfortable few seconds before he disappeared, with his shadow muscle trailing behind him.

The next time they met at the Gutterball, Leo wore the same beret, but a different face altogether.  He did not smile. "OK, that rock? How much of that can you get?"

"You liked it, right?"

"How much? How much, and how soon? You'll have to meet my guy."

Radkin explained that he wanted to do one deal only, completely legit, trouble free, no excitement. They made a deal, two keys, cash, round numbers, no surprises. $30,000 a key was enough to be real, and low enough to attract Leo's boss.

Leo glared ominously when he specified, "No cut, right? Just like the sample?  Remember what I said.  They are all business."

Radkin simply smiled and met Leo's gaze. "That's why I am asking for help.  Same quality, no cut, full weight. Cash, non-consecutive fifties and hundreds only." For good measure, Radkin slipped another bindle into Leo's hand as they shook, some ethnic move that Leo initiated. They set a time.  When Radkin showed up, a couple of guys met him, and after they watched him for a while, they set another time.  Radkin was followed back to his nest by a creeping Ford.  He felt better when he didn't die.

Jude was Leo's guy, and Jude and his goon, a new, bigger button man, were over an hour late to the next and final meeting. Leo was nowhere in sight.  Radkin had made arrangements to pay for his guitar and leave Brooklyn by bus right after the deal, fast. Now he was going to miss his bus, but they ran every couple of hours. When Jude swept into the Gutterball and found Radkin, Jude's eyes were brown and friendly, but they wheeled in two different directions, like search lights on top of the towers at Sing Sing in the old movies. Jude wore a leather coat, jeans and boots, and he chewed on a toothpick. His jumbo body guard stood at Jude's shoulder, with his hands both deep in his jacket pockets. He was as wide as two men and he made a face like something smelled bad. A bag hung down, partly concealed under his armpit. Neither man spoke. They headed for the bathroom, and nodded to Radkin to follow.

Jumbo blocked the door from the inside and handed Radkin the bag he carried, a small zippered diaper bag, patterned in pink ponies and blue unicorns. Radkin made a cursory show of counting the money. Six straps of used $50's and $100's were a little thicker than a brick, since they didn't lie as flat as new money. After Radkin fanned each sheaf of bills and nodded, Jumbo took back the bag and Radkin led them to the bus station. Two more frowning guys waited in the vestibule outside the bathroom, picking their teeth with the plastic cocktail cutlasses that nested in a cup on the bar. The Gutterball bartender shook up a drink and watched in the mirror with professional disinterest as they all left together. Jude's security man swung the bag on his shoulder, and Jude's boot creaked each time he stepped with his left foot. The vestibule guys followed at a distance. At the bus station, Radkin gave them the key to the locker, and waited for them to hand over the bag. After paying Sal for his guitar and agreeing to contact him to arrange shipment of his amp, he headed off the grid, on a Greyhound bus to Woodstock. No one followed him as he walked to the ticket counter.

Although Radkin was relieved not to have been stabbed or arrested during the exchange, he knew better than to assume he was in the clear. He bailed out of the Greyhound in Rhinebeck, where an Amtrak station built like a yellow brick church was visible down the street. He dumped the diaper bag in a trash can in the bathroom after moving the money into his guitar case, packed under the headstock in a tube sock. He bought a ticket on the Ethan Allen Express to Castleton, and stuffed his duffle bag in the overhead rack, as the train began to bump and squeak north beside a line of power poles along the Hudson.

Radkin's grubstake had been delivered by the Antilles current, an arm of the North Atlantic Gyre, a lobe of the Oceanic motor of all kinesis, all salt water, all blood, all wind and tide and luck. He mused on his options as he balanced the guitar case between his knees. Radkin would make certain modest concessions to the prevailing social contract, now that he could afford to surrender some of his sovereign lunacy. He would get a motorcycle, find an apartment, get a library card, and finish his book so he could find his twin. He would surround his mailbox with petunias, and get a cat for each sunny window. He would buy a transistor radio, and tune into the faintest station on the dial.

SECTION V


THE SPARKLEWOOD PROJECT


"About half the practice of a decent
lawyer consists in telling would-be clients
that they are damned fools and should stop."
— Elihu Root

## CHAPTER 19

**RADKIN DECIDED TO TRAVEL BACK** to Adelphi to find some traces of his lost family, and find a spot where he could hide. It took him a few days to settle in. First, he decided he needed to renew his driver's license. The DMV clerk accepted his application without a word, but as she ran her eyes down the page, her gum-chewing slowed, then stopped altogether. Her tag read "Ms. Orleans" and she was a shiny shade of blue black, with ivory teeth to dazzle the impatient public.

"Is this your real name here, this Radkin?" She pointed with a ball point and pronounced his name like a one-word question. He glimpsed a piece of gum, a pale green waffle of minty freshness, a sort of corrugated cud, briefly exposed in her open mouth between prodigious incisors, as she emphasized the first syllable of 'Radkin.' Wrigley's spearmint, he guessed.

"Yes, just the one. Radkin." She stared and he stared back. Then he smiled and she smiled back.

"Just a minute," she said over her shoulder as she headed to the supervisor's office in the back. By the time she got back, with Mr. Wakefield peering out of his doorway to get a load of this curious fellow, Radkin had spread his copy of Judge Pinkerton's Order flat on the countertop.

"It's legal. The Judge entered an Order."

Ms. Orleans summoned Mr. Wakefield, and they stared at the Order. Radkin felt perfectly official, armed with his certified copy of a Court Order entered by an actual Judge. With tentative fingertips, Mr. Wakefield gently fluffed up the gray bird's nest that was his hair, then he smiled wanly and nodded to Radkin and Ms. Orleans before he turned back to his office. Radkin's new driver's license picture was the first and last photograph taken of him for many years, as it turned out. He tilted his head at a jaunty angle, tilted far to the left, with his tangle of red hair touching his shoulders, and his wide smile intended to radiate a sort of force field immunity, to cast a benign spell over any constable who might have occasion to examine it.

Later that same day, Radkin paid cash for a used Yamaha on display at a local garage, and he signed the papers with an R-shaped flourish. The bike was a glorified moped that the salesman called a Fizzy. He bought a bright blue Bell helmet and a basic insurance policy, using his address at the motor court at the edge of campus where he had signed a week-to-week lease. After he completed a brief written test and a basic riding test, Ms. Orleans was quite efficient in issuing another new license bearing his motorcycle endorsement. Radkin decided to tour the town.

His father's father, Horace Seymour Stringfellow, had lived downtown in a colonial brick neighborhood near the train station. He had been fond of walking his dog at dawn and dusk, dressed in his plaid pajamas (a blue, green and yellow tartan favored by the Black Watch, the 3rd Battalion of the Royal Regiment of Scotland, to be precise) and a Yankees cap. During his evening stroll, he would carry a finger or two of scotch over a single ice cube in a chipped glass bearing an engraved "HSS" monogram. His dog was a pugnacious Boston Terrier named Shakespeare, well known for biting any undefended calf within reach. Radkin recalled how, every time a car or bike or pedestrian came into sight, Shakespeare would yap and attack, and often when he yanked the leash, Horace would lurch and stumble, and the ice cube would clank and tinkle in the glass. The neighbors would peer out their windows and from their garages, and wait for this menacing spectacle to pass. Radkin visited the neighborhood on his motorbike, and searched for traces of his grandfather. Just as the highways were spotted where bumps knocked splashes of oil off the undercarriages of a million leaky passing cars and trucks, Radkin imagined that the dark stains he found on his grandfather's old street marked the places where Shakespeare had lunged, and his grandfather had spilled his drink.

Radkin looked up the address of a former classmate who had played Ultimate at Adelphi and who had been part of the tribal full moon ceremony that had prompted Walter to make his fateful phone call. These days, Sherman Klank held himself out as a certified public accountant who specialized in solving the unique problems of farmers. Sherman had a fine reputation, but he had a twitch and a stutter, and he hyperventilated so violently each time he laughed that Radkin decided to cut his travelog short and keep their meeting strictly business, rather than confide about the details of his adventures. After an extended set of hypothetical questions, wink-wink nod-nod, about cash crops and a large hypothetical bag of dirty cash, his new accountant pushed back his chair and exhaled so hard that his haystack of shoulder-length yellow hair shimmied in the breeze. He admitted that he had some familiarity with this scenario, hypothetically. The laugh that followed was so prolonged as to resemble a seizure.

"If I was in this s-s-s-situation, I would open bank accounts at as many different b-b-b-banks as necessary to accommodate all the c-c-cash, but I would not establish more than one account or deposit more than $9,900 at any single b-b-b-bank. OK?" Then Klank either yawned or laughed or just took a big gulp of air, Radkin couldn't tell. "It will be important for us to agree that our c-c-conversation today was purely prospective and hypothetical, and related only to the p-p-p-possibility of legitimate future income from the sale of such legitimate crops as k-k-k-kale, apples, maple s-s-s-syrup, tomatoes, potatoes, soy b-b-b-beans, that sort of thing. Also, I prefer to be paid in c-c-c-cash." Surely, Green Gene would have disapproved of this bank idea, but Radkin had no idea how to handle his sudden infusion of money. Sherman's eyes bulged as he  suggested that Radkin might consider an investment in the local electric company. Sherman counted his fee, and Radkin left without a receipt.

He retired to his apartment, where he resolved to produce three songs and a paragraph of his newest story, per day. He persisted in his fantasy of writing as a form of seduction. Every few days he would roam Adelphi on foot, or ride his Yamaha around the town, scanning the vibrational spectrum, seeking guidance, bread crumbs, clues. There was simply no such thing as coincidence, Radkin knew, and he knew his shining path would be illuminated by some kind of electricity, just as his quicksilver lover would be delivered up to him, in due course of the unfolding world.   Calpurnia had just been a test. Once again, the universe delivered.

Radkin pulled into a cafe by a creek in a likely looking section of Adelphi called Sparklewood Forest. Radkin ordered beans and rice and began scanning his radiant brainwave tuner through the local frequencies as a wizardly chef slid his steaming lunch down the maple counter. Radkin had long cultivated eavesdropping as a vital skill, instrumental to research for his book, so his natural reaction to the fragments of discussion of the newlyweds at the next table was to give thanks for favorable atmospheric conditions.

The new bride, a well accessorized Rubenesque woman, held out her left hand to admire her ring as she poked at her salad with the fork clutched in her right hand. Radkin heard only bits and pieces: "…you never told me…know how allergic I am to dander…didn't realize it was in the sticks so far from town…because the apartment is where I want…dry cleaner, hairdresser…"

The groom was a thin man who wore scrubs with gold spectacles and a name tag that read "Dr. Bauch, DVM." He replied, "…living at the clinic for years was … because I was single...cost to hire a watchman at night and weekends...anesthesia, you see, after the surgeries on the dogs in particular …disoriented and loud and someone needs to keep an eye… receive deliveries at all hours of the night … I just need to find...at least until this buyer...get approval and we can close…". Then he bit his burrito at an angle, leading with his canines.

Radkin's first mouthful of beans and brown rice (with a blast of habanero salsa and sprinkle of sesame salt mixed in) had just begun to warm his core as it dawned on him. He listened more intently until he was sure he understood their situation, at which time he was suddenly covered in goosebumps. A moment like this couldn't be manufactured. Radkin would never forget certain similar moments, like when the curl of smoke had come out from under the RCA TV set before dawn as he watched Agriculture USA when he was five. Or when the rock he threw at that elementary school bully, Dickie Gillem, hit squarely on top of Gillem's head with sickening accuracy. Or his first kiss, when an unexpected scythe of pink schoolgirl tongue had stirred his world, as they sat on the shady steps of the church where she had lured him, by staggering and feigning nausea while the local garage band pumped out Crossroads in the gym downstairs. The same unforgettable noetic sheet of immaculate chicken skin came over Radkin as he turned to this couple at the next table, and the words flowed like jazz. He had his opening.

"Folks, let me volunteer to assist you, I couldn't help but hear. I'm new in town. My name is Fellows, Walter Fellows, and it just so happens that I am fluent in dog, and serviceable in cat, and experienced in soothing the savage beast. If I understand your predicament correctly, I would be qualified and willing to provide capable and reliable after-hours caretaking services at your animal hospital, in return for a modest wage and the most basic lodging."

It turned out that Dr. Bauch owned the Sparklewood Veterinary Hospital, along with a 35 acre parcel of adjacent woods that included some prime frontage on Sparklewood Lake. His new wife was not a pet lover or an outdoorswoman, and he was in the process of gallantly agreeing to move into town to live with her in the deluxe apartment that she had received in her second divorce, and also to take advantage of her zaftig, shall we say, fruits and vegetables. Dr. Bauch obviously had been lonely a long, long time, and he had a special penchant for the voluptuousness that oozed from Georgia Roundtree. Bauch was reassured by this convenient stranger's glib shower of premium words, and since his new wife was his audience, he was pleased to have a chance to display his alpha male skills.

"Here's the deal, Mr. Fellows. The hospital needs to be as invisible as possible, because I will be entering into a purchase and sale agreement to sell all the extra property that runs down to the lake. I thought about bulldozing it, subdividing it, and making a bazillion, but this hospital is so busy, I'll do better flipping the wooded part to this city guy, some doctor from New Jersey who is willing to overpay if he gets the permits or whatever, to put up a fancy nursing home."

Here, Dr. Bauch took another feral bite of his carne asada burrito, and checked his bride to confirm that she was displaying a suitable level of adoration for a man who could have collected a bazillion dollars, but opted for more time at home with her instead, to till her garden, as it were. Georgia had been introduced to him by a friend, an enterprising local chiropractor named Popright who had a lucrative side business operating a combination weight-loss, acupuncture and rehab/fitness clinic. He then staffed the place with herbalists, acupuncturists, physical therapists and a thinly-credentialed naturopathic practitioner, which is to say, hungry and efficient Asian women willing to work for commissions. Popright had spotted Georgia arriving at his clinic in tears, and also in a Bentley. When he learned that her first and soon-to-be-second husbands were both orthopedic surgeons, he thought of Bauch, whose predilection for bountiful women was local legend. Instead of adoring Bauch's gallantry, Georgia was squinting at her ring still, rotating her hand to assess the parallactic twinkle of her new diamond at arm's length.

Bauch continued, "These woods are apparently a big deal, endangered owls, old growth trees, blah blah, and I'm worried this doctor might back out if he gets a lot of pushback from The Audubon Society and Greenpeace and the other tree and owl people. Plus, there are bikers like crazy. So, if you can pass a background check, I will need you to supervise special deliveries, keep the animals quiet overnight, and be my eyes and ears after hours, as the permitting process for the nursing home invites public comment. Otherwise, you would just need to stay out of sight."

Radkin nodded vigorously while the words "old growth trees" reverberated in his ears. It was time to put his education in Green Gene's ganja garden to productive use. The deep Vermont woods would permit Radkin to avoid the obvious problems of the congestion in Humboldt, Trinity, and Mendocino counties, the rain in the Pacific Northwest, the rednecks in Florida and the Piedmont, the short growing season in British Columbia, and the sprawl of suburban surveillance almost everywhere else.  For references, he intended to give Dr. Bauch the phone numbers for Professor Rice, his erstwhile advisor at Adelphi, and Green Gene at L'Estacion Tortugas, but  Bauch did not bother to follow up. Radkin took the job on the spot and, before dark that night, he had checked out of the motor lodge and fixed up a pallet in the loft in the barn behind the hospital.

## CHAPTER 20

**MOST SUNDAYS DURING THE SUMMER,** Freeman Dearborn drifted around Sparklewood Lake in his jon boat. Under the narcotic sun, lulled by the chatter of gulls and the lingering smell of gasoline and oil from his old outboard, he basked beneath a halcyon sky as the anchor tugged the bow into the breeze. Tiny waves rinsed the rocky lakeshore beneath webs of arching cirrus.

The sound of a transistor radio was the next best thing to actually being at a game. He could hear the grandstand murmur, and pictured fastballs popping round dust clouds from the catcher's round mitt, between muted cries of "peanuts" and "cold beer." And he imagined how the pitcher bent over and nodded at the sign, then rocked and kicked in the anticipatory hush, then the bat crack and the white ball arcing out into the green gap and running to the fence, as the crowd's mutter grew to a temporary hullabaloo and the batter slid into second. His batteries were now dying in the sun, as he turned up the crackly signal. Meanwhile, the wash of the lake among the stones stayed steady, with an occasional FOOM, a knee-high wave that raised knee-high spray, and settled in foam. He imagined himself on the bump, rubbing up the ball and peering in for the sign, as the waves whispered down. But the second time he had blown out his elbow had ended that daydream, and this lawyer thing fit him like a noose. And just like that, the spell was broken, and he began to worry about going to hell, and his clients going to jail, and just like every other time, a thousand by now, he saw no escape for either of them.

The law firm of Ratzlaff, Kluger & Bunning had hired Mr. Dearborn right out of law school, at his first interview. The managing lawyer had assigned Freeman to do background work on a variety of low visibility cases at the start. Ratzlaff was short, but that wasn't the whole problem. The problem was the fact that Ratzlaff knew he was short, and he was mad about it. This sense of grievance animated every aspect of his life. Naturally, the practice of law was a perfect setting for his pathology, and his clients benefited immensely from his anger, even as his relationships with colleagues, staff, friends and family were slowly poisoned. It didn't help things that Freeman was 6'5", and had the wingspan of a pterodactyl, the beak of Abraham Lincoln, and the hyperlordotic posture and implied rectitude of a Pentecostal preacher.

Ratzlaff was well regarded in some circles, but mostly he was simply despised. The irony of his specialization in divorce and his scorched-earth tactics became apparent to Freeman, as he served his basic training and waited for his Bar exam results. Ratzlaff had risen to a miserable prominence as the most ruthless divorce lawyer in Adelphi. Despite his sailboat, his sterling Rolls Royce, his Gothic castle on the hill, and his knack for hiring low self-esteem associates susceptible to his abuse, he remained 5'5". His hair was still thinning. He drank expensive scotch, the kind that tasted like a fireplace, but he usually drank alone.

One morning, Freeman was drinking coffee and musing on how these psychodynamics might affect his career when he was summoned to the boss's office by Ratzlaff's secretary, Grace Weatherly, who had been assigned to do Freeman's work too. He watched as Ratzlaff dropped a foot-high stack of files and two Dictaphone tapes on Weatherly's desk, and told her that he needed his dictation to go out that afternoon. Weatherly squinted at this pile of overdue work, and picked up the telephone to cancel her lunch plans. She knew Ratzlaff expected his upcoming safari in Namibia to proceed without a hitch. Ratzlaff had made it clear that for $60,000, he expected to bag at least a couple of the Big Five. The glossy brochures piled on his desk showed elephants, water buffalo, leopards, lions, and rhinos, all dusty and dead, with grinning white men brandishing guns and propping their boots up on their bloody trophies. Cigars and liquor were included in the price of the safari, and the taxidermy options were extra, but very reasonably priced. Ratzlaff beckoned Freeman into his office, as he handed him a letter from the Bar examiners.

"Congratulations, you passed the Bar. We're ordering new letterhead and some business cards for you. I have a new client, a shrink from New Jersey who thinks he's a real estate developer, name of Zuckerman. He'll be coming in at 4 p.m. Take notes, look like you've done it before, we'll figure it out as we go. Follow my lead. Since you've passed the Bar, this will be your client. I'll help you manage him."

Ratzlaff's face was a vacant lot, with mud puddles for eyes, but his cravat was brilliant Italian silk. On the huge mahogany credenza behind his huge mahogany desk, there were pictures of his wife and kids posing with him on a huge mahogany sailboat in the Mediterranean, straight out of some wristwatch ad in a lifestyle magazine. Ratzlaff picked up the safari pamphlet on top of the pile and gazed fondly at the hunter posing proudly with his trophy, a dead Cape Buffalo with a surprisingly long tongue trailing in the dirt. He held it up for Freeman to admire. Freeman nodded, and went to get a fresh yellow pad from the supply closet, before resuming his seat in the library, where he was checking cites in a motion seeking full custody of the children on behalf of a well-to-do medical device salesman who traveled constantly. He had been gone so much that he was unaware that his wife had changed teams until after the divorce papers were served. Ratzlaff had paid $10,000 to retain an apostolic family counselor who would testify, under oath, that lesbian parents were categorically unfit to have physical custody of children. Freeman wondered who would stay home with the kids if the motion succeeded, but he knew better than to ask Ratzlaff about this little contingency.

The Cadillac was battered and funeral black, and muttered into the handicapped space outside the front door at 3:59. Zuckerman was a big man and he tilted from side to side as he walked like John Wayne, like his feet hurt. He was a successful psychiatrist, specializing in talk therapy for mobsters' wives whose boob jobs and facelifts had gone wrong. Sometimes he counseled women whose husbands had been whacked, or worse, had flaunted their mistresses. With his Jersey plates, shiny black leather jacket, thick gold rope chain, gold Rolex, and smoked gradient lenses, he would have been cast as a car salesman who played the greyhounds, or a guy with a fleet of tow trucks and a Jersey City junkyard. April, Ratzlaff's Barbie-of-the-month receptionist, was oblivious, picking at her chipped nail polish and whispering into the phone, until Zuckerman's shadow covered her. She buzzed Weatherly.

Unlike the overcompensating nebbishes who dressed themselves up in Harley Davidson gear every weekend, those black leather batmen who cultivated an ominous image to cushion their egos from the beatings administered by the hands of time, Zuckerman flashed a winning smile. He towered over Ratzlaff, and swung his glasses from Ratzlaff to Freeman like satellite dishes. After the handshaking and name trading was done, Zuckerman tiptoed into the conference room and settled his bulk in the executive chair at the head of the table, where he began drumming his hands on the glass top.

Like a man who was paid by the hour, Zuckerman got straight to the point. His agenda was delivered with a toothy ferocity. "As I mentioned on the phone, I plan to negotiate the right to purchase an attractive parcel of land in Sparklewood Forest, and I will be building a world class nursing home there, if I can get approval. I've heard that your firm is proficient in this work. Can you do that for me?"

The discussion that ensued was a contrast in styles, with Ratzlaff lobbing lofty hypotheticals regarding experts and zoning and wetlands standards and certificates of need, and Zuckerman punching volleys with the declarative grunts of a man accustomed to getting his way. Freeman was unable to suppress a flinch when Ratzlaff named the firm's retainer in the casual manner of a man who owns a 37' sailboat, but aspires to own a 47'. Ratzlaff explained that the process would be technical and time consuming, but that most of the work would be done by Freeman, as an associate at the firm who billed at a lower hourly rate. Freeman was busy scratching his cheek, in an effort to disguise his recoil at Ratzlaff's brazenness.

Zuckerman peeled a check from his wallet and turned his gaze to Ratzlaff after he filled in the numbers and zipped the curlicue that stood for Shlomo W. Zuckerman. "Do you foresee any problems that can't be overcome for this amount?"

Ratzlaff did not look down, but met Zuckerman's eyes and slid the check aside to Freeman like a poker player, to signal that the handling of money and other dirty work associated with the Sparklewood project would naturally be delegated to his subordinate. Ratzlaff explained how a deposit on the property would eventually be necessary to formalize the purchase and sale agreement, and he tapped, for emphasis, a stack of documents he had printed out that morning from the SEC website.

"Closing will be contingent on us obtaining all government approvals for you." As he slid the documents to Freeman, both men turned their gaze to Freeman, who delivered his first words of the meeting. "Leave it to us," he smiled.

Ratzlaff looked sideways at him with raised eyebrows, brief ripples in the mud puddles in his face. Gold fillings flashed in Zuckerman's mouth and his chair squeaked, as he reclined and threw his head back, and roared. "I see virtue when you smile!"

Freeman was unsure how to reply, so he just smiled wider. His first dozen projects had involved runaway teenage shoplifters and repentant drunks and bad debt collections, so this comment on virtue had disarmed him. He could see Zuckerman's Cadillac out the window, bristling with an array of steely armaments, an old-school cell phone antenna, a brand new wheelchair lift, and rusty wire wheels.

Zuckerman flexed his chair forward now, and it squealed again as he leaned forward over the mahogany table, steepled his hairy hands, and peered over his glasses at Freeman. "The Sparklewood project is now in your hands."

# CHAPTER 21

**GRACE WEATHERLY'S EYES AND HANDS** whirled like clockwork for 40 hours a week, operating the buttons and levers and gears of the machinery of the Ratzlaff law firm. She touched the keys of computers, phones, copiers, and postage meters, and wielded hole punches, staplers, glue sticks, envelopes, loaded reams of paper, filed endless papers, signed for deliveries, juggled ink stamps, key cards, rolodex cards, and cleared half full coffee cups and crumpled tissues left behind after conferences and depositions. In the glorious home stretch of her daily virtuosity, at 4:30 or so, while juggling the telephone and a stack of outgoing mail, it was often necessary for her to pop the hidden hatch in the back of the humming Matsumoto copier, when it blinked and bleeped, to pluck out a knot of paper crumpled in the roller bowels of the enormous device, to the relief of the on-looking staff anxiously awaiting their turns. Even as she was posting costs on logs, tabbing appendices, transferring calls, and shooing away salesmen, she would picture the latest earth tone palette to use in her art that night, alone at home with a half-empty tea cup at her elbow, and a red Irish setter named Gibson asleep at her feet.

Weatherly had mastered a studied nonchalance at work, betraying hardly a smirk or twitch, despite the barrage of litigious fuckery rained down on her desk by Ratzlaff and his team of vultures. Admittedly, this new associate was as yet uncorrupted, but she had seen a dozen stronger personalities undone inside the bleak Ratzlaff abattoir of justice. Kluger and Bunning themselves had been driven into retirement by his duplicity, relieved to transition to 'of counsel' status instead of defending against Ratzlaff's sabotage, as he methodically stole their clients and shrank their pieces of the pie.

Freeman's first drafts of Zuckerman's fee agreement, purchase and sale agreement, and petitions for various approvals had each been classic law school stuff, bookish in tone, sesquipedalian monstrosities punctuated with "hereinafters," "now comes," "wherefores," and "prayers for such other relief as this esteemed Court deems fit." Weatherly converted this amateurish dictation into actual writing, free of a wasted syllable, devoid of obsequy or Latinate filler. She knew that Judge Pinkerton had the attention span of a fruit fly, and that any petition with sentences much longer than a bumper sticker would be doomed. But as she watched the pages of the corrected documents flutter into the printer tray in a cloud of ink vapor, Weatherly's facade was atremble. Sparklewood Forest would be bulldozed for Zuckerman's nursing home?

## CHAPTER 22

**JESTER'S DAILY DANCE BEGAN BEFORE** first light. He stooped as he worked alone, leathery and angular and fuzzy, bent over the maple cutting boards and the wide countertops of The Molecule, his vegetarian restaurant and café in downtown Adelphi. Jester started by separating beans from stones, straining rice from cloudy rinse water, milling and sifting coarse wheat berries and rolling out dough, as flour dusted his beard and the bandana tied around his dreadlocks. Shortly, the ovens ticked and the gas burners hissed, and he was wreathed in aromatic clouds of steam and spice. Jester didn't chop vegetables, he sculpted them, rangiri style, so that his flashing knife exposed the fibrous structure, the architecture of the carrot, the onion, the pepper and ginger root and others. He flicked perfectly sized bits to one side, and the stems and skins to the other, in time to a quiet stream of throbbing dub. Jester peeled ping-pong ball sized bulbs of garlic with the flat side of his cleaver, blam, in one stroke.

Picasso would have admired the designs of the crooked wheaten pizza pies he extracted from his ovens, with zig zag bolts of red and green pepper, splashes of red sauce, browned buttons of mushroom, and a web of melted Cabot cheese speckled with black olive hieroglyphics. After he'd spun the pies, and approved of their charred crusts, he slid them from the wooden peel onto a marble slab dusted with flour. There he cut them savagely with a sort of curved cutlass, according to his own inscrutable Pythagorean lumberjack geometry, each crooked piece shaped differently, and yet congruent somehow, in foldable triangles. His breads had the same dramatic rustic quality, like topographic maps of steaming western lands.

As his customers flowed in and out of The Molecule during the breakfast and lunch rushes, the dishes moved in a circular path, counterclockwise, from the drying rack to the clean stacks to the clanking pots on the stove, to the serving line, to the tables, to the bus station, to the dirty stack beside the soapy sinks. Jester learned to count as one particular chipped bowl made the rounds, to estimate the day's take. During his turns at the sink, he didn't so much wash the dishes, as he baptized them in a right to left operation, as if he was performing a solemn blessing. There was both art and science in this hot water ritual, in which he brandished a bristled brush to gather up a steaming cloud of soap bubbles that he applied with a swooshing movement, starting in the center and swirling out to the brim of each plate and cup and bowl, top and bottom, followed by a rotary rinse at a steep drain angle, top and bottom.

The Molecule became his timepiece, a constellation of people and food and dishes spinning like a solar system. The original Molecule had been in Stinson Beach, but by 1974, San

Francisco had grown too weird for Jester and his partner, Dixie. Too much speed, and too many tweakers made the Bay Area dirty and crowded and dangerous, so they sold their small bakery and traveled east. They found a crumbling stone mill that they could afford, beside a creek in Vermont, where they could live in the loft, and serve food on the ground floor, where the walls were 2 feet thick and the windows looked out on the rocky creek bed full of water talk. Their son had been born back in California, and they named him Banjo. In Vermont, browned by outdoor summer life, Banjo grew feral, and his hair reached his waist.

Eventually, they sold enough rice and beans and bread and pizza to the college kids to build a bar on the second floor, using wood salvaged from a local barn that had been flattened by years of heavy weather, sun and shower, wind and snow. They called their bar The Rumble Seat. A natural division of labor developed. Jester worked at The Molecule from dawn until the lunch rush ended in mid-afternoon, and Dixie took over The Rumble Seat every afternoon, managing the bar, the booze and the bands, bartending and mopping long past midnight. The fact that she disdained booze and regarded it as an ugly but profitable poison made her perfect for the job. Dixie ruled The Rumble Seat the same way Jester degloved cloves of garlic, blam, with blunt gestures.

## CHAPTER 23

**THE DAY THAT NEWS OF** Freeman Dearborn's admission to the local Bar association was published in the Adelphi Gazette, listed with several others in a short item under the fold, Weatherly stuck her head into the library and announced that Freeman had a phone call. On the line was a local lawyer named Leonard Dreyfus who informed Freeman that he would be taking him to lunch as part of his traditional practice of welcoming newly credentialed lawyers to the professional community.

The next day they met at the quiet little restaurant that Dreyfus had selected, in a house behind a picket fence on South Main Street, the kind of place where the wood floors squeaked and potted geraniums lined all the windowsills. A grandmotherly waitress shuffled up and bent over their table as she pulled a pencil from behind her ear. She whispered about the homemade salads of the day, chicken, fruit and spinach, like some hush-hush conspiracy. Mr. Dreyfus wore a bright bowtie and had a fuzzy wreath of electric white hair and a bushy white mustache that made him look like Einstein.

There was an initial exchange of biographical niceties. When Dreyfus asked what he was working on, Freeman explained that a new construction project in Sparklewood Forest was his first real file. Once the food arrived, Mr. Dreyfus cleared his throat. He began by explaining his belief that, as an officer of the Court, every private attorney must clearly understand his role in shaping and serving public policy, which required a vision extending beyond the urgencies of a client's immediate needs. Freeman was unsure what he had gotten himself into, as Mr. Dreyfus's lecture took on a scolding, peremptory tone.

"Now, there's a practical side of the practice of law, so you'll have to learn the business side of it," he continued as the Blessed Mother of Luncheon poured coffee for these important two men in suits. "Your friends will ask for your help. You must charge them. Your enemies, if you have any, will not hire you. So you will learn to charge your friends, if you want to be in business."

Here, Mr. Dreyfus paused to eat a heaping forkful of chicken salad, in an effort to keep pace with Freeman, who had quickly filled his mouth to hide his apprehension. After a slurp of coffee and a ceremonial dab of his napkin, Dreyfus resumed.

"In the old days, when the frontier was growing towards the west, there were no police departments or 911 emergency operators, so people turned to gunfighters to solve their private problems. Now, as a lawyer, you can think of yourself as a sort of modern gunfighter when you are asked to help people by using civil law to solve problems that criminal law and the police can't address. Your private work will have public effects. These must be considered."

As Mr. Dreyfus waved his fork back and forth, and leaned closer to Freeman to emphasize this point, he knocked a red grape clean out of his salad. Freeman pretended to rub his forehead to disguise his attention to the grape's wobbly course, bouncing off the table and rolling across the floor, coming to rest under a cast iron radiator beside the window where the geraniums rested, leaving behind a faint shiny track of horseradish and mayonnaise. Dreyfus continued.

"Now I wish someone had told me what I'm about to tell you back when I was your age, because I'd be retired by now, instead of still on this treadmill." Dreyfus's demeanor suddenly softened here, and his scowl gave way to a more benevolent mien. "Why did you decide to join Ratzlaff?"

Freeman sputtered, confused by this shift of topic and tone. He wiped his mouth with the back of his hand. "He offered me a job right off the bat, and um, their practice seems varied enough for me to find my own niche, and uh, well, my baseball career was clearly over when I tore my ulnar collateral…"

Here Freeman's eyes bugged out, as Dreyfus loaded a forkful that included two grapes wobbling precariously on a small beige pillow of cabbage, studded with bits of carrots and chicken. Once this cargo had been safely delivered, whisked beneath Dreyfus's broom-like mustache, Freeman resumed.

"When I tore my elbow up a second time, I knew that I couldn't bounce back."

Dreyfus was evidently not a baseball fan, and his scowl returned. "I'm talking about Ratzlaff, not your elbow. Why did you pick Ratzlaff?"

At this point, Freeman made a tactical choice to fill his mouth with food, and shrug, waving a white flag of surrender.

Mr. Dreyfus shook his head from side to side, gravely. "He hired my right hand away from me. He nearly ruined me. Is Grace Weatherly doing your typing?"

Freeman nodded, chewing more vigorously than was necessary.

"Well," Dreyfus relented, "you should be able to learn quite a bit from her. I taught her everything. She knows more than most lawyers. Including your boss." He trailed off here, unable to conceal his disdain. "I'm sorry about your arm." After a deep breath, Mr. Dreyfus returned to his coffee.

"Now, imagine that two ranchers, two neighbors way out on the range, both had rustlers stealing their livestock. With no police department to help them, way out on the fruited plains, the grazing lands, they each needed to hire a gunfighter to protect their herd." Mr. Dreyfus put down his fork, and leaned in again for enhanced effect, as he waxed all Mark Twain.

"One gunfighter would need three months, dozens of bullets, and would shoot up half the town before he would solve the problem, at last. But the other gunfighter would take only one day, one bullet. Problem solved." He blew on the tip of his index finger, and paused as he holstered his imaginary Colt. "Who should charge more?"

Freeman was unprepared to be called on, especially with a mouthful of tabbouleh, the cheapest thing on the menu, but it didn't really matter, because Dreyfus' question was rhetorical, and he had no intention of yielding the floor.

"Never charge by the bullet," he inveighed, as he wagged his pistol finger over his plate like a Rabbi of Lunch, like the Wyatt Earp of Trial Practice. "If you have learned to be surgical, if you have learned to be efficient and to go directly to eliminate the root of the client's problem, your service is more valuable than the service provided by the sort of lawyer who wastes time, wastes paper, and fires shots in the dark to look busy and important. Never charge by the bullet. Charge by the job."

Here, Freeman found himself hoping that Mr. Dreyfus might whack another grape across the room, and lighten the atmosphere a little bit, but he was disappointed. Leonard stared at him with the intensity of a man whose zeal about getting paid was hard won. Freeman nodded, and mumbled several forms of "ah." Dreyfus rambled on about the importance of declining to represent dishonest clients, how to fire them once they showed their true colors, and other ethical challenges, but his moment of drama had passed. He then cleaned his plate, as he eyed the half-moon of tabbouleh that Freeman had failed to successfully hide under a generous sprig of parsley and a lemon slice.

Dreyfus reached for the bill, and perched some half-round Ben Franklin reading glasses on his nose to calculate the tip, while Freeman wondered how long it would take for the grape under the radiator to shrivel into a raisin. After shaking Freeman's hand in the parking lot, Dreyfus climbed into a diesel Mercedes, and crunched across the gravel as he wheeled off to solve the next client's problem with a single shot. Remembering her look as she had announced Dreyfus's phone call, Freeman avoided Weatherly's inquisitive gaze when he returned to the office.

SECTION VI


PARAGRAPH 13


"Quiet minds cannot be perplexed or frightened,
but go on in fortune or misfortune at their own
private pace, like a clock during a thunderstorm."
— Robert Louis Stevenson

## CHAPTER 24

**THE NEW NIGHT WATCHMAN AT** Sparklewood Veterinary Hospital was pleased that the dogs seemed to like his music. In the evenings, after all the animals had been fed, and the boxes and pens all cleaned up, Radkin would tune up his guitar. He had run an extension cord up to the loft, so he had a light and a place to plug his amp in. As the tubes in the Deluxe began to glow, Radkin would open up the big shutters where hay bales had once swung in and out of the barn, and he would extemporize a stream of musical inventions. Most cats would stretch and blink and yawn, and a lucky few dogs would tilt their heads, and their ears would twitch and swivel, and choruses of yowling and howling would begin. Behind the line of cages and kennels, lined up on concrete pads covered with sloping tin roofs atop chain link enclosures, a ridge of tall whispering trees would wave in time and conduct his compositions.

The clearing where the barn stood was surrounded by coils of barbed brambles and a drooping woven wire fence that had been flattened by a fallen tree trunk in one spot. A neglected orchard stretched across the lawn beside the hospital, a ragged troop of Giacometti men, with wild wooden arms spread in the knotty asymmetry of apple tree agony. A skinny stripe of black dirt led through a gap in the fence, through a stand of scrub pines, and into an overgrown fire road that disappeared over the top of the ridge. The remote location of the hospital, and the steep bank of the ridge, barricaded by the wire fence, brambles, and deep dark stands of cedars, combined to make this trail inaccessible, except for the occasional insectoid cyclists flashing in and out of the woods. Radkin investigated.

Branching off the fire road, just over the rise, he found another stripe of dirt that led to a series of C- and L-shaped divots in the floor of the forest, like the base paths in a weedy baseball diamond, but winding through pine needles, leaves, branches, limbs, and knee high logs. Overhead spread a green canopy so thick that he couldn't tell how high it reached. The few tilting beams of sunlight that touched down were glowing medullary ropes, stretched through the murk. He lost his sense of direction quickly, as the trail twisted from side to side, and snaked through what must have begun as trails used by the deer, fox, bear and assorted other varmint populations. Radkin turned back  and welcomed the light when he emerged at the fire road.

Some nights, after he had quieted the kennel, Radkin would take a dog on a hike through the woods, once he had learned the way.  At first, he found himself hurrying through the darkness for no good reason. From the faint jingle of tags and leashes, and the pattern of the dog's steady trot, a martial rhythm emerged. But when the dog halted to snuffle a curious smell, and lifted his leg to RSVP, Radkin became aware of the waving canopy above him, the shivering limbs and muttering leaves and hissing needles. Radkin's mind gradually assumed the size and shape and sound and smell of the dark woods. He then resumed his circuit around the lake, but more slowly.

When he was in the mood, he would walk down to the dark water and strip, and slip into the lake and swim out to the middle where she would meet him, if she existed. He would dive down and reach out for her, with a faith as devout as any true believer. No one could deny that if a woman shared this notion and if she floated nearby, or dove down and reached out for him, they would be quicksilver twins, joined perfectly by synchronicity, that infallible matchmaker.

His search had led him down a long and twisty detour at Adelphi, on to the road with the Funnybones, and into the refuge of Culebra, but his resolve had been reinforced by a diaper bag of lucky money, and he was determined to find her, just like he had found the key under that doormat, by sheer immaculate coincidence. Never mind how foolish he appeared to others, if she existed, if she was covalent, she would be there. Radkin drew a deep breath, and dove down, kicking at the moon. When he came back up, he looked up into the thicket of branches that formed a natural roof to the forest cathedral, and felt the familiar tingle of an electric shock. Of course. He would grow his crop in the treetops, close to the sun and hidden from view, above the dense ceiling of pine, spruce and juniper.

He slung a hammock as high in the trees as he could climb, to observe the inhabitants of Sparklewood Forest, their routines and their numbers. As Radkin swayed in the treetops, he drew a map of the woods like the map he remembered from 'The Wind in the Willows,' indicating the veterinarian's hospital, the line of kennels, the barn, and the various trails, fire roads, fences and streams that split the tract, and the lake. On every bright Saturday and Sunday morning, small groups of cyclists could be heard making egg-beater noises, ticking and whirring, rattling over roots, and curling around bermed turns, leaving behind only a line of waffled dirt and the occasional stray water bottle.  The hikers seemed more attentive to the tree canopy, and a few had binoculars, scanning for birds. He decided to grow his crop at the crown of the densest part of the forest.

## CHAPTER 25

**MAXWELL NORTON HAD PLAYED LEFT** tackle in high school, and a scholarship had paid his way through two years of community college in Albany, even though he only played on special teams, blocking and defending on punts, extra points and field goals. He had majored in weightlifting, which is to say, criminal justice. Instead of pursuing a career as a cop, private investigator or prison guard, he interviewed with a federal recruiter on campus, and ended up at Quantico in Basic Training for the DEA. After serving as an agent for three years, he had only succeeded in setting a government car on fire, while bungling a bust of a Hungarian bodybuilder.

Igor Blavatsky's black market steroid business had been exposed by amateur packaging. When a couple of Blavatsky's outgoing shipments broke open in a postal sorting facility and resulted in hazmat incidents, Norton had been assigned to investigate. Like any new agent, Norton was expected to memorize the dossier that provided background for his investigation. He learned that, before coming to America to seek his fortune selling performance-enhancing drugs, Blavatsky had served time in prison in Hungary, in a charming medieval dungeon outside Budapest.

The hulking Igor had been convicted of attempted murder after he botched an attempt to take revenge on his prospective girlfriend, Erz'ebet Lakatos, who had spurned his advances. At trial, Ms. Lakatos testified about her first (and last) date with Mr. Blavatsky. At a fancy restaurant, he had attempted to impress her by twisting two tall pewter candlesticks into a knot, as they were awaiting their entrees. She excused herself to powder her nose and never looked back. Naturally, Igor decided to blow her up with a bomb he hid in the bushes where her dogs liked to pee, but the bomb had fizzled, barely singeing the poodles with just enough smoke for her to notice. Erz'ebet went directly to the police and identified Blavatsky as the obvious suspect. His fingerprints were, as it turned out, clearly visible on the sticky side of the duct tape that he had used to attach a stolen cell phone and fuse to a Bambi soda can filled with a blasting cap and roofing nails. Igor didn't confess exactly, but he had to be subdued by a dozen officers and transported in an armored car, after he snapped their handcuffs and tore the door off their patrol car. Consistent with local practice, the bench trial took two hours and the judge rendered a guilty verdict before lunch, and that afternoon, he sentenced Blavatsky to five years in prison.

Once he got to prison, Blavatsky sought to advertise his weightlifting prowess by commissioning a tattoo (actually eight tattoos) from one of the gang leaders and alpha bullies of the cell block, Josef Doomzac, who was serving life for multiple kidnappings, assassinations, and briefly escaping from prison. (He was also a hip-hop artist and beatmaker.) By having Doomzac tattoo his knuckles with the letters that spelled out "PUMP IRON," Igor hoped to call attention to both his strength and his affiliation with Doomzac and his brutal stooges, and protect himself from attacks during his sentence. Blavatsky initially demanded that the letters should be arranged so that he could read his tattoo himself, but Doomzac insisted that knuckle tattoos were meant to be oriented so that he could menace his rivals by holding up his fists with his thumbs together. Igor relented, but insisted that the words be spelled in English, since he already planned to travel to make a new start in America as a trainer.

After studying the dossier and staking out the suspect, Norton got approval of his plan to hire the perp as his personal trainer, and maneuver until he could make a few controlled buys of the illegal steroids that were suspected. After all, Norton was slightly overweight, according to DEA administrative regulations, so his interest in training was sincere. He assumed the cover name of Watson Tubman, a name he was proud to have picked himself. Norton saw no conflict in identifying "improved erectickle power, weight loss and climbing El Capitan" as his primary objectives when he filled out Blavatsky's new client paperwork, with his tongue and right thumb protruding just as they had since 2nd grade, where he had first adopted his primitive pencil grip.

Blavatsky did not have his own gym yet, he had explained, so they worked out at the local YMCA. Sure enough, after just a month of sessions in the gym, Igor offered to provide Mr. Tubman with something he called "strong injection," pronounced as one four syllable word, a bilabial fricative with a hard 'g.' Blavatsky assured Tubman that this miraculous supplement would speed up his progress, at a cost of $200 per shot, in cash. Agent Norton handed over the marked bills and, as Blavatsky prepared the syringe, Norton tried not to stare at the tattoos on Blavatsky's knuckles. Norton dutifully pulled down his shorts in the empty locker room for the first shot, which hurt like a bitch, but made him feel like an actual undercover agent, taking one in the gluteus maximus for the Agency. Blavatsky was a casual operator, throwing the syringe in the trash where Norton would easily collect it later. Out of curiosity, over the next month Norton took three more shots, even after Blavatsky's fingerprints were confirmed on the first bit of evidence that the lab processed. Norton felt like a new man. This stuff worked.

The Agency had a 98% conviction rate, but at trial things went bad. The jury acquitted defendant Blavatsky of possession with intent to distribute a controlled steroid, after a laboratory technician was forced to admit that the product had actually tested as adrenal gland extract from an orangutan. Blavatsky was still convicted of a lesser offense, conspiracy to engage in cruelty to animals, but the real cruelty was during cross examination when Igor's public defender, Donald Stanky, forced Norton to admit that while on the Blavatsky program he had lost 30 pounds and measurably improved both his overall fitness, his aerobic capacity, his strength, his VO2 max, and his lactate threshold. Stanky took special pleasure in introducing additional evidence establishing that a government-owned and maintained Ford LTD Crown Victoria had been damaged in the course of the investigation, catching fire while Agent Norton and Mr. Blavatsky were driving up the road leading to the top of Mount Chittenden.

Generally, Judge Pinkerton found public defender Stanky repugnant, due to his plaid thrift store wardrobe, his mumbling oration, his casual relationship with rules of procedure, and his utter disregard for military time and military posture. However, in this case Pinkerton exercised his discretion to overrule the government's relevance objection, just so that the courtroom could be entertained by Stanky's introduction of Norton's reluctant testimony that the Agency had determined that the car had caught fire because he had left the emergency brake on as he and Blavatsky had driven up the mountain to find a boulder to climb. With a special delight, Stanky waved around the application in which the undercover agent had listed his aspiration to climb El Capitan.

As this line of questioning proceeded, Norton glared fiercely, and Judge Pinkerton leaned back in his chair with his hand over his mouth so that the jury couldn't see his smirk. Things only got worse as Stanky cross-examined Norton. The jury snickered openly when an exhibit listing Norton's ambition to improve his "erectickle power" was displayed on the big overhead monitor that was visible across the courtroom. When Igor was sentenced to probation and a fine, Norton's regional chief, a former Border Patrol officer named Deputy Edgar Milgram, sat bolt upright and red faced at the counsel table. Blavatsky's misdemeanor conviction became a whispered DEA legend, and Norton became a pariah.

## CHAPTER 26

**WEATHERLY WORKED AT NIGHT IN** her home, drawing and painting in chalk, ink, watercolors, and pencil. Her eyes were grey, and she rarely gazed directly at her subject. Her focus was diffuse, encircling the model and the page where her hand flickered. The process was medicinal, an open-eyed meditation during which the clock ticked, her dog twitched at her feet, and her work gradually assumed the precise shape of the object at hand. This took time.

Her favorite subject was an object that was almost always at hand, a glass tea cup, usually half full. When her drawings were inventoried, a few years later, her curator mapped a virtual Universe of the Glass Tea Cup, its taxonomy and anatomy, complete with studies of glinting gradient light bars inside the curved handle, columns of liquid tea coated in glass, the half-dark half-circle base, a crescent of bubbles, and the silo of the prismatic cup itself, where light rested in curly effulgent shavings.

Weatherly found it unnecessary to accessorize the tea cup tableau with so much as a lamp, window, or bowl of chubby fruit. No sleeping dog, no coaster, no spoon. Admittedly, the edge and corner of the table appeared eventually, details that emerged from the developing tray that was the Weatherly brain pan, filtered through lapidary eyes. Once her meditation was complete, on restless nights she would set her work aside and lead her big red setter, Gibson, out onto the fire road, and they would walk a long loop through Sparklewood, the forest around the gleaming lake.

On one of those summer nights, when she was walking Gibson under a square yellow smudge of moon, a fish or beaver or bird or something slapped the surface of the lake and sprinkled the light way out in the middle. Weatherly paused and stared for a few seconds, waiting for her eyes to compose the dim picture, but she couldn't see what was out there, splashing the moon. Some faint bell chimed in the darkness, perhaps a night bird. Gibson grumbled and tugged her back into the woods.

## CHAPTER 27

**IN HIS SPARE TIME, FREEMAN** composed an essay compiling all his pitching theories, and he submitted it to The Sporting News.  They ran it without a single edit, and paid him $250. This small triumph brought him more joy than the Sparklewood project ever could, but the syllogistic genius of his essay did not attract any lucrative pitching coach offers. He had been secretly hopeful that his analysis would go down in the annals of the game as a primary text.

"ON DECEPTION AND THE STRIKE ZONE

Consider the role of deception in connection with four comprehensive categories of pitched baseballs. Every single pitch either:

1) appears to be a strike as it leaves the hand, but crosses the plate as a ball. This is the most common and essential deceptive pitch, which can be used to induce a swing and miss ('or weak contact) in many counts, but it may not be advisable to a disciplined hitter in a three-ball count.

2) appears to be a ball as it leaves the hand but crosses the plate as a strike. This is the second most common and

essential deceptive pitch, best used to generate a called strike early in the count, or with less than two strikes.

3) appears to be a strike as it leaves the hand and crosses the plate as a strike. This pitch must be thrown in many adverse counts to avoid walks, and may be thrown to contact, or to overpower weak hitters. This is the most dangerous pitch to throw, as it lacks the full power of deception, and it can be avoided by favorable count management.

4) appears to be a ball as it leaves the hand and crosses the plate as a ball. This pitch may be thrown in favorable counts as a set-up pitch, to invite expansion of the strike zone by the umpire, or to tempt an undisciplined batter. It is not deceptive, and should rarely be used.

Combining these guidelines with several ancillary principles of deception will serve the pitcher's goal of maximizing called strikes and swings and misses, and minimizing contact with the barrel of the bat. The deceptive pitcher must learn to:
    a)   vary pitch speeds and locations,
    b)   vary arm slots,
    c)   mix similar pitches with dissimilar delivery and arm slots, and dissimilar pitches with identical delivery and arm slots,
    d)   throw to the edges of the strike zone, both inside, outside, high, and low, while rarely delivering a center-cut pitch,

145

e) reliably begin each count with some form of strike one, the most critical pitch,

f) field his position on every pitch, including covering first base on hits to the right side and backing up throws to third and home,

g) warm up and pitch equally well from both the stretch and the wind-up, and

h) hold runners on base.

Pitch selection (fastball, both 2 & 4 seamer, slider, cutter, curve, change-up, sinker, screwball, etc.) is a function of the original four categories and principles a-e. Variable manipulation of speed and location, as well as variable types of movement, are combined with the crucial deception goals described in categories 1 and 2 - deceiving the batter, when the ball leaves the hand, as to whether the pitch will arrive as a ball or strike. At 60 mph (90 fps+/-) the slowest pitch crosses the plate less than .67 seconds after release. At 90 mph (135 fps +/-) the faster pitch crosses the plate in less than half a second. The batter has a split-second to commit either to swing, or to take the pitch. There can be no tip-off in any aspect of the pitcher's manner of receiving the sign, gripping the ball, handling the glove, or delivering the pitch. The role of the catcher in calling, setting up, and framing each pitch will be the subject of a separate article. Deception is central to the pastoral American game."

Freeman had originally intended to include photographs of suggested grips for use with each type of pitch, along with a diagram of arm slots and divergent paths of the various pitches delivered from the same slots, but he was unhappy with his artwork. He framed the check on his office wall, but no one noticed.

# CHAPTER 28

**FREEMAN DID A DOUBLE TAKE** back at his desk, as he began to edit the Zuckerman dictation, when he found a couple of unfamiliar paragraphs in the draft of Zuckerman's Contingent Purchase and Sale Agreement for the Sparklewood Forest parcel. Like any young lawyer faking his way through his first few years, Freeman was smart enough to know he did not know everything that he did not know, but he was still naive enough to assume that what he didn't know wasn't going to be missed by anyone else. He tried to set aside his resentment of Weatherly's presumptuous edit, and the fact she had not discussed, flagged or italicized the chunk of boilerplate she had added.

He was offended particularly by paragraph 13, as he read it several times. There was clause after clause detailing all the contingent machinery of prophylactic weaseldom necessary to protect the client from Murphy's Law. The list included Acts of God, asbestos, sinkholes, hurricanes, floods, toxic waste, endangered species, nuclear events, famine, plague, along with a catch-all basis for rescission of the contract and refund of Zuckerman's deposit "upon discovery of any other undisclosed hazards or circumstances rendering the property unsuitable for its intended use as a nursing home." He winced at the next subsection too, providing for the award of costs and fees to the prevailing party in the event of litigation of any disputed provision. He raised his pen, and after clicking the ballpoint into its locked and loaded position, he deleted paragraph 13 with a phalanx of emphatic X's. He reasoned that failure to obtain the necessary government approval, as set out in paragraph 12, was the important clause that would protect Dr. Zuckerman.

Just then, Weatherly swept into his office and placed a stack of files on his desk. "I meant to bring these files with the drafts. Sorry. I added a few paragraphs of contingencies we always include. These form files are organized alphabetically in the cabinet behind my desk. We try not to reinvent the wheel every time."

He nodded as she left the room, and then Freeman clicked his pen shut, and paged through a few of the most recent examples of the firm's Purchase and Sale Agreements that he found on top of the first file. The imaginary horribles from paragraph 13 clashed with his natural optimism, but now he began to worry that these contingencies were included in every single form for an important reason.

The problem was that his X's were bright and blue, and he couldn't very well cross out his cross outs without looking indecisive, so he left the edit as is. Once he was done looking it over, he put the draft in his outbox so it would be redone before Zuckerman came in to sign everything in the morning.

After she gathered the edited documents from his box and looked them over back at her desk, Weatherly shook her head. It was her professional duty to disregard this inexperienced edit, so she ignored it, fully aware that Freeman would resent it, if he noticed at all. Paragraph 13 remained.

The next morning Freeman was pressed for time and as he and Weatherly sat down with Zuckerman, he simply assumed that his revisions had been faithfully carried out. Weatherly handed him a series of stacks of fresh documents, one by one, and collected the signed originals. Zuckerman made a big show of initialing and signing the papers with flourishes, with dramatic indifference, and without reading a single sentence. Some clients expected to have every paragraph explained, and experienced lawyers insisted on doing so, but Freeman was green. He tried to act casual as he slid page after page of the various documents across the table to the Doctor, muttering "radon" and "waiver of conflict" and "certificate of whatever" as a formality before he gestured to the pink flags that Weatherly had placed, marking where Zuckerman was supposed to initial, and the blue flags where he was supposed to sign.

The defiant doctor made the same mark at each flag, a triple slash like Zorro, with a fancy Cross pen he pulled from his shirt pocket. The pen had been a gift from Joey "Pocket Meat" Serruto, a made-man in the Baldini family from South Philadelphia. (Zuckerman was tempted to tell the story about how he was given the pen because he had convinced Mrs. Serruto not to divorce her husband after she learned how he got the nickname "Pocket Meat," but he knew better than to spill family secrets in violation of HIPAA, not to mention omertà.)

Weatherly returned from the copy room with Zuckerman's stack of signed copies in a dark blue folder emblazoned with the Ratzlaff, Kluger & Bunning logo, some generic golden lion's head thing, just in time to see Freeman flinch as Zuckerman dramatically pronounced his blind faith in the Ratzlaff machine. "I'm sure that you've reviewed every page under a microscope, at your full hourly rate, am I right, Mr. Dearborn?"

Freeman had no choice but to reprise his virtuous smile. His soul shriveled just a bit as he repeated his new theme. "Leave it to me."

# SECTION VII


## KEY 74


"Don't tell me the moon is shining;
show me the glint of light on broken glass."
— Anton Chekhov

## CHAPTER 29

**IT TOOK A HALF DOZEN** false starts, lasting through mud season, before Radkin figured out how to grow his chosen strain of marijuana – an underexposed sativa he called 'Velvet Manhole' - in the Sparklewood treetops.

A systematic approach to treetop cannabis cultivation had never been perfected, as far as he could find. In Culebra, Green Gene had imported Green God dirt, and firmly believed in five gallon pots, so Radkin began there. He had scouted a spot, not far from the hospital, in the thickest part of the woods, atop a cluster of spruces with dense crowns. He learned to scale their branches like a monkey, flashing up the spiral staircases they formed, to the top of the trees. The benefits of full sun and hidden-above-plain-sight security were complicated by one major problem: irregular rainfall. A half dozen discarded hoses that Radkin lifted from a derelict concrete mixer operation in town were then patched, linked and covered by pine needles and leaves in a shallow trench, running from the last dog wash faucet behind the kennels to a metal drum he buried beneath his new tree farm. He rigged a pulley to hoist green buckets of water to the top of the trees, with green rope.

Radkin started with a dozen seedlings in burlap pots. He mixed rice into the dirt to hold extra moisture. Just above each pot, he rigged one of these high tech watering devices, called Greenwells, which were these absorbent bladders fitted with fancy valves that opened as they dried out, and shrank and closed as they swelled up with rainwater. The first few batches ended up getting thrown down to the forest floor, just dry sticks. But once Radkin gauged the rainfall, learned how to manage the Greenwells, and discovered the magic of crossing an auto flowering strain of cannabis sativa with a strain of the fast growing cannabis ruderalis, he was in business. These plants were sturdy, required less water, and grew and flowered much more quickly in the full sun in the treetops, unmolested by hikers, bugs, deer or rabbits. He remembered his lessons from Green Gene, and gradually grew so adept that his seedlings grew into purple-haired bushes every ten weeks or so, yielding multiple harvests of impressive quantity and quality.

After he had confirmed the quality of his crop and spent enough unobtrusive face time at The Molecule to demonstrate his harmlessness, Radkin decided to make his move. One slow afternoon, covered in dog hair and bearing the amiable grimace of Buddhist gratitude, he quietly asked Jester if he'd be interested in working out an arrangement. Saying nothing as he came out from behind the counter, resettling his bandana and plopping down in a puff of flour, the baker trained his eyes on Radkin like a hungry owl regards a quiver in yonder grassy meadow. And moving grass was indeed the topic. Radkin proposed to discreetly deliver a small but steady and exclusive stream of fresh cannabis sativa buds, a powerful variety of sinsemilla grown locally from royal roots, at a very reasonable wholesale price. Plus, he requested occasional free meals and a position washing dishes, to get him through the winter months.

As he made his pitch, Radkin slid a small matchbox of Velvet Manhole to the center of the table. Jester tilted his head to scrutinize Radkin's sunburn, his red pony tail, his boots and jeans, and his freckled hands, precise as science, brown as wood. After years of baking fragrant breads and preparing spicy food, Jester had the acute sense of smell of a Tibetan yak who could detect the first fresh mushroom of spring sprouting in the next valley. The aromatic terpene genie that rose out of the matchbox made Jester's nose dilate like the nose of the famous cartoon skunk, Pepé Le Pew. Jester smiled with approval as he put the matchbox in his apron pocket. Radkin scratched out some terms on a paper napkin, and Jester read it and nodded, before balling it up and throwing it into a trashcan. They apparently had a deal.

By fall, there was a steady uptick in The Molecule's carry-out business, consisting mostly of Dixie cups of "skunk salad" and brown paper parcels of "nitrogen cookies" and "helium bread," cash only. Tight lids on the cups and heavy gauge plastic wrap inside the parcels confined the dank genie. Most days, Radkin watched from his favorite table at lunchtime, stirring his beans and rice. By the time the days grew shorter and the growing season ended, he had harvested several kilos of resinous Velvet Manhole buds, a blend that became a sort of religious sacrament for certain customers.

Radkin was blessed with a rapid instinctive diagnostic reflex, and he was also cursed by this same reflex. His knack for fashioning ready solutions to the common riddles that bedeviled incurious potato people endeared him to some, and infuriated others. Sometimes, he was wrong. In addition to his musical inventions, his cat and dog whispering, his green thumb and his aptitude for tuning and fixing pianos, he cycled through numerous fevers collecting broken things cheaply, and selling them at reasonable prices after fixing them. He had an aptitude for  TR7's, guitars, amplifiers, bicycles, motorcycles and small devices like fans, toasters, lamps, radios and the like. He relied on Occam's Razor, a bias in favor of the most obvious diagnosis, to his great advantage, but after he had ruled out the first few obvious solutions, he pursued differential diagnoses with a persistence that ignored the principle of diminishing returns, and embraced the sunk cost fallacy. People looked at him funny when he quoted Sir Arthur Conan Doyle about how "when you have eliminated all which is impossible, then whatever remains, however improbable, must be the truth."

It was in this ambitious spirit that he established a new enterprise that he named "The Foundation." For a flat fee, tailored to the task, Radkin would guarantee his ability to find lost items. The pleasure he derived from this form of detective work was incalculable, and he rarely failed. On his first paying job, he charged $250 to locate a missing diamond ring, which he found hooked onto a stem on a tomato plant within 20 minutes. When he found a lost kitten asleep inside a recliner within 7 minutes, he charged $20. The second time, when he found a different kitten inside a different recliner, he charged $30. (Leonard Dreyfus would have applauded his calculus.) Once, he tracked down a nocturnal ghost for $400. This job required him to stake out the supposedly haunted house beginning at midnight. Just over an hour later, Radkin apprehended the punctual ghost, a clock radio that had fallen behind a bookshelf with the alarm set to play the radio at 1:15 am and the channel tuner stuck between AM stations, where electromagnetic interference sounded like lo-fi cries from limbo.  He found dozens of lost sets of keys, mostly in couches, dirty clothes hampers, and jacket pockets.  To his surprise, the more obvious the places he found the lost objects, the less likely the customers were inclined to contest his fees.

As winter descended, Radkin blended into the landscape, tuning pianos, washing dishes at The Molecule, working his side gigs, and planning the purchase of an actual bed to install in the barn loft at the hospital. This turning point, his arrival in a bed of his own, would call for a new attempt at writing the story that he would present to his muse.

## CHAPTER 30

**EDITH ZUCKERMAN'S CHIHUAHUA WAS NAMED** Pancho. He was all eyes and ears and teeth, and almost small enough to fit in a teacup. Before she had been forced to move in with her son, Edith had relied on Pancho to serve as her doorbell, personal trainer, vacuum cleaner, heating pad, and alarm clock. His vocabulary included a yip and a yowl, but his best tool was a snarl that started as a rolling, sub-guttural grumble that suggested a much larger animal, then morphed into the sound of a blender grinding a mixture of ice cubes and light bulbs, and finished with the phase-shifter sound of a cavitating outboard motor. Pancho used these warning skills to great effect on welcome and unwelcome visitors alike. If given the chance, he had a vicious bite. Not long after Edith and Pancho moved in with him, Zuckerman nearly lost a toe when he nudged Pancho with his foot to silence the dog's unruly response to the clank of the mailbox. After some experimentation, Zuckerman discovered that pelting the little bastard with pretzels was a better approach, much safer. From then on, his pockets were full of salty crumbs.

Early one morning, Pancho started snarfling up a chainsaw, making a persistent ruckus at the front window even after Zuckerman fired two pretzel nuggets over his head. By the time Zuckerman cinched up his bathrobe and opened the front door to investigate, his garbage can was rolling in the middle of the street, rocking back and forth on a dented spot, perfectly empty. Zuckerman thought it was strange that he hadn't heard the screaming diesel of the garbage truck. Sure enough, all his neighbors' trash cans were still full and more or less in line, up and down the block. Zuckerman retrieved his can, as he pondered this strange event. A little later, Pancho launched another fusillade at the window, when the garbage truck roared around the corner and screeched its brakes at the first cluster of full cans.

## CHAPTER 31

**WEATHERLY LIKED TO READ AT** The Molecule during her lunch hour. She ate colorful legumes, and minded her own business while reading biographies of dead artists. She was practiced, like many women, in the use of body language, mainly the denial of eye contact, as a sort of martial art force field to manage men and protect her virtue and peace. She had mastered quiet control of all her visual moves, her full gaze and her passing glance, and all the levels between, including her sparkle, her 100-yard stare, her scan, her laser cannon, her coming-up-for-air refocus, etc. Inquisitive men were at her mercy, in general, in a small town like Adelphi. Yet, despite her considerable talents, a situation developed.

A new customer, a scraggly red-haired hermit, had gradually become a regular at a table in the corner. Coffee and a steaming bowl of rice and beans were supplied to him without the formality of any audible order or payment, a circumstance which was barely remarkable in itself. What qualified this as a genuine situation was a form of sophisticated seduction to which Weatherly had never been subjected, and from which she had therefore never learned to protect herself. His tactics were infuriating. He ignored her. He ignored her furtive gaze, he ignored her tactic of ignoring him, and he was mistake free in managing his own gaze, which he trained on a notebook in which he slowly inscribed printed words with what appeared to be a small black lacquered fountain pen.

Over the centuries, predatory men propagated the species by learning to stalk their fecund prey. Angular women, hourglass women, endless women, wounded women, pale freckled women, Delta women, Saharan women, women with bee stung lips, long legged women, sturdy women, women with Wedgewood eyes, women with French braids and Cleopatra eyelashes, nurses, women with tattoos peeking out, black Marias with handbags, ladies with umbrellas, with hats, with books and reading glasses, in suits and tutus, serapes and sundresses, in robes and habits, all the women were measured by these men, the frat boys, handsy pastors, salesmen wearing big watches, red-faced drunks, lonely husbands, farmers in straw hats, cops, the fossilized remains of once bold towel-snapping high school linebackers and center fielders, creepy clerks, doctors with stethoscopes, Casanovas and Romeos, soldiers in camo, businessmen in suits, and well-coiffed dandies. Most men were full frontal hunters, direct and conspicuous with their eyes and their patter and lines and jokes. This guy was different. It was not only his strategy in ignoring her that disarmed her. Weatherly was also undone by his table manners.

Grace Weatherly had never seen a human mouth and a spoon fitted just so, in the graceful intercourse, with rhythm and pleasure, displayed by this man's epicurean stylings. His spoon flickered from beans to rice, then proceeded to the edge of the splash of salsa and pepper, plus a mere touch in a half-moon of Tabasco, followed by a gentle tap at the edge of the bowl to settle the contents in the center of the spoon. What intrigued her, despite her studied immunity, was the manner in which this tender steaming freight, this precise spoonful, was then conveyed to his parted lips and savored with stern but deliberative pleasure. There was no conspicuous indulgence or self-conscious display of superior discernment, as he removed the spoon. There was no slurping, and his cheeks never bulged with a hint of gluttony. He stood apart from the legion of American men who had been ruined by fast food and the barbaric urgency of the shrinking lunch hour.

Between the time she lifted her head from her pillow in the morning and the time she returned to sleep at night, Weatherly carried herself like a scythe, moving through every tangle, every knotty scrimmage, with a sharp whoosh. Her manner of dressing, of eating, of driving to work and discharging her duties, all had become samurai choreography without a wasted gesture. Of course, when she considered her palette, inhaled her vaporous tea, or tickled her dog to sleep, she was fully capable of dallying, dithering, and digressing. But even as a master of the efficient mechanical machinery of housekeeping, of clerical logistics, of any workaday errand, Weatherly was enthralled by this spectacle, this hobo laureate, managing his rice and beans. Weatherly found herself reading the same sentence over and over as she struggled to resist this spectacular stranger. Her eyes turned to slits, and he ignored her.

It had  become unnecessary for Radkin to order, or even to speak, on the mornings he went to The Molecule to write. His coffee greeted him, and the woodgrain topographic map on the maple tabletop in the corner, by the window, would swallow him and his notebook for an hour, give or take. As his pen heated up, a gelid black stripe of ink would lead him further and further into the rag paper wilderness. Like the cloud of flour that surrounded Jester as he moved through the kitchen, Radkin's visions would orbit his distracted globe like translucent moons.

Weatherly had no way of knowing how Radkin cloaked himself, every day, in pages of calibrated cuneiform scribble, a weave of breath and melody, the rise and fall of dactyls, iambs, and spondees, studded with occasional surprises, a left turn, a Chinese adverb, a golden cat's eye noun set upon a black velvet clause. Radkin had never permitted anyone to read his work although, back in school, Professor Rice had required everyone to read an original piece at the outset of the course, and again at the end. Even if his dream girl never turned a single page of his story, his loneliness was cushioned by the prospect of an imagined reader whose breath would obey each comma and whose pitch perfect ear would true every syllable. As caffeine bubbled up in his percolator mind, with hints of chocolate and smoke, black ink would crawl across the page and Radkin would vent the accumulated steam from his brainpan until the dregs in his cup went cold, and the spell would end. On the synchronized days when the cover clanked on Jester's iron pot and Radkin's book slapped shut in perfect tandem, their glances sparkled.

At the end of his daily writing session, Radkin would lay down his pen and re-read whatever passage had alighted on the page. He would inevitably itch to edit, to make the words gallop, to scratch out a superfluity, or add a glinting detail that would fine-tune the image, like Chekhov's broken bottle glinting in the moonlight. Even when he closed the notebook without making a single edit, he reconsidered every line on his next visit to the page, and he often ruminated as to whether his chief loyalty was to the actual vision, or to the process of squinting ever more closely.  No one would read his story until it was done, and in a moment there was second-guessery that another moment would expose as overwrought. On Sundays, he would say a repentant prayer to T.S. Eliot, and crumple up every page that failed to ring true.

Radkin grew skilled at overlooking the pathetic futility of his undertaking, since there had not yet appeared any languid muse to bring him tea and fan him with ostrich feathers, nor had he identified a prospective lover who would read his book and swoon at his triangulated architectural penmanship, in which the capital 'Y' was a tiny radiant yogi with arms outstretched in the Sun Salutation, and the '4' was a sailboat bending across the bay, and the lowercase 'a' was a whistling sparrow on a clothesline. He had the same problem with his music. He played best for the dogs.

## CHAPTER 32

**ZUCKERMAN DID NOT KNOW WHY** his mother had stopped responding to his nightly piano recitals. Even when he played what he thought were his best bits, like his Guaraldi and Evans impressions, she had begun turning away and motioning to her bed. When he came home one afternoon to find the fallboard closed over the keyboard, he decided to find a new teacher or buy a synthesizer or something. Thumbing through the classifieds in the back of the Sparklewood Gazette, Dr. Zuckerman tore out an interesting ad.

> PIANO TUNER AND "tone regulator," specializes in tuning and adjusting the finest pianos, all makes and sizes, reasonable rates, money-back guarantee. Also, lessons for select students. Ask for Walter at Sparklewood Veterinary Hospital.

Radkin agreed to take a look and showed up right on time. He was not interested in any small talk, even after he had snapped his fingers and tossed a morsel of bacon to quiet the tiny dog that had been throwing himself against the front door. Radkin proceeded by removing a full bottle of cold mineral water from his coat pocket, and tapping it sharply with his wrench. Instead of a tuning fork or pitch pipe, he preferred to rely on the surprisingly precise bell-like tone of the glass vessel. Radkin had determined that a 12-ounce bottle of Topo Chico served as a sort of accidental reagent, and would sound a near-perfect 440 Hz A note, when full and chilled. Given a chance, Radkin could rattle on about the Railsback Curve, the cult of 432 hertz, the Schumann Resonance, and the Nazi conspiracy that had interfered with global chakra harmony, but he avoided these topics with new clients. Each calibrated swallow of water raised the harmonic of the tapped bottle, and Radkin worked quickly from the 49th key, the A4, down to the F3 and F4, keys 33 and 45, and then up to key 64, the high C, tapping the bottle, tuning a string, matching fifths, cross checking octaves, and tilting his head sideways as the notes decayed, like the Victor Gramophone dog. Every adjustment was performed by raising the string up to pitch, never down. The first half hour was ugly.

Zuckerman had excused himself, and sat working at his desk in the other room, shaking his considerable head at the clinking sounds and the sickening microtones. His mother remained seated in her recliner beside the piano, where she rocked and twitched, making tiny bird noises as the pitches wavered, and then began to ring true, one by one. After an hour or so, when he had the instrument in provisional tune, Radkin began voicing the hammerheads by stabbing certain felt heads with a needle tool, and by heating and bending the hammer shanks to tighten the attack on a few keys. Eventually, he slipped paper punches under the same keys (one punch under the low G, two punches under an F, and one each under a C# and D#) and adjusted the weights on each key until they measured 51 grams at the bass end and 47 grams at the treble end.

The tone regulation process proceeded gravely until an unpleasant Bb presented a riddle, to the obvious concern of Mrs. Zuckerman, whose rocking abruptly ceased. There was no mistaking the problem with the metallic, plinky tone of key 74, Bb6. As Radkin made fruitless adjustments and played this offending note over and over, Ethel furrowed her brow, beaming her disapproval at Radkin's backside. He was oblivious to her scrutiny and worked with absolute diagnostic concentration, using a tiny flashlight as he leaned inside the piano, closely inspecting the hammer action, scowling at the pin block, and pressing on the bridges. After plucking the string by hand, and then striking it with the handle of his wrench one last time, Radkin cocked his head and murmured as he slid beneath the Steinway with his flashlight in hand, like a mechanic submerging beneath a limousine. When he emerged to strike key 74 and sound a beautiful Bb, Mrs. Zuckerman resumed her rocking with vigor. Radkin turned, in a glimmer of temporary triumph, to show her the stray stainless steel pan head screw he had found rattling on top of the soundboard.

Once this Bb had resumed its natural stance, Radkin closed his eyes and felt his way into an unrecognizably primitive "Giant Steps," rubato, testing the overtones. He paused to fine tune a few flat strings and soften a few strident hammerheads, then drained the last swallow of his water before resuming his etude, which worked into a passage of pounding block chords, intended to flush out any more slack strings that might go flat.  Radkin played "Giant Steps" again, achingly slow now, so slow that each halo of harmonics had time to bloom and die in sequence, and every pleasant interval could mesh, at last.

When Radkin looked up from his final recheck, fully satisfied with the piano, he smiled at Mrs. Zuckerman, who was patting her grey hands together like two mockingbirds fighting. Zuckerman had come to stand in the doorway to witness this development, which is to say, his beaming mother. Radkin counted the cash, $300, and gathered his tools to leave. But first, he stood off to the side respectfully as Zuckerman settled himself on the bench and played a short version of his finest original composition, a diatonic ballad in F he had named "Felonius Monk." The mockingbirds celebrated his performance like old times. The little dog sat at Radkin's feet in total submission, an acolyte of bacon. Pleased beyond words, Dr. Zuckerman made arrangements for some lessons with his new piano tuner.

## CHAPTER 33

**THE CASE MANAGEMENT CONFERENCE** began with Judge Pinkerton grimacing at this young new lawyer from the Ratzlaff firm, and his Mafioso client. The Judge put Freeman through his paces, just as he welcomed every other uninitiated lawyer into his creaky courtroom, confirming his local rules,  his ritual approach to marking exhibits, using the lectern, observing strict adherence to the timing of sessions and  lunch breaks, observing the standards for a variance and wetlands certification, the applicability of historical district criteria, and the rigorous procedures associated with the public comment stage of the preliminary hearing. Beasley, the red-faced town counsel, never even looked up from doodling on his yellow pad, having grown catatonic over decades representing the little town of Sparklewood in every sort of dispute. He was pop-eyed, a feature that was magnified by his thick glasses, and a black bush protruded from each of his nostrils. In contrast, Freeman eagerly nodded in assent, took notes obediently, and signaled his readiness by citing his familiarity with <u>Foster v. Town of Sparklewood</u>, the seminal case with a nearly identical fact pattern, in which a condominium complex (dressed up in frilly colonial trim and surrounded by extensive retention ponds and marshland remediation) had been approved by Judge Pinkerton, and affirmed on appeal.  Beasley yawned and put the final touches on a primitive still life of the pitcher of water and stack of paper cups on the clerk's desk.

It wasn't until Freeman and Zuckerman made their way into the hall afterwards that Freeman understood the Judge's increasingly pained expression as he had concluded the hearing. It seemed that Ratzlaff had asked an old friend to monitor Freeman's performance in court. Out in the hall, Richard Burgess, a local lawyer specializing in riparian rights, with a face creased by many years of litigation, offered his hand to Freeman. Burgess then pulled Freeman aside as he whispered, sidebar style, with his hand over his mouth so Zuckerman couldn't hear him.

"Burgess, Ratzlaff's old fraternity brother. Look, good work finding the <u>Foster</u> case, but two things. Always hand the Judge and opposing counsel clean copies when you cite a case, even if they handled the case. And for fuck's sake, get yourself a pen that you can't click open and closed 75 times per minute." Freeman's face burned as he thanked him and guided his client away to the elevator.

SECTION VIII


OVERDRESSED VISITORS


"Kenneth, what is the frequency?"
— Dan Rather's assailant, William Tager

# CHAPTER 34

**NORTON'S NEW ASSIGNMENT WAS TO** stem the tide of powerful cannabis that was now an open secret in Adelphi. His supervisor spoke to him bluntly, offering this case as Norton's best chance for redemption after the Blavatsky debacle. Milgram explained that resolving the task should be quite simple, based on basic detective work. A radiometric image collected by routine hyperspectral drone surveillance had revealed a faint red blob that indicated a patch of cannabis growing on private property in Sparklewood Forest. The prospective owner of the property was from out of town, a guy rumored to have mob connections. By staking out the operation, and pinning the tail on the bad guy with direct proof, Norton could salvage his career.

On his initial casual reconnaissance outing, Norton only found grim, slim cyclists rattling along twisty trails through the woods. There was an orange sign and a surveyor's stake beside the trailhead, advertising an upcoming hearing on the petition that the Ratzlaff law firm had filed to permit the construction of Zuckerman's nursing home. Norton had expected something obvious, some farmer tending a garden full of pot plants mingling with tomato plants or rosemary bushes, but he saw no such crop, nothing suspicious.

At Quantico, Norton had received mandatory classroom training concerning the criminal drug culture, which covered the best legal means of surveilling suspected sites, identifying various drugs, investigating users and dealers, and the prescribed approaches to infiltrating and disrupting their distribution networks by recruiting informants, and collecting and processing admissible material evidence. Their instructor had passed samples of the pot around the room in baggies and jars, along with the most popular pills, powders, and paraphernalia. At the outset, Norton had taken extensive notes using fancy Roman numerals and all. But as the weeks of training droned on, he was gradually overwhelmed, and glazed over. He ended up doodling under his arm, so the other agents-in-training around him couldn't see what he was doing, and so they wouldn't be able to see how he gripped the pen like Fred Flintstone, with a jutting thumb.

Because this assignment in Sparklewood Forest was his remedial test case, Norton decided to dig out his outline from the advanced course called "Field Investigation Techniques and Tactics - Domestic Edition," to see if, in a fleeting moment of insight, he had recorded anything useful. Among the tiny drawings of tiny guns spurting tiny bullets, smokestack-studded skylines, and Dick Tracy portraits, Norton found what he hoped for. Under the heading "Building Blocks and Buried Bones," he found a drawing of a garbage can, with little clouds of W's signifying flies, and these words scribbled beneath:

> Garbage cans – Greenwood  SCOTUS  "no expectation of privacy"

White collar - follow the money

Dope - follow the hippies

Norton's lips moved as he read and re-read this revelation. Garbage cans and hippies would save his career, and he would stare at Judge Pinkerton in triumph and fury, as the jury's guilty verdict was announced by the clerk.

But as Norton pawed through a rancid heap of Zuckerman's trash spread out on sheets of newspaper on his kitchen table, he was no longer so sure of his approach. He frowned at a tangle of catheters, tubes, and empty IV bags, wondering if pot was now taken that way. There were pill bottles with words he didn't recognize, and empty boxes with pictures of flowers and fish. He set this stuff aside from the obviously innocent stuff, like sodden tea bags, fouled diapers, junk mail, empty cans of Campbell's tomato soup, and small knotted plastic bags of dog shit. He rooted through an assortment of rotten foodstuffs like stalks of broccoli, eggshells, wilted lettuce, avocado skins and seeds, Cheetos crumbs, and mysterious compost-in-progress. As he sorted through the bottom of the biggest trash bag, he found a half dozen crumpled bags of Digby's Honey Mustard Pretzel Pieces, which had once been "bursting with Old Tyme Pennsylvania Dutch flavor." As he noted the number of bags, and balled them up to save space, he felt something powdery in each bag. Was this evidence? Agent Norton emptied the bags into a pile on a fresh sheet of paper.

Close forensic examination revealed that each bag contained bits of crushed pretzel pieces and a fine powdery amalgam of pretzel dust, salt and honey mustard spices. When Norton leaned down to scrutinize this pile, sufficient to fill a small coffee cup, he grew curious, but in an off-duty sort of way. There were many half pieces, and they had been kept perfectly crisp and dry inside the bags, untainted by the slop that he had set aside. Boldly, he sniffed the pile and detected irresistible Old Tyme flavor. Tentatively, Agent Norton placed the largest fragment of pretzel nugget in his mouth. It was good.

Of course, Norton had no way to guess that Zuckerman had deemed these half pieces insufficiently aerodynamic to discourage Pancho from yapping at every noise outside the front door, relying instead on the bigger, intact, acorn-sized nuggets that flew straight and packed a meaningful Chihuahua-sized punch. Norton had heard of pothead "munchies" and he considered the possibility that this pretzel stash was circumstantial evidence, even if it was not directly incriminating. Without appreciation of any irony, he ate the big clues and left some strategic dust in a few bags to conceal his unofficial research.

DEA operating procedures called for each field agent to maintain a contemporaneous written inventory of all evidence collected during an investigation. To ensure a proper chain of custody, Norton was required to wear latex gloves, to photograph every item of evidentiary value, and to store it all in such containers (baggies, boxes, Tupperware bins, manila envelopes, etc.) as suited the evidence. He was fresh out of latex gloves when he processed the Zuckerman evidence, so he wore plastic Wonder Bread bags, with rubber bands around his wrists. Each container was to be labeled with black

Sharpie, numbered sequentially and listed along with the case number and date, the identity of the collector, the source of the evidence, and a physical description entered in a computerized database. When evidence was deemed susceptible to decay or deterioration, it was to be kept airtight and refrigerated. If his superiors learned he had collected evidence and failed to inventory and preserve it, he would be in trouble.

Norton suddenly realized that if he followed the rules literally, his refrigerator would be packed with bags of garbage, the disposal of which was prohibited without advance approval by his regional supervisor. Asking for permission to throw out dozens of freezer bags of trash was out of the question under the tenuous circumstances of his employment. Norton pictured himself forced to eat from cans, unable to even open his refrigerator. He considered Campbell's tomato soup a very satisfying snack, and he knew that Spaghettios also made a fine meal, but he sighed when he thought of his nice clean refrigerator, stocked with cartons of milk, Wonder Bread, hunks of cheese, and containers of bacon and eggs. He made a mental note to check the butter compartment to see how much of the adrenal gland extract from the Blavatsky case was still left in the half pint mason jar.

As he examined the rest of the garbage, Norton found himself unable to distinguish conclusively between several suspicious substances. He poked and sniffed at several different clumps, a few composed of dry brown stems, and a few composed of wet green leaves. His training suggested these plants could be marijuana, but he wasn't sure. Either that or basil, parsley or tea, like the loads of loose tea his mother used to brew, or maybe just rank celery trimmings, or oregano. One clump looked like the stems left over from bunches of grapes, he really couldn't tell. Or possibly the tufts of the same kind of green soapy-tasting stuff that he pushed to the side of his plate at Taco-Rita, whatever it was called.

Agent Norton considered taking a proper field trip to the local supermarket to examine various leafy spices and vegetables, but, of course, the herbs in the store were uniformly crumbled and colored, and sealed for freshness in little jars with plastic caps and seals, so he could only guess at their aroma. As he bent over his kitchen table, he concluded that one particular clump was so unusual and irregular, compared to regular garbage, that he suspected it might be illegal contraband.

As he used a folded piece of paper to push this pile of evidence towards the edge of the table to transfer it into a baggie, he noticed a red circle on the paper. Someone had circled an ad by a piano tuner named Walter, who worked at Sparklewood Veterinary Hospital, which just happened to be located in the shadow of the marijuana operation. Norton decided this was a bonafide clue, and he calculated that if he saved just a few baggies of garbage, he could put the newspaper clipping in a manila envelope and label it Exhibit #1. Remembering his notes, and suddenly swollen with the unexpected success of his garbage-picking strategy, Norton made plans to infiltrate the local hippies, after he assessed this piano tuner fellow. He found a few more pretzel nuggets that were big enough to eat.

## CHAPTER 35

**AT THE MOLECULE THERE WAS** a circle of big soft chairs inside the front window, and the same group of old men would claim these thrones every morning to nurse their coffees for hours, as sun and shadows crept across the floor. Because they were mostly deaf and set in their ways, most of their discussions were repeated from day to day, too loudly and with slight revisions. There were tales of glory days, sports news, groans about stock market dips, old grievances about ex-wives, details of their latest aches and related medical treatment, and half remembered scenes from old movies. Once a week or so, one of them would sing a snatch of an old song, and their eyes would all briefly twinkle.

But Jester had heard it all before, and he had grown weary of the way this group was always monopolizing his best seats all morning. Although these men were mostly harmless and genial, many of his other customers had gradually been rubbed the wrong way by the nonsense they would occasionally bellow. Jester particularly disapproved when one of them would leer and stage-whisper lascivious commentary on the shapely college girls who would come and go. Jester decided to shuffle their deck one day, by leaving a scientific plate of Manhole-infused cookies for them, in what he considered a benevolent experiment. He hoped that low doses of this fine medicine would enliven these grumps, and brighten up the place, or maybe even just send them home in mild confusion to take a nap, so others could enjoy the prime window seats. Instead, after about an hour of gradually mounting hilarity, the men lapsed into episodes of laughing which left them so breathless that their shoulders shook and they coughed and rocked and gasped for air. After tiring themselves out in this manner, they grew quiet and quieter and more thoughtful. One by one, some chins tipped forward and some heads tipped back, and their eyes grew lidded, slitty, and finally closed. The cafe was then filled with loud snoring, like a chorus of leaf blowers being pull-started on a cold day, with the inhales generating rheumy kah-kah-kahs and the exhales producing phlegmatic wheezes. General Cleveland, the leader of the group and once a wartime bomber pilot of great distinction, had fallen asleep ramrod straight in his chair, with a silver filament of drool staining his golf shirt. Jester just stared at this obvious waste of quality product. This development would be bad for business, so he asked his dishwasher to roust them and call their wives.

## CHAPTER 36

**WHEN RADKIN SWAYED IN THE** high treetops, he could hear bike riders from far away, the faint whirring sounds punctuated by rattles of chainslap, as they would bunny hop the logs and big roots. Inside the crown of the spruce canopy, he reclined in a nest of hammocks and camo tarps. There was a trailhead less than a hundred yards away, where he could sometimes hear the riders stop to drink and catch their breath, or wait for stragglers to catch up. Sometimes he'd smell the unmistakable Manhole bouquet and hear coughing, and then Radkin would settle back into his rocking cradle and smile. These were his people. But he knew these sweet days were about to end, when some new visitors appeared on foot one day, in silence. They were overdressed.

Ratzlaff had suggested that Dearborn should visit the proposed site with Zuckerman, to check its suitability. It didn't go well. There was a stream that presented a problem because wetlands were protected from development. When Zuckerman asked, "Why can't this be our little secret?" Freeman felt the crackle of looming hellfire. He remembered, with some irony, Zuckerman's comment on his smile and his virtue. New lawyers were often plagued by these troubling twinges of ethical conscience, he guessed. He thought of Mr. Dreyfus, but only briefly. There was no creek or brook or spring marked on the site survey he unrolled, but here was an unmistakable brook, or at least a spring or rivulet bubbling out from under a log on one side of the trail and disappearing under a bank of pine needles at the other edge. Considering this inconvenient trickle, maybe just standing water, Freeman began to rationalize. His reply was intended to sound matter-of-fact, but echoed strangely in his own ears. "Leave it to me."

Neither man noticed the tiny flash in the trees, as Radkin trained his army surplus binoculars on them. Radkin watched as these men gestured back and forth, taking turns shrugging with outstretched arms, and pointing to the ground, and then pointing to a big sheet of light blue paper. After a while they left, and Radkin descended, eager to get a look at whatever they had been talking about. To his relief, he concluded that there was no major problem, just a leak where a thirsty critter had bitten through his hose again. He could fix that right away. Then a fluorescent bit of orange tape flapping from a steel rod in the brush stopped him in his tracks.

## CHAPTER 37

**THE ONLY TIMES FREEMAN HAD** actually been invited inside Ratzlaff's office were when he was hired and when he was assigned to the Sparklewood project. This time, the invitation was ominous, and when Ratzlaff closed the door with a bang like a gavel, Freeman's collar got warm and tight.

"I wanted to speak with you before your meeting with the Doctor today. I understand we have an issue with the Zuckerman property." Ratzlaff began, pronouncing the word like an Englishman, "iss-you," and wringing his tiny hands. His big chair swallowed him up as he settled back and reclined. "How will it be addressed?"

Freeman assured Ratzlaff that he had already called Burgess, that Zuckerman was unaware of the gravity of the problem, that no wetlands were identified on the survey, and that he was in the process of arranging an inspection by a wetlands mitigation expert who was known for "getting things done." Burgess had recommended this guy, called him a real asset.

Ratzlaff spread his hands, and turned up his palms. "Actually, the Doctor understands better than you think. He called me after you visited the site, in a bit of a panic." He paused here to glare at Freeman, and watch his reaction. "Burgess called me too. He has some ideas if we need to, um, divert this surface drainage. Be sure to keep your time on the wetlands angle, I expect it will take an extra couple dozen hours to, ah, research and arrange things with the expert so this 'iss-you' is not an obstacle." His grin was a rictus.

Freeman smiled with the exact same smile that Zuckerman had once found virtuous. He wondered if his virtue would prevent him from making Zuckerman pay for going over his head to Ratzlaff.

The stream could be the end of the project, and now he knew for certain that Zuckerman would not understand at all. Weatherly lived near Sparklewood Forest, and Freeman knew she rode her bike and took her dog out there, so he decided to ask her a few quiet questions one day when Ratzlaff was at a "conference," rocking his sailboat with a  half-beautiful divorce client who was quite lonely. No, Weatherly reported, after he showed her the spot on the map, she couldn't recall ever having seen any water in that location, even when the spring rains came, but she agreed to take a look on Saturday. For the first time, Freeman noticed a wrinkle in the shape of an asterisk between her eyebrows, a small crack in her neutral façade, as she frowned at the map.

# CHAPTER 38

**MOST SATURDAYS, AS WEATHERLY RODE** her bike through the trails in Sparklewood Forest, she leaned and curved through the turns behind her big running dog and her worries disappeared. Her single-track mind was pointy, clear and quiet. As she followed Gibson onto the stripe of dirt that twisted and turned through the woods, winding over leaf litter, pine needles, logs, streambeds and tree roots, she merged completely into her line. But the prospect of construction and Freeman's request that she check for this spring had given her a strange feeling, and she got off her bike, wandering in circles where the spring, or whatever, was supposed to be located. There was nothing. Meanwhile, Gibson wandered off into the brush, rooting out some smelly morsel. He had run this trail with her almost every weekend for years, and he had never alerted on this spot before, but she found no stream or spring, not even a mud puddle.

They resumed their full routine, circling the lake counter-clockwise, and by the time they got back to the truck, Gibson's tongue was wagging a little more than usual. When Weatherly unloaded her bike at home, she noticed that Gibson was unsteady, scrabbling to jump out of the truck and belly flopping onto the kitchen floor, then rhythmically splashing the contents of his water dish all over. When Gibson rolled onto his side in the middle of the kitchen, panting, and his eyes rolled back and his tongue spilled out, Weatherly immediately loaded him back into the truck and drove directly to the vet, wondering if dogs had heart attacks. She barged into the waiting room with her arms full of limp dog, and there was the redheaded stranger who had been tantalizing her at The Molecule.

Weatherly swallowed down her heart as a warm flush spread across her cheeks. She asked if the vet was available, but he ignored her and lifted Gibson from her arms. He laid him down gently and kneeled over him, murmuring into his ear, and combing his rusty coat with the same sure hands that had carried the spoon that had launched all those ships surging in her bloodstream. He shined a light into Gibson's dreaming eyes and felt between his damp toes, and then murmured in his ear again as he pressed a stethoscope to his belly and throat. Gibson's tongue was now spooled out on the floor like a pink fish out of water. The stranger examined the dog's chest, legs and face, closely, and looked up.

"Has he eaten anything strange in the last hour or two?"

After telling him how Gibson had rooted around in the brush at Sparklewood, and how he had emptied his water dish, Weatherly renewed her question about the vet, which he ignored again, scrunching his eyes and calculating. He turned his gaze onto her in a different way now, and spoke with a more deliberate solicitude.

"He's not in the office this late on Saturday afternoons, but I can get him on the phone. Give me a few minutes. How long ago were you in Sparklewood Forest?"
She strained to hear the murmur of his voice through the wall. By the time he came back to the exam room, Gibson's breathing was slower, almost normal, and his tongue was partly reeled in.


"Doctor Bauch says to give him some time and all the water he wants, he might have eaten a toadstool or something, but if he's not throwing it up, it'll probably pass. I find no sign of snake bite, his pulse is within the high range of normal. There is no heart murmur or flutter, no arrhythmia. We can watch him overnight, if you'd like."

Weatherly found that if she looked at his whole face with the same sort of diffuse vision that helped her "see" teacups and the line she followed down the trails at Sparklewood, she could act naturally. Radkin wrote 'Walter' and his phone number in black fountain pen on the back of the vet's business card, and asked her to call him directly if there were any problems. He said there was no charge, and offered to help her carry the dog back to her truck, but she declined and gathered Gibson up by herself, while strange feelings clattered in her mind. Walter? At home, after she settled Gibson on his bed, she looked more closely at the card, and noticed how the letters and digits that he had written were symmetrical, precise and angular pictograms, like a string of Hammurabi code. Toadstool?

## CHAPTER 39

**NORTON FLASHED HIS BADGE AT** the receptionist at Ratzlaff, Kluger & Bunning, and asked to see the lawyer involved with the nursing home project in Sparklewood Forest. When April reached out to take his wallet, Norton pulled it away and struggled to stuff it back into the inside pocket of his suit jacket, which was a bit too tight now that his training days with Blavatsky were over.

"Whatsit about?" she inquired.

April wore a golden curlicue thing on her left middle finger, maybe a snake, which served to call attention to the absence of a wedding ring on her ring finger. Norton told himself that this sort of observation was proof of his investigatory skill, not creepy at all. Accordingly, he felt fully professional as he noticed she was rather well put together.

"Can you just let them know that Agent Norton wants to see them about their work in Sparklewood, please?"

"'Course," she replied, "but what sorta agent? Insurance?" She was expected to screen salesmen, and she wanted to be sure this guy wouldn't try to sell them life insurance or a copier or phone system. The last girl had been fired after she let some guy fake his way into a conference with Ratzlaff, when he turned out to be a tailor with a briefcase full of tape measures and catalogs and fabric swatches and buttons. Norton had been comfortable dealing with the sub-literate Blavatsky, but lawyers and their staff always made him nervous, with all their funny words and procedures and stuff. April's designer glasses made her eyes look like Wedgewood kaleidoscopes in full hypnotic flower, as she stared at him and awaited an answer.  Norton made a mental note that she chewed tiny gum, with perfect teeth except for one or two, and her eyes might have been crossed, but the glasses made it hard to tell. Norton hissed to start, and spit to finish.

"Just say Federal Agent Norton, DEA, needs to speak to them for a few minutes."

"Why dintcha say District Attorney in the first place?"  April picked up the phone, and pushed a button and whispered something.

Norton just sighed, and let it go, as she gestured to the loveseat and chairs in the waiting area where a gallery of gold framed plaques and certificates showed what big shots the lawyers were. He did not sit, but remained standing at the corner of her desk, in the hope that his impatience would confer an impression of pressing urgency and ominous power. April snapped her gum as she crossed and uncrossed her flowers, and then she got up and sashayed down the hallway on tapping heels, swaying back and forth with an audible zip-zip-zip of nylon friction.

A few minutes later, Freeman swept into the reception area and smiled with what he hoped was obvious virtue. He gestured to the open door of an adjacent conference room. Norton took his time and walked slowly through the door and down to the opposite end of the room. He looked out the window to gather his wits. Freeman closed the door and sat in the chair at the head of the table, the one he had intended to offer Norton, and spread his arms.

"Mr. Ratzlaff is busy, but I'm his associate, Freeman Dearborn. I'm working on the nursing home project. How can I help you, sir? You are an agent of some sort with the District Attorney's Office?"

Norton had practiced in the mirror for hours, early in his training, but he still fumbled to get his wallet back out of his jacket pocket. As he displayed his DEA badge upside down, a Friday Night Margarita Club card from a local Mexican restaurant fluttered to the floor. Norton acted casual, and pretended not to notice, hoping that the lawyer would be intent on his badge, but Freeman openly stared at the pastel colored card, which had landed with the business-side up. It had nine out of ten boxes punched with little sombrero-shaped holes.

"Agent Norton, DEA. Coupla questions about a property belongs to Misser Zuckerman."

Freeman cocked his head. "DEA? Drugs?"

He steepled his hands here, and did not conceal his annoyance. "We are providing legal advice and assistance with the permitting and construction of a top quality, full service state-of-the-art nursing home. Our client, Doctor Shlomo Zuckerman, has an option to buy the property if his proposed project is approved, but he doesn't own it yet. What's the issue?" Freeman hoped Ratzlaff couldn't hear him through the wall of the conference room, but Norton reacted exactly as he hoped, wincing and narrowing his eyes as he labored to stuff his wallet back into his jacket pocket.

"Isss-what?"

Freeman leaned in. "Iss-yu, iss-yu. What's the problem you're here to discuss?"

Norton strained to appear casual, explaining that he was the agent responsible for investigating a "hot spot" that showed up as a possible marijuana patch on routine aerial scans of the Sparklewood Forest property. As he spoke, he stepped forward and placed a big black shoe atop the card from Taco-Rita, and he schemed how he would pick it up as he left, in a casual swipe. Only one more punch until he'd get a free margarita, no sense wasting it, especially since his pay was being garnished to repay the Department for that defective fucking Ford that had burned up. Of course, he was not proud that he was still driving what was left of the car, but he hadn't had time to repaint it yet, so he had backed in at the end of the parking lot, with the blistered back end hidden under some overgrown bushes, so he wouldn't look like a redneck or have to explain his bad luck. When Freeman just stared in disbelief, Norton went on, explaining how the Department operated routine drone fly-overs when certain tips were received, and this hot spot was suspicious.

Freeman spread his hands again, even wider this time. "You feel free to poke around the property, Agent Norton. I've been through Sparklewood Forest several times, and all I have seen are a bunch of mountain bikers skidding into logs and trees and such. Doctor Zuckerman is no pot farmer. He's a very successful medical doctor, a psychiatrist. I'm sure your scanner just had a bad day."

Then his tone changed, and he dropped his voice. "By the way, does that drone thing show water, by any chance, streams and springs and puddles?"

Norton was busy balancing on one leg and pulling the Taco-Rita card back with his other foot, and as he did so, the tip of his tongue had begun to protrude from the corner of his mouth. He looked up. "I'm not sure, but I'll look into it."

Both men stared in a brief silent deadlock that signaled the end of this phase of Norton's highly technical investigation of a sensitive and dangerous "iss-yu." Visions of a free margarita danced in Norton's head as he quickly bent and snatched the card from the floor like he was gathering some vital evidence. After he replaced this valuable token in its place in his wallet, he extracted a business card and handed it over to attorney Freeman. "This is how you can reach me, if you come across anything that might be helpful."

Freeman stood to take the card, but Norton ignored his offer to shake hands, and shouldered past him with what he hoped was a menacing efficiency. He flashed his finest friendly federal face at April's blue flowers on his way out.

Weatherly was standing at April's desk as Norton left. She had invented a reason to scout the conference room for a peek, after word rippled through the office that someone from the district attorney's office was asking questions about Zuckerman's project. When Weatherly had arrived at the reception desk to pretend to check for phone messages, Freeman was seated with his back to the glass windows that flanked the conference room door, and his hands were spread wide. He appeared to be whispering to this fugitive from the Big and Tall Store, who was pawing the carpet with one shoe like a prosecutorial bull about to charge. His tongue stuck out a little bit just as their eyes met. It was not love at first sight, and Weatherly quickly turned back towards April. Freeman seemed spooked by this visit when he returned to his desk, but he did not confide in Weatherly as to the nature of the investigation. He tossed Norton's business card onto his desk, and decided that Ratzlaff and Zuckerman didn't need to be bothered with such a frivolous inquiry.

## CHAPTER 40

**RADKIN LIKED TO PARADE AROUND** naked, a practice he had cultivated in Culebra on his days off. He had what he thought were compelling reasons, having to do with the manner in which the epidermis had functioned as a bioelectric organ in the course of phylogenesis, as fish first crawled onto land. Radkin realized he scared most people when he explained this stuff, the course of Paleozoic evolution and the link between modern homosapiens and electric eels as suggested by Haeckel's recapitulation theory, which treated embryonic ontogeny as cellular alchemy. He had to admit that these discussions went especially poorly when he conducted them while he was naked. It had ended badly the first time that he had mowed a cow pasture by Sparklewood Lake, perched on a horse dragging a big sickle mower. The local police cited no actual authority and declined to cite him for any infraction, but they urged him to wear britches when he was in public. From then on, whether he was technically "dressed" or not, he resolved to carry himself through the world with an attitude of perfect, immaculate nudity.

194

Accordingly, Radkin strutted inside his clothes when he first attended the Fourth of July picnic, open to the public, at the Adelphi VFW Lodge #231. As he approached the VFW faithful and the spread of patriotic food, there was a particular arch to his low back and an unmistakable roll to his hips, to his gait, that conveyed his jaybird freedom. Radkin ignored the veterans' wary looks as he opened up a bag of cookies to donate to this celebration. He proceeded to help himself to the free food, concentrating on the piles of steaming corn-on-the-cob, and the big pot of baked beans studded with chunks of pork. The locals were slow to accept him, but he was persistently cheerful, and his cookies were all gone by sundown, when the fireworks began. It was quite a show, most of the locals agreed, far more vivid than any previous display. A few celebrants fell asleep on their blankets and didn't wake until they felt the morning dew.

Within a few months of his installation as night watchman at the Sparklewood Veterinary Hospital, Radkin had mastered the sounds and gestures that soothed the cats and perplexed the dogs. He found that the cats responded to a series of bilabial clicks and kissing squeaks mixed in with long blinks and sighs and subtle motions, while the dogs responded better to big blunt gestures, like thumping his hip with his palm, followed by presentation of the back of the hand while kneeling at eye level, as a petition for acceptance to the pack. He carried a toothbrush on a stick for the cats, to impersonate the grooming affection of their family tongue at a distance to start, and having found bacon too messy, he now carried a supply of jerky for the dogs, recognizing their brief and transactional attention span.

Late one Friday night, after the music ended and The Rumble Seat closed, Radkin's heart continued to thunk in his chest, so he decided to take a walk around the lake. The hospital had a regular guest, an Australian Shepherd that was often boarded by a local shopkeeper who took frequent extended buying trips to Thailand to stock her store with treasures of teak and silk and brass and silver. Radkin had taken a liking to Bodhi, a blue merle with rusty patches on his grey, black and white coat. After his close call with Gibson, the one that had drooled all over the waiting room floor, Radkin decided to take him out for a walk  to see if he could sniff out the scant traces of Manhole trimmings that Radkin had been dropping from the treetops. Sure enough, Bodhi alertly backtracked as they walked along the section of the trail that passed close beneath the crop, and circled, counter-clockwise, sniffing among the brush exactly where the cuttings had fallen, exactly where Gibson had been rooting around before his spell. On his next trip to the treetops, Radkin resolved to rig a green trash bag beside the plants to collect his trimmings.

When Radkin and Bodhi reached the edge of the fence, a truck was beeping and strobing as it backed up to the barn. Radkin was worried that he was supposed to sign for this delivery or unload it but, as he watched from the shadows, the truck driver just rolled a pallet jack of steaming boxes down the ramp into the barn and took off into the night without a word. Radkin  eventually took these curious deliveries for granted.

## CHAPTER 41

**THE PUBLIC HEARING ON SPARKLEWOOD**
Manor was scheduled for a Saturday morning. Freeman spent
the week outlining his order of proof, tabbing his exhibits,
and phoning his witnesses to review their opinions. The
petition for approval had attracted all the usual NIMBY
objectors, the advocates of owls, trees and turtles, the sky-is-
falling conservationists with data about traffic and green
space shrinkage, and the local nursing home operators who
opposed competition. But it was the group of cyclists that
concerned him most.

Zuckerman had called him about the protests, and Ratzlaff
acted gravely concerned, but actually he had been eyeing a
bigger boat. These bike people were vigorous and articulate.
They had spent years creating and maintaining the trails that
wound through Sparklewood Forest, cutting and dragging off
treefall, adding crushed rock to stabilize eroded wash-outs,
naming and marking the trails cleverly, and rattling through
the single track on their expensive carbon fiber and stainless
steel and aluminum contraptions, weaving a network of thin
brown stripes through the thick forest, leaving hardly a speck
of litter.  Freeman anticipated their LL Bean flannel, their

militant Sierra Club talking points, and their xenophobic hostility to Zuckerman, with his out-of-state plates, and his gruff talk and greasy vulgarity. Pointing out that the cyclists had been trespassing on private property was likely to inflame matters, and invite heated rebuttal, since Dr. Bauch had never objected to their presence.

Ratzlaff had not confided in Freeman about how Judge Pinkerton had been boinking Mrs. Silver, his tax accountant for years. She was the same accountant that Ratzlaff relied on, a plain librarian-type lady with a liberal view of deductions, a hidden streak of naughtiness, and a penchant for having her hair pulled. The Judge feared that his indiscretion would eventually come to light, an inevitability in such a small town, especially because her office adjoined a row of lawyers' offices, and she yelped during their kinky dressage, no matter how he tried to muzzle her. Pinkerton had already paid a hefty retainer to Ratzlaff, to reserve his services for the anticipated divorce. He had also provided Ratzlaff with a collection of receipts and prescriptions and medical records to document Mrs. Pinkerton's OxyContin habit, and her doctor shopping. Sparklewood Manor was sure to be approved, but Freeman suffered as he prepared for the worst, unaware of his illicit advantage.

On Saturday morning the gallery contained the usual assortment of locals, the Gazette beat reporter eating candy, the town counsel's law clerk paging through the agenda, a group of slim bikers in the front row, the owner of the local Sweet Chariot Nursing Home and his sweaty lawyer, and a frowning cohort of crusading townspeople who could be counted on to oppose every single request for variance and every single petition for waiver of environmental impact study ever filed in the clerk's office. Hidden in the center of the squirmy gallery was a heavy-set man, eyes shifting left and right, wearing the most obvious pair of black federal shoes that ever clomped into a courtroom. Norton tugged at his suit coat and muttered to himself, scanning the room for criminal horticulturalists. Just as the hearing was gaveled to order, the heavy wooden doors in the back of the courtroom creaked open to admit a slight man in faded denim and a backwards baseball cap, wearing big sunglasses patterned like compound bug eyes. Freeman was oblivious, as he rearranged his notes and prepared to speechify at the lectern, but Zuckerman swiveled in one of the rolling chairs at the front table and squinted at this late arrival, who slid into the back row and ignored the bailiff's half-hearted attempt to order him to remove his hat.

Freeman had decided to present his experts first, all the dry technical witnesses, and save Zuckerman for last. Professor Ronald McKernan, Ph.D. explained demographics, certificates of need, and the strong demand for more nursing homes and "end-of-life" care in greater Adelphi, as the Baby Boomers grew old. As Dr. McKernan twiddled his goatee and tweezed his bowtie, he reeled off an impressive set of government statistics without notes, and scrutinized the gallery, ready to glare at anyone who rolled their eyes at him. The Sweet Chariot Nursing Home had experienced a declining census for years, and the owner shook his head as he heard this testimony. His lawyer looked glum. His advice about the need to increase staff, and improve compliance with standards governing training, timely patient checks, and record keeping had been ignored for years. Sweet Chariot smelled like formaldehyde and the risk manager had their attorney, their malpractice claims line, and the ambulance service on speed dial, in that order. On the other hand, the steady stream of claims for bed sores and medication errors was putting the lawyer's kids through college, as he settled case after case confidentially, rather than risk the adverse publicity of a trial.

Freeman had discarded his retractable ball-points after Burgess' scolding, so now he was reduced to straightening and restraightening his notes, and pressing them flat on the lectern. Judge Pinkerton rocked and swiveled and cleared his throat with a croak like a grey heron during Dr. McKernan's testimony, but asked no questions. No objections were voiced by City attorney Beasley, who just waved McKernan off the stand instead of challenging his testimony on cross. This decision prompted a series of agitated stage whispers between Sweet Chariot's lawyer and his client. Judge Pinkerton stared them down until they got quiet.

Freeman's next witness had an early flight to catch, and it showed. Lacey Stickler hurried through her architectural compatibility opinions in a tremulous voice that modulated from soprano to contralto, in a practiced form of testimonial opera. Her hands fluttered along with her voice, as she explained the colonial antecedents upon which Adelphi's Historical District standards were based, mesmerizing Judge Pinkerton and leaving Freeman to shift from foot to foot and steal glances at his black plastic Casio watch. Had he taken the chance to turn around and scan the gallery, he might have been curious about the bug-eyed stranger in the back row, whose glasses and hat remained firmly in place. Instead, he became preoccupied with Beasley's perfunctory cross-examination, challenging Stickler's thin credentials, consisting of an undergraduate degree in Art History at Slippery Rock University, and a correspondence course doctorate, during which she had presented her thesis on "The Influence of Ergotism on 17th Century Salem Architecture." She batted her eyelashes at Pinkerton, as Beasley wearily moved to strike her testimony for insufficient predicate. Distinguishing between the admissibility and the weight of her opinions, Pinkerton denied the motion and peered vigilantly as Stickler flashed some leg stepping down from the stand.

Over the lunch break, Freeman gently urged Zuckerman to smile and act friendly during his testimony, going so far as to suggest that he tighten up the sloppy knot in his tie and button shut the wide and furry gap in his collar. Zuckerman just stared at him, and regarded Freeman's anxiety with pity. Zuckerman wondered why Ratzlaff had not favored his young associate with the reassuring news about Judge Pinkerton's accountant and their monthly "audits," hi ho Silver. Dr. Zuckerman reassured his young lawyer, but made no adjustments to his clothing.

When Freeman called him to the stand that afternoon, Zuckerman activated his secret superpower. He turned to direct his testimony to Judge Pinkerton with the gravity of a sumo, an oracle of municipal rectitude. As Zuckerman launched into an explanation of his intentions in building the nursing home, Freeman could barely mask his amazement. Zuckerman's voice boomed in every corner of the courtroom, and rang true as any fairy tale. Zuckerman had hidden from his counsel the true reason he wanted to pursue the project. His testimony was compelling and masterful.

Except for his brief flicker of interest in Ms. Stickler, Judge Pinkerton had been inscrutable during the morning session, lazily rocking his chair, clearing his throat, and cleaning and re-cleaning his thick glasses. After lunch, the courtroom usually matched his somnolence as he settled into his customary postprandial torpor. But Judge Pinkerton was stirred by Zuckerman's testimony about his years of psychiatric practice, his fellowship in Vienna, and his wife's tragic death due to heavy metal poisoning, as she was learning to paint Impressionist landscapes in France.

Dr. Zuckerman warmed to his subject as he began telling the tale of his mother's illness, explaining how some creeping form of undiagnosed dementia had caused her gradual decline into mute childishness, aggravated by malnutrition, secondary to her loss of appetite and depression, after her husband's slow submission to cancer. Zuckerman explained his original resolve to care for her himself, in his own home, and his subsequent fears about her plight if he was unable to provide more skilled care for her as her needs changed. At this, Judge Pinkerton quickly grew rapt, visibly moved. He resumed rocking, but in an almost imperceptible, tight, determined jiggle, quite different from his lackadaisical wobbling earlier in the day.

Zuckerman took in the gallery and waved around his hairy hands as he explained how Sparklewood Manor would serve as a state-of-the-art model of high quality multi-level residential end-of-life care, suitable to his own mother's protection, since it would be her final home. The cyclists in the front row slumped like their tires had been deflated. In the back row of the gallery, the man in the hat and sunglasses pulled a camouflage bandanna out of his pocket and swabbed his face. Radkin had an idea.

# SECTION IX


## THE MELACHRINOS


"There's man all over for you, blaming on his boots the faults of his feet."

— Samuel Beckett

## CHAPTER 42

**SOMEHOW, JESTER SEEMED TO ALREADY** know everything that Radkin told him about the businessmen in the woods, the surveyor's stake with the orange ribbon, the nursing home sign, and the public hearing. Jester showed no reaction to Radkin's description of how the public commenters, even the rabid bikers, had been disarmed by Zuckerman's testimony. He just shrugged at Radkin's questions with the type of shrug that was his specialty, the primary existential calisthenic, the Godot signal, the Buddhist gesture of resignation and acceptance. When Jester got up to wait on a couple of college students in tie-dye t-shirts who had called in a take-out order for Nitrogen cookies and Helium bread, Radkin helped himself to a bag of cookies and headed to Zuckerman's lesson to test out his idea. Radkin was on his own, he figured.

The piano lesson began like the first few had, with Radkin winding up a small spring-loaded metronome and inciting Zuckerman to tap his foot, rock in place, and pat his hands together in a Bo Diddley stomp that gradually built up momentum, until the untouched piano reverberated faintly, and the critical voice in Zuckerman's head was silenced. They sat side by side on the bench as the metronome clacked, and they rocked together to that syncopated hambone rhythm.

Next, Radkin directed the way they each would touch any white key, any one at all, as long as they obeyed the beat, with Radkin on the left holding fat bass notes, and Zuckerman answering with tinkly high notes, careful to take turns and mind the start and finish of each note.

There can be no mistake, Radkin assured the Doctor, as long as their tapping feet synchronized with their fingers either landing on or lifting off the white keys. In time, a simple melody emerged, two birds calling from adjacent trees in Congo Square, Radkin down low, donk-donk-donk, uh-boom-boom, and Zuckerman plinking high, tink-tink-tink, uh-tunk-tunk. As this clavé pattern emerged, three paradiddles followed by a rest stroke and two flams, Zuckerman's mother edged crablike from her room, and alit on her chair where she watched with blinking concentration.

By the time the spring ran down, and the ticking slowed, Zuckerman looked up to see her shining eyes. He began to explain her illness to Radkin, and his fears about her care, her descent. His mother had been shrinking as her condition worsened, and neither mega doses of B vitamins, jellyfish-based brain potions, high-calorie supplements nor intravenous TPN had succeeded in slowing her decline. The way things were going, he had begun to question whether Sparklewood Manor would even be approved before she withered away altogether. Radkin waited in silence each time Zuckerman paused in his confession, and each time, Zuckerman resumed, eventually explaining his plan for Sparklewood Manor just as he had at the hearing, how he knew she would be safe, and how he could be sure of her quality of care.

Here was the exact opening that Radkin had sought. Like a bent modern version of Johnny Appleseed, he calmly explained the virtues of a new, old, organic, vegan, locally grown herbal supplement that would quickly and safely solve each of Edith's problems, by stimulating her appetite, boosting her sensorium, and tickling every worthwhile fancy in her slumbering spirit. And when he drew forth a bag of innocuous cookies and explained the modest necessary dosage, Ethel held out her hand directly, and looked at Zuckerman with a kindling spark. Here, Radkin touched on the importance of keeping this plant medicine under their hat, since it was not yet completely legal. With his ears full of the primitive music they had just played, and his mother looking on with desperate hope, Zuckerman acceded, and asked if he could eat one himself. Or three. In light of his size.

Two hours later, after a four-handed concerto of increasingly groovy variations, stoned Ethel was smiling at stoned Radkin, who was smiling at their grilled ham and cheese sandwiches and tomato soup, and stoned Zuckerman was smiling as he peeled a few hundred dollar bills off his roll, and arranged weekly guided sessions. It was a nullifidian miracle in the making.

## CHAPTER 43

**IN RESPONSE TO THE BREATHLESS** reporting of the local TV news teams about the efforts by the Sheriff's office to address the new scourge of powerful marijuana in Sparklewood, and fresh off several sessions of his promising pilot program rehabilitating Edith Zuckerman, Radkin decided to submit an anonymous essay to the local newspaper, in which he would extoll the virtues of the judicious, medicinal use of cannabis, and the means by which it could serve healthy, beneficial, and constructive purposes. Dressed in his insect sunglasses and tucking his hair up under an orange hunting cap with earflaps, Radkin found an unattended computer terminal at the public library. He had watched an older woman gather up her shopping bags and totter out the door, without closing her search for information on Himalayan salt lamps, essential oils, and colloidal minerals. Using the account she had left open, Radkin quickly cut and pasted a letter to the editor of The Sparklewood Gazette from a thumb drive, and signed it 'William Pickard' before pressing send.

An editor with an eye for marketable controversy published this piece on the Gazette's webpage overnight, and it caught fire. Christine Glassboro was an apple-shaped chain smoker, whose head swiveled atop her frozen shoulders like the head of an owl. The newsroom revolved around her and the sound of her keys clacking, because she was indefatigable and omniscient, and could not be swayed by any distraction or inconvenient circumstance. Her prescient articles on lawn mower robots, hemp seed paint, laboratory meat farms, professional lunch and dinner date companions for hire, tiny houses, and the menace of talk radio echo-chamber tribes had each set records for reader engagement, measured by online click-meters that spun almost as fast as her fingers could move. New interns lingered near her desk to marvel at her keyboard itself, which was bereft of any markings whatsoever, except for the exclamation point, the only key which had not yet been worn completely smooth by her blurry prestidigitation. When she made a decision to print a submission, her staff took notes.

Glassboro saw potential in Pickard's essay, which explained how, contrary to the recent alarmist news articles in the Gazette, modern cannabis, due to its robustified cross-pollinatory terpene intensification, could be useful in the clinical treatment of anorexia, aggression, boredom, anhedonia, lassitude, depression, anxiety, chronic pain, and alcoholism, without major safety concerns or adverse side effects. The author explained how small doses could be utilized as an adjunct to healthy flow state activities, like aerobics, badminton, jogging, swimming, bridge, etc. 'Pickard' wrote how he preferred to play a ukulele for kittens during his sessions. Of course, he included other suggestions, like Kundalini sessions with a willing and flexible yogi or yogini, drawing with colored pens, assembling jigsaw puzzles, rhythmic stretching to a well amplified cello suite by Bach, riding through the woods on a bicycle, gardening, telephoning an old friend, throwing a stiff flying disc (he recommended the 175-gram model) across a grassy and sunny field with a skilled partner, or combining a cup of strong coffee with a fresh gel pen and a piece of paper. His letter rattled on in this colorful manner, explaining how no surfer ever rode a purer line than the one who surfed a wave of lava, and comparing the smooth hot air balloon ride of the gentle vape with the exhilarating rocket blast of heroic combustion.

The resulting flame war lasted for weeks and delighted the editor and most of the Gazette's advertisers. Many experienced readers posted comments debating the extent to which the author embraced the philosophies of Kesey and McKenna and Ginsberg, and the extent to which 'Pickard' seemed to subscribe to the public Prankster model instead of staying within the cloistered academic 'set and setting' guardrails of the Leary School. Frightened skeptics griped about how rampant criminality was contributing to the crumbling mores of society.

After the essay on cannabis prompted this firestorm of controversial commentary that nearly crashed The Gazette's servers, Glassboro tried to email the author to solicit a defense of his position, hoping for more eyeballs. She was not entirely surprised to receive a confused reply from an older woman who protested that she was not the author of the piece, and suggested that her email account seemed to have been hacked. On the other hand, she was pleased and intrigued by the possibility that this natural herbal remedy might serve as an adjunct to her new regimen of colloidal minerals, fermented turmeric juice and essential oils. Glassboro quickly ascertained that there was no phone listed for anyone named William Pickard in Adelphi, and she published a short bulletin inviting the author of the "Guide to Modern Cannabis" (as it had come to be known) to step out from behind his assumed name and explain his reasons for anonymity. Within an hour, this piece arrived in her inbox, and she published it as drafted, like so:

> "Because I am bashful and like to hide in the recesses of the book, where words serve as exquisite joinery, crushed diamond alphabet pavé,  fitted to the wrinkles in our dovetail brain with a sharp pen, and because of the way these private scribbly machines echo, icy tongues of "s" and kettledrum "m," just as the wind shapes smoke signals despite our desperate wet blankets, and slipclick open the mystic lock on skullcastle chambers of the secret sovereign soul, where the table is set with silvery talon fork and knife, reptilian cutlery and swan-necked candelabra, or plain chopstick tatami, and we can linger over the imagined feast of choice, her pale throat, a Tangiers fog full of spies, troubadours wreathed in tavern smoke, dusty cowboys and bronze Indians, stone wall moss codes and, with each portable wonderland, a new light shines in the window to reshade the story, whether read on a train, a sofa, in a snowstorm tollbooth or cumulus bed pillows, to mask scars and cruelties or just escape flat light and dishes and dogshit, or middle age mirrors where my mother and father have begun to peek back at me, instead I can

taste Marcel's transportational tea and madeleines, play hide and seek under turtled dinghies, or in short pants shrubberies where a long-gone girl once taught me to kiss her back, down dappled paths that led to school and to brooks that disappeared into concrete sewer netherworlds, and soon, the noble silvery indignities that will lead to slate blue rooms where I will await the footfall of my nurse and her cruelkind needles and pills, where I will show humor and sportsmanship to the rusting thieves, gravity and her thermodynamic friends, who will finally take my last book from me and leave it to be opened by children."

Comments critical of this run-on word salad outnumbered favorable remarks by an overwhelming margin, but editor Glassboro regarded any form of reader engagement as the most vital indicator of the health of the Gazette, so she offered this writer a regular column, in order to give her readers a colorful and provocative piñata to bash. At irregular intervals, she received and published odd bits from porchkey@hush.com, but the author never identified himself. He was, however, secretly elated, and bought a 3-pack of new gel pens to celebrate.

## CHAPTER 44

**RADKIN'S NEXT BIG BREAK WAS** the result of a beautiful disaster at The Rumble Seat. Dixie had booked Red Johnson and the Choir Boys, a traveling bluegrass gospel quintet from Georgia, for Saturday night. Radkin decided to attend. Earlier in the day, during an unusually hectic lunch rush, Jester had forgotten to remove a pan of Helium cookies that he had set aside to cool in the closet that also served as a green room for the musical acts that performed at night. He had also failed to anticipate the manner in which the band's honest hunger would lead them into temptation and sin.

The Choir Boys' set began innocently. They took the stage right on time, cradling their instruments as they stepped into a single spotlight with straight back solemnity. The band wore matching Western suits and black cowboy boots, and everyone but Red wore a white Stetson. They encircled a single old timey microphone at the center of the stage, with no amp or monitor in sight.

Red was a minor bluegrass legend, with a big gold ring on each hand, and a big gold watch on his wrist. He had a high silvery pompadour, and a broad preacher-style grin. The Martin guitar that he wore up high, almost under his chin, looked like it had been dragged behind a tractor for forty miles. It had a deep crescent that had been etched into the spruce top by forty years of sanctified strumming. Red acted surprised by the smattering of sleepy applause as they gathered around the mic. His grin got impossibly wider as he nodded, and his tall hair nodded with him, as he counted off the first number.

The sound that Red and the Choir Boys produced was high and lonesome as could be, with the band members stepping to and from the central microphone in Opry-style choreography. Now three faces surrounded the mic in angelic harmony, Red's clear tenor pitched above the baritone and bass, now the banjo was centered on the mic, clanging, chiming, ringing, now the fiddle and bow slipped in between the banjo and mandolin to let loose the horsehair-tearing fiddleflow, now the mandolin barked like a dog. As each solo ended, and the next player waltzed into the sweet spot, Red played rock-solid back-up, leaning his battered guitar into the mic briefly to punch the iconic Flatt g-run that framed the solo spots. But gradually things began to go wrong. As Radkin watched Red's decline, he imagined Sigmund Freud at a slapstick version of a faculty party, where he started out in a tweed jacket and an ascot, sipping Chablis, pinky extended, and an hour later, he was disheveled, wearing a toga with a lampshade on his head as he lunged at the French teacher.

Like all good Southern Baptists, Red had always abstained, not only from tobacco, alcohol and coffee, but also from the diabolical drugstore nostrums including lotions, vitamins, aspirin and Pepto Bismol. The employment contract that Red offered all his Choir Boys expressly proscribed impure exhibitions such as smoking, chewing gum or tobacco, sinning, cursing, drinking, womanizing, wearing sunglasses, t-shirts, sandals, and a dozen other well-known Satanisms. About half an hour into the set, when his head began to float like a balloon and his ears began to whoosh and then to roar, Red paused mid-song to take his bearings, and looked around for the source of this disconcerting noise. When he tilted back and looked overhead for a fan, or overhead duct, or a golden host of trumpeting angels, his stance and his time wobbled, and his band exchanged side-eye glances. Red's flawless six string drive was the durable engine of the Choir Boys, and now it had coughed for the first time in their collective memory.

Things continued to go downhill as they prepared to begin the next song. Red's usual grin had tightened into a grimace, and the band watched as he fumbled with his capo. Red began to laugh, and as his shoulders shook, his arms shook, and his shoulders shook harder as he stabbed at the neck of his guitar with the capo, helplessly. Red doubled over, breathless, defeated by the capo he had been using for years without incident. At this point, his senior sideman, a longtime mandolinist named Harry Mutterman stepped into the breach. Although he had attended Bible college in West Virginia, wink-wink, and had passed seedy joints in the woods at Bean Blossom, Harry had been a model of sober rectitude while he served his apprenticeship in Red's band, an anointed gig which clothed him in all the vestments of hillbilly royalty. But now, feeling a familiar wobble in his own brain, remembering the pungent sheet of cookies backstage, and sensing that Red was faltering because he was unprepared for lift-off, Mutterman stepped to the mic and began to play his best song, a fast instrumental étude he warmed up with every day. The rest of the band quickly joined in, with a combination of fear and exhilaration.

This development caused Red to throw his head back again, not to find a chorus of winged cherubim this time, but to laugh at the way his band had spit the bit to rescue him from whatever spell had come over him. As the music sped from Kentucky into New Orleans, careening through the outskirts of Storyville, Red's laughter echoed in his own ears as he stumbled offstage to find a glass of water. Mutterman and the band took this as a license to proceed, and they plowed through another improvised instrumental, even after Red came back on stage without his guitar, swabbing his face and fanning their instruments with his hanky like a vaudeville clown, laughing uncontrollably. Harry was now running out of steam. His legs had suddenly grown 10 yards, and there was a strange sound in his ears. He announced a break, and he and the band guided Red out the stage door, down the back stairs, and onto the shiny motor coach idling out back, next to the dumpster and grease barrel.

Just as Mutterman had converted disaster to opportunity, however briefly, Radkin saw his own chance. There were no signs of resistance when he knocked and slipped onto the bus. Radkin introduced himself as a good friend of the owners of The Rumble Seat, and began to assess the Choir Boys' capacity to finish out the night. After confirming that they had all eaten some cookies, Radkin gave them a closer once-over.  Red was a total loss, but the mandolin player was salvageable, and Big Clyde, the bassist, was a bear of a man who appeared so robust that Radkin was confident he could withstand a dozen more cookies without missing a single G, C, or D. Jethro Stoneman, the fiddle player, insisted he could play fine, but he worried Radkin, because he was staring at his hands in wonder, and mumbling about spiders and the Holy Ghost. He used to be a drinker before he joined the Choir Boys, and he explained that he felt a little funny, but was ready to play.  The banjo player was puking in the bathroom, but assured Radkin that he'd be fine, after he came out and toweled off his face.

Radkin calmly explained that, by mistake, there had been some medicine in the cookies, but it was just mild organic medicine that would pass. He likened their situation to a modern parable, just an updated test like the apple from the Garden of Eden, and explained how he would help them finish the gig and get paid, so everyone would be just fine. Red did not object. He had begun shivering, and now was giggling under the blanket that Radkin had spread over him, drinking water from a paper cup and praying aloud, confessing that he had actually eaten four cookies, falling prey to Satan's trickery, have mercy. The Choir Boys were game, and after Radkin passed cups of water all around, and announced a simple strategic plan, they grabbed their hats and instruments, and returned to the stage.

Then ensued a bold musical adventure of the sort that Radkin had imagined for months. He lowered the microphone and arranged a semicircle of chairs for everyone but Clyde, who stood up and clung to his bass. Relying on the band's intimate relationship with the key of G, and hoping that their bluegrass chops, although surely scrambled, had not been obliterated, Radkin used Red's guitar to conduct a series of improvisations that carried the band until the end of the night. By capitalizing on the band's stout muscle memory and converting the fast boom-chick of bluegrass to the deliberate boom-chick of reggae, Radkin anchored an instrumental journey through the stuttering one-drop rhythm of stony dub. He counted off an irie "Sittin' On The Dock of the Bay" which melted into a pigeon-toed "Turkey in the Straw" which dissolved into a stately "Friend of the Devil" which segued into an original waltz he had not yet named. Meanwhile, Red snored softly, back on the bus. Judging from the manner in which the tip jar was overflowing at night's end, Radkin was not surprised that Dixie asked if he would run a regular open mic gig every Friday night. Of course, he agreed, and he warned her that The Choir Boys' bus would be spending the night listening to the river sing sweet songs out back. He decided not to speak to her about the cookies.

## CHAPTER 45

**RADKIN TOOK HIS NEW RESPONSIBILITIES** at The Rumble Seat quite seriously. He had always believed that he played his best music alone at the hospital when the trees waved in the turbulence that stirred up the lake at night, but how could he be sure? He had played only for the dogs since his duets with Calpurnia had come to an end. But now, with a regular gig to cover, Radkin began to practice with a new purpose. Sparklewood Forest seemed to resonate in the awkward key of Bb, and Radkin learned to obey his conductors, the swishing pines and spruces and oaks, and the faint boom and hiss percussion of the waves coming across the lake onto the rocky shore, when the west wind was stiff. It was on such a night that the melody of Radkin's plaintive joy in Bb drifted through the forest and reached, faintly, to touch Weatherly and Gibson as they perambulated deep in the woods. They paused and listened. Was it the wind?

Radkin held an audition to try to assemble a group of local musicians to back up the weekly open mic. It was tricky. He found a few local amateurs who wanted to play, but between the harmonica and accordion and their yodeling cacophony, he knew these primitives would clear the room in minutes. When Mutterman tracked him down at The Molecule one day, Radkin closed his book and listened.

Mutterman reported how Red had retired from performing the morning after his fall from grace. He had released his band from their contracts, and paid each of them a small severance, apologizing for the way his gluttony and shameful embrace of the sinful cookie medicine had disqualified him as a sanctified leader. He had learned that The Choir Boys had participated in playing a song about the devil or his friend, either way, it was grounds for dismissal. Red told Harry that he planned to sell his guitar. He had been told that he could get a lot of money for his 1934 herringbone D-28 from some old guitar professor in Nashville, probably enough to buy a nearly new John Deere 3386 KMC combine that would double his peanut yield on the farm, and let him spend more time at home outside Valdosta.

Mutterman had already talked to the rest of the band. Their banjo player, Yonder Stanton, had agreed to help Red at the farm, after he had some sort of bad dream about hell and liquor. But just like Mutterman, Stoneman and Big Clyde wanted to shift from gospel-driven bluegrass to music with a broader appeal. After the night of the medicine test, they felt ready. Mutterman and Stoneman wanted to play without suits and hats, although Clyde wanted to stick with his outfit. They were pretty sure they could play better if they moved around a little bit in place as they played, and they hoped to make some more money, too. And as for girlfriends, they had never had any, so far… He trailed off at this point, and Radkin knew he had found his new team. He agreed to handle the bookings and arrangements, with each man to share equally in the money. Radkin announced, without explanation, that they would be named The Melachrinos, and he convinced Dixie to let them play The Rumble Seat twice a week on a trial basis, for a modest fee and tips.

Radkin called Red on the landline at the farm, and purchased his vintage microphone for $500, boom. The Shure 55 was older than Red, and as Red felt obligated to point out, it was designed to resemble the iconic grille of the 1937 Oldsmobile Six convertible coupe. When they gathered at their first practice one afternoon before the Rumble Seat opened, Harry, Clyde and Jethro gaped at the surprise microphone like it was a graven image of Red. His new band mates did their second double-take when Radkin pulled out his electric guitar. They expected, of course, an American round-hole, flat-top guitar made in Nazareth, Pennsylvania. Things got even more confusing when Radkin pulled out an amp that had been abandoned by another band, more of a side table than a musical device, covered in full ashtrays and empty beer bottles. Radkin took a look at it and, with a smile, bent over this neglected machine and cleared it off. He snugged up the loose hex nut on the input jack with his fingers, and he sprayed the jack and the shafts of all the knobs with a little aerosol can he pulled from his bag. Then, before he turned it on, he plugged and unplugged his cable a dozen times, and he rolled every knob back and forth a few dozen times. An hour later, The Melachrinos marveled at the filigree that he drew from this Babylonian appliance. Radkin  insinuated his electric guitar into the band's mix like the smell of wood smoke in a lumberjack's coat.  After they worked up a few sets, and they began to learn how to work the resonances of the old mill, to entrain their sound with the slamming door woofer and the gamelan ring-a-ding of the pinball machine tweeters, they were encouraged by a regular group of receptive listeners who assembled every Thursday and Friday night. Harry Mutterman shocked his bandmates a few weeks later, when he showed up in sandals, with his left ear pierced.

It was Radkin's routine to appear just before the gig started, with his electric guitar in a tattered bag over his shoulder, along with a leather strap, two cables, and something he called "The Bulb," a small boost device he had built inside an antique metal cigarette box that his grandfather had given him. Radkin had worked by trial and error to develop a tiny FET preamp by soldering different resistors and an op-amp chip to a piece of circuit board he had removed from a broken flashlight. It was powered by a battery he had made from a bit of copper and two small magnets from a Lionel HO train, wrapped in a metal strip from a Campbell's tomato soup can. The Bulb made his guitar sound big and glassy, and Radkin eventually produced a few dozen versions for his friends, for a nominal charge.

For a few months, their music covered The Rumble Seat like pretty wallpaper, ornate, or at least patterned and decorative, but flat. Over time, on those natural nights when the wind was fair, on those happy nights, The Melachrinos ran on automatic, and their flow would unfurl in casual ease. With the residual benefit of Red's training, Radkin had assembled a crack outfit, and on certain nights The Rumble Seat would seem to spin, to the delight of both the band and their listeners. Musical doors would open where there had been no doors before, and they would be admitted to the inner sanctum, to their own unique form of modern mutant chamber music.

Stoneman, it turned out, played fiddle like a grass fire burned, advancing in crackling destruction, almost too bright to behold. On the other hand, Stoneman's renewed consumption of booze increased gradually, by degrees, and Radkin's effort to substitute Velvet Manhole for the fiddler's beloved moonshine was  revealed to be a failure, as Jethro developed a taste for a compound form of intoxication that obliterated any vestiges of bluegrass discipline. Mutterman, on the other hand, was a mandolin metronome, marking precise meter to propel Stoneman's combustible excursions. Big Clyde insisted on continuing to wear his western suit and Stetson hat, and he disapproved of Stoneman's promiscuous departures from the pentatonic scale at first. However, a few months into The Melachrinos' tenure at The Rumble Seat, Clyde's ears expanded a bit and he was amazed to discover that, even if he dispensed with an occasional root or fifth, the music would not collapse. As Radkin encouraged Stoneman to extend his hoedown ragas, Harry and Big Clyde grew bolder in following Stoneman and Radkin into the exhilarating wilderness of flat-five bebop and other chromatic heresies.

A local festival promoter heard some buzz about this new band, how they were developing a fan base that traveled, so he decided to check them out in person. It was his practice to watch a few sets before making up his mind, because he had been burned so many times by bands of sketchball one-trick gypsies. Stanky Pilferton had no way of connecting The Melachrinos with The Funnybones, who he had never actually seen before they absconded with his credit card years earlier, despite his estimable promotional services. His capacity to suspend disbelief long enough to fully evaluate the crooked genius of The Melachrinos' chaotic compositional approach was sorely tested on his first exposure.

On the first night Pilferton scouted the band, he became alarmed when Stoneman launched a solo on the eleventh bar of a 12 bar set of changes. His phrasing was in nines, based on some perverse but precise and intentional logic. From the start, the sensation of flat-tire dissonance created by the clash between the meter of the rhythm section and Stoneman's solo was uncomfortable, and the tension only grew in unbearable and malicious increments until the rhythmic planets all finally aligned on the glorious downbeat of measure 372, when the groove re-emerged like a 4/4 bomb had exploded inside an out-of-balance washing machine filled with sneakers. A bolt of recognition struck Pilferton between his beady eyes. Years earlier, driving through the deep woods of Alabama in search of a blind albino banjo prodigy that he wanted to sign, Pilferton had experienced a similar epiphany when the forest blur at the edge of the road, a seemingly random flickering of pines, suddenly lined up for a split second to reveal perfect parallel rows of a tree farm which had been planted at an oblique angle to the road. Then, just as suddenly, the angle changed and the random blur resumed. Measure 372 had the same effect, leaving Stanky Pilferton pleasantly amazed.

The Pilferton Agency signed The Melachrinos, and Stanky promised to book them in every bar and festival in New England. Radkin was modest and played the fool, giving no hint that he had been a member of The Pilferton Agency's esteemed roster in the past, along with the magicians, bearded ladies, and flea circuses that groveled for gigs. Of course,

Radkin agreed to continue hosting the open mic nights at The Rumble Seat when his schedule permitted, so Dixie took the news pretty well. She agreed to book them on the new terms that Pilferton imposed, paying them more money, doing some advance local promotional advertising, and reserving a little room for an exclusive merchandising table where they could sell t-shirts and bumper stickers and hats, squeezed between the pinball machines and the bathrooms.

As directed by their new manager, The Melachrinos began traveling to out of town gigs year round. Radkin bought a bread truck for cash, and built in a few bunks. His installation of a chemical toilet beneath the hinged driver's seat was a source of controversy in the band. Everyone was relieved after he demonstrated how he had engineered a set of nesting Tupperware bins to provide an airtight and slosh-proof seal when the driver's seat lid was closed. Clyde was most impressed when Radkin demonstrated how a roll of toilet paper could be conveniently stored on the turn signal.

The nature of Melachrino music lent itself to a certain type of listener, spinners, whirlers, and symbolic dancers who plucked imaginary fireflies from the air around them, or pulled invisible streamers back and forth in cosmic boogaloos, unconcerned with lyrics and fond of extended aerobic trances. The Melachrinos had arrived, and their regional tribe began to grow, with the mercenary backing of Stanky Pilferton. Radkin had not had a drink in years now, and he was confident that he would not lose the truck and all the gear again.

## CHAPTER 46

**NORTON WORE CAMOUFLAGE THE SECOND** time he scouted Sparklewood Forest, having expensed a woodland pattern jumpsuit at an Army-Navy store downtown. His black shoes still gleamed like a pair of hearses, ill-suited for the woods. He unfolded his shiny copy of the thermal aerial picture that was supposed to show a field of marijuana, and rotated it round and round, as he stood beside the same sign and staked ribbon which had marked the limit of his initial excursion.

Freeman's dismissive treatment had upset him, as had his strange question about water. This picture didn't have a compass rose or any recognizable landmark other than the roadway and the lake, and once Norton started to follow the narrow twisty bike trail away from the road, the tree canopy became so thick that he promptly lost his bearings. He stuffed the paper into one of the many zippered pockets in his waxy new nylon outfit. Barely any sunlight passed through these dense cedars and pines, and within an hour, Norton was completely lost and thirsty, having seen no sign of narcotics or streams, just trees and bushes and logs. At intervals, small groups would come skidding around the curly trails on chattering bicycles, and Norton would be forced to lurch into the bushes at the edge of the trail. Finally, he decided to wait in an opening where several trails converged, to flag down a biker and get help finding his way out. When a large red dog came charging into sight, pink tongue flapping in a toothy grill, followed closely by a rider, Norton started waving his arms wildly. A ruckus ensued. The dog snarled and began barking ferociously, as Norton backed into the brush and bellowed, "Federal Agent! Federal Agent!" digging in his cargo pockets for his badge.

Radkin heard this drama from his crow's nest in the treetops, and by the time he had focused his binoculars, the big guy was running in place, just beyond the maw of the barking beast who was now spraying the agent's footwear with foamy clouds of slobber. This camouflaged fellow was waving his wallet around like a crucifix, and his "Federal Agent" refrain had now died down to a whimper. Radkin watched as the biker gestured and the hiker gestured. As the hiker began to leave, walking briskly in the direction that the biker had pointed, the biker bent down and picked something up off the ground where this guy, presumably a Federal agent, had been tap-dancing. In her helmet and sunglasses, Weatherly was impossible to recognize, but the dog drew his attention. Radkin knew this red dog.

**SECTION X**

**MAKING THE BED**

"If you want to change the world, start off by making your bed."

— Admiral Wm. H. McRaven

## CHAPTER 47

**RADKIN HAD SPENT HIS SPRING** and summer days in the trees, conjuring his fragrant crop, and he practiced his music for the dogs and cats at night, when he wasn't playing with The Melachrinos. Radkin had a lot to think about, as the weather changed. He had been spooked by the nursing home project planned for Sparklewood Forest, and now this Federal Agent was poking around in the same spot. His job at the hospital had served its purpose of giving him a low-profile place to live, and by chance, a convenient source of water for his crops. But after he was awakened one night, late, by another unmarked truck that beeped loudly as it backed into the barn, he made plans to leave his position as night watchman. He had peered over the edge of the loft as two swarthy men in white overalls rolled a half dozen light blue coolers down a ramp and into the barn, before sliding the door shut, putting the idling truck in gear, and groaning off into the night.

The coolers steamed, and were marked with red stenciled warnings, both in English and what he assumed was Chinese. "HANDLE WITH CARE- DANGER- Liquid Nitrogen Inside- Biological Substance, Category B." Covered in a thin layer of frost, each box was latched and secured with a tamper-proof zip-tie lock, and a plastic bag hung from each latch, containing papers with more foreign writing and red biohazard symbols. Radkin jumped straight up in the air the first time one of the boxes made a burping sound as a little jet of vapor shot from some sort of vent, but in time he got used to it. Radkin didn't sleep well, and decided not to ask the hospital staff about this mysterious freight. By the next night, the boxes were gone.

Tired by his itinerant years traveling the countryside with the Funnybones, sleeping in the van and playing bar room music, then counting turtle nests and getting his heart broken, Radkin decided it was time to get away from the hospital and settle into a domestic routine. Winter was coming, and he couldn't grow any Manhole for a while anyway, and Jester had another dishwasher lined up. Radkin had been saving most of his income from his various side businesses, and his last harvest had been his best, so he decided to follow Sherman Klank's advice and buy a piece of land, with some sturdy shelter and a wood stove.

The first few auctions were depressing affairs, with red-faced farmers and their hand-wringing wives sniping on rusty milking machines and disc harrows. Radkin was afraid that if he scratched his head or adjusted his sunglasses, he could buy a horse trailer by mistake. Eventually, he won a dilapidated farm outside of Adelphi, a foreclosure complete with a crooked rhombohedron barn, and a stone house full of junk. He moved his scant belongings to the second story of the farm house and quit his job at the vet, which is to say, he disappeared. Bauch wouldn't notice for weeks.

Radkin immediately found a new job as a lift attendant for the winter, monitoring the skiers riding the topmost lift to the peak of the most remote mountain in the Northeast Kingdom, Crazy Creek Glen. Radkin had been the only applicant for the job, and he agreed to start work the next day. After tucking his truck into the service garage at the bottom of the mountain, he loaded the truck battery, a bicycle without wheels, and a few boxes of odds and ends onto the lift and into the crow's nest, the small cabin that would be his new home for the winter. The antique single chair lift was built of iron, with a series of drive terminals, an enormous boat wheel, 158 chairs, a wire rope, and 23 towers positioned at zigzag intervals on the steep slope. The terminal at the top, beside his cabin, creaked like a galleon in a storm. It only took two nights, with the gusting wind playing the cracks in the wooden cabin like a whistle before he hooked the bicycle crank to a repurposed garage door opener motor wired to feed a charge to the battery. This setup gave him electricity for a radio, a small reading light, an electric blanket, and a hot plate. His volume of Emerson's collection of essays, including "Self-Reliance," was a slim hardcover, and Radkin found that it fit perfectly into the biggest gap beneath the single windowsill in the lift shack, where snow had drifted inside during the first storm.

Radkin took baths in the snow when it was sunny, and loved to play his trumpet naked, to the shock of 99% of the skiers who dismounted the chair lift. Unfortunately, on the very same day that a Mennonite family from Ohio complained to the safety patrol about Radkin, a portly skier from Germany suffered a cardiac incident induced by the naked trumpet ambush. His symptoms were reported to have been significantly aggravated by Radkin's attempt to perform mouth-to-mouth resuscitation. Radkin was promptly fired for "risk management" reasons, despite his protests that nudity was not unlawful in Vermont, technically.

Anyway, he had work to do at the new house. Using bills peeled from one of the stacks of money that had filled the diaper bag, Radkin splurged and bought himself a double bed, a set of fitted sheets and wool blankets, a couple big chairs and a halogen floor lamp bright enough to banish the blues, so powerful it could be seen from space. He also bought a brand new Swedish wood stove, three cords of kiln-dried ash, beech, and white birch, and some used copies of his favorite books by Proust, O'Brien, Joyce, Kotzwinkle, Casady, Stevens and Farina. He started a junk hauling business with his truck, and he collected a half dozen rust-ravaged, skeletal Triumph TR7s. He salvaged enough working parts from these junkers to assemble one semi-complete car, which coughed, belched and refused to start, but came tantalizingly close. His line-up of rescued pianos in the front yard was a scene from Bosch or Dali, as the snow, sun, rain and local critters transformed each piano into a grotesque caricature, with swollen and peeling sheets of maple, ebony, birch and spruce, curling ivory veneers, and fan-shaped arrays of high carbon steel strings that he would never actually harvest, despite his irreproachably fine intentions.  Radkin liked to feed the squirrels and chipmunks that took shelter in his barnyard pianos, and he heard music in the random sprangles and plinks that could be heard as the critters chased the sunflower seeds he would broadcast over his collection. As his junk business paid off, Radkin began converting his savings to coins, mostly American Eagles and gold Krugerrands, but also sovereigns, doubloons, and every manner of silver nugget, as well.

As his hands began to wrinkle and brown, like any honest farmer's hands, and his copper hair turned rusty with silver streaks, Radkin almost lost hope that his magic book would serve the purpose of wooing a girl, as he had long dreamed. Only a telepath could ever decode his semaphore journal, where he inventoried his worry closet, and recorded his dreams of coconut surf, boom-hiss, and the comforts of negligence, the necessity for a sharp blade, and his plan to gracefully surrender to creeping chaos, weeds, rust, and sleep. He faithfully maintained his daily stance, bent over the page awaiting his muse with reverent attention, with a pen full of wet ink at his fingertips, and white rag paper pages spread before him, but the flow had run thin. Who would be interested, much less enthralled, by his electric meat science, his precious allegorical bed-making and his wordy mind-at-play?  Inside all the Corinthian decoration, all the acanthus alphabet stylings, was there an actual story being offered? What was the story? Boy meets girl? Boy fails to meet girl and whines about it? On the other hand, he took some solace in the improvement in his blues guitar, as his out-of-tune bends began to sound like authentic agony.

## CHAPTER 48

**WHEN HE WAS POSTURING IN** meetings with his lawyers and when he testified in court, Dr. Zuckerman put on a good show, gruff and jovial in equal parts, just as he had handled his patients, slap and tickle. But when he was sitting alone in the waiting room at Ratzlaff, Kluger and Bunning, he was like any other solitary middle-aged man who was paying for services by the hour, which is to say, he was patting his hair into place, what was left of it, tweezing his trousers out of certain crevices, and checking his watch. He watched April out of the corner of his eye, stealing glances at her confectionary lips and cantilevered bosom, while he paged backwards through the fancy car and boat magazines piled on the side tables.

As Dr. Zuckerman waited to be ushered into the conference room for an update, Weatherly appeared in the reception area to offer him some coffee and to explain that a hearing had run late, and Mr. Ratzlaff and Mr. Freeman would be delayed 30 minutes or so. When Zuckerman tossed his magazine onto the top of the stack and gestured to the next chair, Weatherly felt obligated to sit down. She primly folded her hands over her knees and listened to the standard-issue awkwardness that often spilled from clients, a stream of observations that veered predictably from weather to current affairs, requiring only that she nod and make demure sounds and crinkle her eyes occasionally, with appropriate signs of interest in

Zuckerman's glib wisdom. However, she was unprepared for a sudden confessional shift in Zuckerman's soliloquy, when he lowered his voice and began to describe his mother's recent cognitive improvement, her restored appetite and enthusiasm, her weight gain, and his new optimism about her prognosis.

April glared each time she had to punch the hold button to park Weatherly's incoming calls, even after Weatherly slid forward in her seat to signal that she was ready to resume her work station. Zuckerman whispered that he was having second thoughts about Sparklewood Manor, now that his mother was more suited to run the place than to live in it. Obligated to say something other than "hmm" and "I see" and other deferential pleasantries, Weatherly took a chance. "This is a good problem to have, right?" Zuckerman was uncharacteristically tentative. "Sure, but what would I do with the property if she's recovered? Can I back out? Do I still have to close on the property? Will I get some of my deposit back?" Remembering the price she had paid for giving quasi-legal advice in the past, Weatherly stood up and cheerfully suggested that these were the sort of questions that he should bring up with the lawyers. She promised to make them aware of this development.

April was relieved as Weatherly returned quickly to the blinking phone on her desk, but a black cloud of worry trailed behind Weatherly, as she thought about paragraph 13 and the Federal Agent snooping in the woods. She typed up a memo to the file and added it to the pile of paper that was stacked on Freeman's desk.

## CHAPTER 49

**AS A YOUNG SOLDIER, IN** his search for a brand of cigarette so disagreeable that no one would bum them, Radkin's father had discovered Melachrino No.9s. Melachrinos burned like cylinders of camel hair rolled in tubes of green Egyptian papyrus. Mr. Stringfellow gagged on their hideous spume the first time that he tried these smokes, but he never ran short, so he got used to them. Even though they were rank, he smoked Melachrino No.9s until his wife died of lung cancer. She had smoked Tareytons until the last day.

A few years later, right after he turned 75, Mr. Stringfellow was hospitalized with pneumonia and COPD. When he reached his 80's, and his emphysema had progressed to a grave rattle, he was not surprised to be diagnosed with lung cancer. Having watched his wife's miserable and ineffective treatment, he was unwilling to subject himself to the same plight, so Mr. Stringfellow telephoned his younger son and left a message, hinting around that he could use some help dying, without delay. He had never reconciled with Walter Jr. after his name change.  They had barely spoken at his grandfather's funeral, where Walter Jr. had looked so lost, red as a lobster and wearing a stiff white button down shirt that he obviously bought at the airport, with the plastic stays sticking out of the collar.

Wyatt was well paid as a senior claims adjuster at the Special Investigations Unit of the Golden Peanut Insurance Company, where he worked at the headquarters in Des Moines, Iowa. Wyatt had become rewarded for his cold-blooded ability to locate an errant or misspelled entry on virtually every insurance application, to serve as a pretext to deny practically every claim on the basis of some form of colorable fraud. Golden Peanut adjusters like Wyatt were emboldened by the sad fact that peanut farmers were typically undereducated and functionally illiterate, and many had been stupefied by a toxic airborne mixture of pesticides, fertilizer, and dust, which rendered them prone to misreading the fine print of the applications for coverage. It turned out that peanut farmers were also almost universally reluctant to pay money to consult with lawyers by the hour, when faced with Wyatt's infamous certified letters, strategically mailed from Golden Peanut's Philadelphia office, all of which denied coverage and warned of the felonious nature of the material misrepresentations contained in their applications.

 The underwriting department had conducted a careful audit of the Golden Peanut books, adding up premium dollars received, and subtracting dollars paid out for advertising, postage, paper clips, computers, rubber stamps, ink pads, rent, light bulbs, printing costs, phone bills, lawyers' and investigators' fees and costs, registered mail expenses, and also the rare and paltry amounts actually paid in claims. The accountants ascertained that, by simply identifying all their adjusters as members of the Special Investigations Unit, they could reduce the severity of paid claims by 17%. After comparing the effectiveness of all the denial of coverage letters signed by all their adjusters, and noticing Wyatt Stringfellow's shameless penchant for reducing claims payments by alleging fraud in every single file, Wyatt won the company's prized Golden Peanut Award every year he worked for the company. Even though the plaques were just laminated walnut, and the mounted golden peanuts were just gold colored, he lined his awards up on his cubicle wall and became a Special Investigations Unit legend.

Eventually, every single denial of coverage letter mailed out by Golden Peanut was first reviewed by Wyatt Stringfellow, and signed by the company's Philadelphia lawyer, Rudy Goldblatz, Esq., whose brutal signature subliminally resembled a peanut harvester tractor rake, scratched onto the page like an array of serrated blades dripping black blood.

When Wyatt was unable to reach Walter in Puerto Rico, he asked a colleague to perform a skip-trace investigation which revealed a listing of Radkin as a musician represented by The Pilferton Agency, some outfit that mostly booked novelty acts like polka bands, sword-swallowers, and talking dogs. Wyatt wrote a short letter to his older brother in care of Pilferton, suggesting that Radkin might check on their father. Wyatt reasoned that Radkin was probably underemployed and in a better position to help, timewise, but he omitted this rationale from his note. Instead, he included a copy of their mother's obituary in his letter, an unhappy development which he had not yet seen fit to share with his long-lost brother. In the letter, he pointed out that their father was alone and struggling with lung cancer now, and he asked Radkin to step up and get him some help.

Of course, when Wyatt wrote to Radkin, he used official Golden Peanut stationery and, out of habit, he described their father's fatal predicament as terminal lung cancer having been diagnosed by an imaginary pulmonologist from Philadelphia named Rudy Goldblatz, M.D. Radkin reacted exactly like the underwriting department research suggested. He set up a comfortable spot for his father upstairs by the stove, packed up his truck and drove straight to New Jersey to pick up their father. Because the last phone call he had placed to his parents' home had gone so poorly, Radkin dispensed with the formality of an advance phone call.

Mr. Stringfellow was clearly confused by the unannounced arrival of his estranged oldest son after so many years, but he welcomed Bean inside like he would welcome any neighbor or fellow Rotarian, with a handshake and backslap. In response to Radkin's offer of help, Mr. Stringfellow admitted that he was sick, but denied any knowledge of a Dr. Goldblatz, insisting that he had never been treated by anyone with that name. He described Wyatt's plan to move him into a nursing home with disdain, and Radkin could tell he would flatly refuse any attempt to bring him to Sparklewood for convalescence. Even the prospect of a to-be-constructed world class "retirement community" with full end-of-life care on site would not interest Mr. Stringfellow in the least.

Declining to comment on his father's savage cough and audible rasping, Radkin shifted tactics, describing his farm in such restful and pastoral terms, apple orchard, lake view, woodstove, maple sugar, etc. that his father agreed to take a ride to see the country around Adelphi. They packed up his calendar of medical appointments and his sheaf of medical records, some warm clothes, a shoebox of photographs, a few books, and his glasses and medications, and they drove north in the bread truck. At first, Radkin didn't mention the toilet under the driver's seat and Mr. Stringfellow didn't ask about the toilet paper on the turn signal, but after an unfortunate curry at an Indian restaurant in a converted Dairy Queen in New Paltz, both father and son agreed that the driver's seat toilet innovation had some useful advantages.

## CHAPTER 50

**RADKIN WAS TEMPTED TO TRY** to ease his father's fear of mortality with a  cookie or two, but instead he made the decision to quit using his precious Manhole in solidarity, as long as the old man could hang on. Before he had departed to pick him up, Radkin had gathered an extra bed and a recliner, a heating pad, a bright reading lamp, and a few blankets, and he had constructed a sort of throne stationed in front of the best window in the house, on the second floor, looking west towards the distant lake where all his father's literal and figurative lights were sure to drain away before too long.

Once Wyatt learned that their father had been relocated to Radkin's rural home, instead of being installed in a nursing home, he regretted involving his brother. Picturing his father mired in some drafty yurt in a commune overrun with a bedraggled tribe of dirty-foot hippies digging carrots and garlic and potatoes, and surrounded by earth mothers suckling communal babies, Wyatt decided to request a wellness check from the Adelphi Adult Protective Services Agency. He requested anonymity on the phone, and claimed that his infirm elderly father was being subjected to poor hygiene, inadequate nutrition, and a lack of medical supervision. Golden Peanut investigators had finally succeeded in finding Radkin's new address by rusing their way into the public database of electric utilities, an ironic means of tracing that Radkin would have considered profoundly funny, given his penchant for apophenia and his conviction that electricity ran through everything.

Within 24 hours of Wyatt's report, the lead screening officer for Protective Services determined these allegations were facially sufficient to warrant an investigation to protect a vulnerable adult, and an experienced staffer named Glorious Lincoln was dispatched to perform a field screening. Ms. Lincoln found scant history of legal activity associated with Walter Stringfellow Jr. when she searched her database, just an court order regarding his name change, a report of lost and/or stolen property, to wit, an Econoline van, and a missing person report filed by his parents. Agency protocol required that the screening must be unannounced to increase the likelihood of an accurate evaluation of the actual conditions under which the reported victim was living. From the road, Radkin's farmhouse looked like most others, but when Glorious pulled through the gap in the tree line and circled to the side yard, she feared the worst. A row of broken down cars and disintegrating pianos formed an unsightly rampart guarding the side of the peeling house. There was not a chicken or cow or dog or cat anywhere in sight. A box truck and a Japanese motorbike were visible through the open barn door, but there were no tracks in the fresh snow that covered the barnyard.

When Investigator Lincoln made her way to the back door and knocked, she found that the door was ajar, too swollen to close, so she pushed it open and called out. When she heard faint voices she edged inside, entering a maze of junk, piles of chairs, boxes, bookshelves, fans, toolboxes, rolled up carpets, lamps, refrigerators, pieces of a pipe organ, bales of blankets tied with string, spools of wire, rusty dairy cans, buckets of rusty nails, and every other thing, piles of newspapers, stacks of firewood, and walls of black trash bags. Investigator Lincoln called out again and walked toward the voices, up a groaning staircase, announcing herself as required, "APS Investigator Lincoln, here to see Mr. Walter Stringfellow."

A voice called back, "Come on in. He's up here." At the top of the stairs, she turned and saw two men silhouetted against a bright window at the back of the house. The recliner was occupied by an older man and a stuffed wingback chair was occupied by a younger man, and there was a Scrabble board on the table between them. The older man was triumphantly placing tiles that spelled "sovereign" and shared the "o" with "foxglove," and crowing about his score. After the clutter of the first floor, Glorious was impressed by the sparse simplicity of the second floor. There was a pot of steaming water on a glowing wood stove standing inside a stone fireplace. There were two beds flanking the stove, and some fancy looking carpets were spread out on the floor. On the table between the men was a bowl of fresh fruit and a cutting board with a knife beside half a baguette, some cheese, and a hunk of salami.

The younger man sprung up to introduce himself and offer her tea, and his chair. Ms. Lincoln explained her purpose, and after she asked Radkin to leave them to talk for a few minutes, he nodded and disappeared down the stairs. He knew Wyatt would be behind this meddling. It became apparent to Ms. Lincoln that Mr. Stringfellow was in no danger. He was coughing into a handkerchief at intervals, but there was a serviceable bathroom, the stove threw out waves of warmth, and Mr. Stringfellow reported that the big claw foot tub in the bathroom, when filled to the top with hot water, was the best remedy for his medical condition.

"What is your condition, Mr. Stringfellow? Our information is limited."

"Oh, I'm dying of lung cancer," he announced brightly, "but I've been to a local doctor to get my records transferred and reviewed, and before I'm gone, I will be warm and well fed, and my son will let me win a certain percentage of our games. I was too proud to go into a nursing home like my younger son suggested, but this," he gestured out the big frosted window at this point, "this is what I needed." Under his breath, he made a short confession. "My older son here changed his name to Radkin years ago, and we thought he had lost his mind, but we were wrong. Now I see he's actually very responsible."

Glorious looked up from her notebook, after confirming that this tip had been anonymous. She asked for the younger son's phone number. Out the window she saw stone walls slanting across the snowy fields in the distance, and maple and apple trees coated in ice, and across the distant frozen lake, she saw the Adirondacks glinting in the morning sun. After Radkin returned, there was a perfunctory interview. He sat cross-legged on the floor and apologized for the clutter on the first floor.

"I just bought the place a few months ago, and I haven't had a chance to clear it all out. We live up here," he said. "It's warm and I only leave him alone when I go shopping and take care of my business. The water heater is brand new, and fills that tub. My father and I were out of touch for a time, but things are better now. He's agreed to sell the old house, my brother will handle it, and he'll stay here. Mom is dead, also lung cancer. We've already seen a local cancer specialist. I think he's gained some weight, and we're going to take a walk every day after the snow melts. If he makes it 'til then… "

Ms. Lincoln closed her notebook and decided to close the case. Wyatt Stringfellow was aghast when he received her phone call. She explained that her call was standard procedure, and that all family members had the right to appeal the Agency's decision. She gave no indication that she had deduced that he was the anonymous caller who had requested the check. Wyatt requested a copy of the redacted report. There was no appeal.

Since he was going to be home for the winter helping his father finish his race, Radkin looked for something he could do at home to make money. He knew he was probably on the spectrum, and he was proud of his affinity for technical, intricate, repetitive tasks. He had heard that a solar panel manufacturer across the lake would pay cash for tiny battery charger controller circuits that he could assemble in bulk at home. Radkin made a work bench near the woodstove by hammering the pins out of the hinges that held up a closet door, which he laid across a few sawhorses that he brought in from the tilted barn. Using the same car battery and extension cord that he had used at Crazy Creek, he dangled an extra light bulb, and rigged a soldering iron and transistor radio.

After studying the schematic for the controller circuit carefully, he engaged his superpower of mise en place, lining up a row of coffee cans to organize his mail-ordered stock of tiny circuit boards, resistors, sensors, sockets, coils of wire, switches, mosfet transistors and LED bulbs. Through the winter nights, warmed by cup after cup of hot black tea, and twitching to faint jazz from the Adelphi College radio station, Radkin assembled thousands of these tiny wafers to the rhythm of his father's breaths. He sat up straight in an industrious form of dhyana, his breath and hands cycling like waterwheels, the only clocks in the house. Eventually, he learned how to assemble these devices without the intervention of a single conscious thought. In the mornings, he would test each controller for continuity with a multimeter. The ones that failed were set aside for reconditioning, and the ones that tested okay were stacked for delivery in egg cartons he rescued from the recycle bin at The Molecule. The receiving clerk at the solar panel factory frowned when he eyeballed the first few egg cartons that Radkin delivered, but he dutifully pushed a check across his desk after punching his calculator buttons. Over time, as the production supervisor reported the flawless quality of Radkin's output, the clerk grew downright cheerful when Radkin made his deliveries, usually on his motorbike, even in snow and rain.

When Radkin first made his request to be paid only in gold or silver coins, based on the paranoia about banks, inflation, and market crashes that had been instilled in him by Green Gene, the clerk sighed with a doleful bulging cheek. But the next time Radkin delivered a batch of controllers, he received a small sleeve of gold half-ounce American Eagle coins that had been specially requisitioned from the bank. Over time, Radkin began to fill coffee cans with these clanking nuggets, and he eventually built a set of bookshelves, setting planks on stacks of coffee cans filled with coins and spray-painted gold.

It only took Mr. Stringfellow a few months to die, but neither man was troubled by a sense of impending doom. Radkin had no objection to being addressed as Bean. Radkin won most of their chess games, his father won most of the Scrabble games, and they were evenly matched at backgammon and setback. Radkin kept the stove warm, learned to make every type of soup his father could think of, and told every old story he could, to stir and tickle the roots of his father's faint rememberings.

Bean's life as a young boy had revolved around school, sports and books, so he told his fading father his best stories, in random order. He began with the one about how the big kids played baseball in the street, using a manhole cover as home plate, and opposing curbstones as first and third. Second base was marked with chalk. The big kids assigned Bean to play "sewer" position, responsible for catching the ball before it disappeared into the depths of the iron grate at the edge of the road, where subterranean pipes yawned and gurgled. This was the same street where he later learned to ride a bike, coasting down a slope that had seemed so steep at the time. He told a series of tales about walking to elementary school, taking a shortcut through the fragrant woods that the kids had named "Vietnam," because it was overgrown like the jungles on the evening news. When Radkin struggled to explain the smell of the woods, the rank smell of the weeds in the spring, his father smiled and nodded. There was no hurry.

During recess, Bean learned to play Red Rover, faking out the others long after he was the only one yet to be tagged. The basketball court was also run by the big kids, most of all by Marty Katzburg, the owner of the basketball which had once been pebbled, but now was pure smooth rubber and therefore slightly smaller than regulation and easier to handle. The games were half court, make-it take-it, winners stay on. After Walter realized that the winning team stayed on the court, he learned to dribble with both hands, to steal the ball and throw no-look passes, and to make the ball do exactly what he wanted. Eventually, Bean learned to play with what passed for elementary school playground swagger, throwing bounce passes between defenders' legs and banking shots off the perforated metal backboard so the chain net clanked.

He told his father about the first magical word he had learned from Mrs. Lenzen in third grade, how "sovereign" had burst in his mind like a flashbulb. Self-governing, autonomous, no synonym could convey the grandeur of sovereign, a word that stretched from London to Philadelphia and sounded like bright brass trumpets in his mind's ear. He lingered on this detail, and said the word again. He remembered the smell of the public library, of all those cellophane covers on the hardback books, and of the ink and paper and those gummedon labels with Dewey Decimal System numbers, all the books in their precise order. *Sabre Jet Ace* was his first favorite book. Mr. Stringfellow had served in the Air Force and flew the F-86, a fighter jet, and he had suspended a plastic model with decals on a piece of fishing line over his desk in the basement. Bean had been mesmerized by the picture of the snub-nosed fighter plane on the cover of the book, and the librarian laughed each time he checked the book out again. He recounted how his father would use his hands to demonstrate how his jet could outmaneuver the MIG by using the tighter turning radius of the F-86 to bank sharply and snap a fast roll straight back over the top of the MIG, and then drop in on its tail, hiding inside the glare of the sun. When Bean used the model plane to imitate this maneuver and broke it, he remembered how his father had just fixed the model, and hung it back up, but not out of reach.

He recalled reading all the Hardy Boys and Tom Swift books, and the Adventures of Tom Sawyer and Huck Finn. As the Hardy Boys solved their first dozen mysteries, Bean realized that he needed tools, mostly a flashlight and a pocket knife, and he learned how to blink SOS in Morse code. Tom Swift required more advanced tools, and Wyatt and Bean began gluing antennae to their football helmets, yelling into toilet paper tube microphones, and building robots from cardboard boxes with scissors and tape, using paper towel tubes for arms, and cutting ping pong balls in half to make eyeballs in shoe box robot heads. He confided how his friend had saved mercury from a broken thermometer and hid it in her pencil box, and how she liked to pour it in her hand and watch the globs separate and merge when she poked it.

The end of each elementary school year meant summer, which meant that Bean and his brother packed their shorts and t-shirts, and loaded into their mother's family station wagon to head to the shore where they rented a cottage by the bay, a different cottage each summer, in a grid of twenty rectangular blocks running from the Atlantic Ocean to Barnegat Bay. They skinned their knees, learned to swim, bike, played wiffle ball, threw frisbees, blew bubbles with Bazooka gum while they read the comic wrapper, and used white Elmer's glue and popsicle sticks to make small ashtrays. Their father stayed home to ride the Erie-Lackawanna to Hoboken, and then took the tubes under the Hudson River to Penn Station where he'd take the subway to Wall Street. On Friday nights, their father would drive to the shore, pull into the driveway, crunching on the yellow stones, and he would stay until Sunday night.

One Saturday morning in May when Bean had just finished 5th grade, instead of driving them straight to the shore, Bean's mother detoured to a dingy gymnasium in Newark where folding tables were covered with test forms, face down, and boxes of sharp #2 pencils. His mother waited in the car while a big group of kids were instructed to fill in little circles on the test form after the test monitor said go. He and Wyatt didn't recognize any of the other kids, and they were both so eager to get to the shore that they gave this surprise test no thought. Wyatt and Bean and their friends spent the next two and a half months bodysurfing, catching crabs along the bulkheads using long-handled nets and selling them to the black-toothed lady down the street, rowing dinghies across the little harbor and back, playing hit-the-bat in the street with a tennis ball, and riding bicycles in a pack, from the beach to bay, looking for short pants trouble.

Once or twice a summer they got to go to the boardwalk in Seaside, to slide down the steep wooden ramps on burlap mats, shriek in the fun house where the mirror made them look one foot tall and four feet wide and mechanical ghouls popped out of hiding places, spin in the teacups,  hold tight on the rollercoaster, ride the Ferris wheel into the night, high above the lights and smells of tar and popcorn, throw heavy balls at weighted bowling pins that never tipped over, and pinch clumps of vaporous cotton candy that would melt on their tongues.

Walter had forgotten about his test altogether, but near the end of August, back home, in scratchy new school  clothes, he was surprised one Monday morning to be walked to his first bus stop, to stand beside some kids that he'd never seen before. The green bus was a diesel, driven by a bald bus driver everybody called Eddie, who slung that tippy motor coach up and down the short, steep hills, using his left hand on the big wheel while he gobbled red pistachios from his red right hand, periodically throwing handfuls of the empty shells down into the stairwell, so they would fall out and mark every bus stop when he opened the doors.

That afternoon, shells crunched underfoot as Walter wrestled a stiff and heavy new bag of new books off the bus. His mother attempted a breezy inquiry about his first day at the Hillside School, but a furious Bean just clomped up the stairs. She  wisely held her fire, and left the debriefing for Mr.

Stringfellow after he got home from work. A few hours later, Walter's father knocked and came in. His dark suit smelled of newsprint and the railroad.

"I understand we have a problem," he observed, but as more of a question.

Walter was ready, and he vomited up his anger. "I'll tell you the problem, there's more than one, you send me to this egghead school, the bus stinks, I don't know anyone, and I have five homework assignments. FIVE, in all these textbooks, due tomorrow." He kicked at the book bag, on the brink of tears.

Mr. Stringfellow slid open the top drawer of his desk in the corner of Wyatt and Walter's bedroom where he did his taxes and paid his bills, and he took out a fresh yellow legal pad. "Make a list of your assignments on this page. I'll be back in a little while, when you've pulled yourself together."

This moment shaped young Walter's life in ways not anticipated by father or son. Writing down the assignments on the paper served to instantly diminish them. When his father returned and asked which of the five assignments was the hardest one, Walter pointed out the one that he dreaded the most, but the truth was that by making an inventory of the work, the list had already given him a powerful form of leverage. His father simply said, "Do that one first, then call me."

When Mr. Stringfellow returned, he said, "Now cross that one off the list, and do the next hardest one, then cross that one off, and keep going like that." As Radkin told him this part of the story, Mr. Stringfellow made a fist and punched the air like an umpire calling strike three, with a flash of stank face. Radkin's other stories seemed to please him, but none as much as this one.

The story about the sleepy silver haired black orderly at the hospital came close. Young Walter had been found by his mother, groaning and doubled over on the cold bathroom floor one night. (He had probably eaten a whole can of salted peanuts that day, he confessed as he told the story.) The Emergency Room doctor diagnosed Bean with pyloric stenosis. As he was being admitted to Orange Memorial in the middle of the night, the orderly handed him a bottle for a urine specimen and pointed to the bathroom. Walter took a quick inventory of his bladder and shook his head, signaling an empty tank. The orderly just nodded and held Walter's hand under a stream of warm water in the sink beside his work station. His young patient promptly filled the bottle, and never forgot. This gentleman knew things.

Mr. Stringfellow dozed in and out of most of these meandering storylines, on his way to his final rest. Radkin improved some of the stories as he went, taking advantage of every opportunity to invent a better tale through the process of telling. As the rattle in his father's chest got slower and louder, his oldest son grew more calm and quiet, and more selective in his stories. Their routine was no longer indexed to the sun. Walter Senior slept, and grew confused, but he faded and rallied on his own schedule. After talking to Wyatt, Walter called hospice, and his father accepted the advice of the hospice nurses who promised to help him make a dignified exit. He was able to competently explain his desire for purely palliative care, and Radkin monitored his father's responses to the various patches that they placed behind his ears, to ease his pain and reduce his nausea and gurgling respiration. Radkin ran completely out of stories before the end came. Walter Senior gradually stopped eating and drinking. Radkin kept the fire burning, offered spoonfuls of tea and soup, and played his own kind of quiet ragas on the guitar, accompanied by the metronome. Father and son never discussed Radkin's phone call from college, nor did they contend over their years apart or Radkin's absence from his mother's funeral.

One night, Radkin was not sure of the day of the week or the date, he paused his playing after his metronome ran down and stopped.  He realized that the rattle had stopped. What remained in the recliner was not his father any more. He made sure, whispering to him, touching his hands and face, and feeling for any faint pulse. His spirit had fled. His race was run. Radkin finally allowed a black shiver  to overtake him, traveling the length of his vagus nerve and releasing his long-suppressed grief.

It was late, and Radkin decided to wait until daylight to call for help. He had looked at his list of things to do, which he had clipped to the funeral home pamphlet, the hospice package and the "do not resuscitate" directive. He called Wyatt at work and left a message on his answering machine. Finally, he put some more wood in the stove, and carried a candle into the closet where he bent over a stack of shoe boxes, muttering to himself as he searched, "box three, tape five." He put the tape on, low, and watched the shadows rise and fall until morning.

The ambulance arrived without any lights or siren, and the crew was very efficient and professional. Wyatt handled the estate, and the details of their father's cremation.  Mr. Stringfellow left them each an equal and modest bequest, after deduction of Wyatt's 3% executor fee.

## CHAPTER 51

**AGENT NORTON WAS ALL ATINGLE** with investigative caffeine when he pulled into the Sparklewood Animal Hospital, but the ginger lady behind the desk was no help at all. She was trimming a big unhappy poodle slung in a tabletop hammock, and the shaver she was using was so loud, she didn't even realize Norton was there until he finally slapped the little bell on the counter. She was new on the job, and was bleeding from her free hand where the poodle had nipped her. No, there was no such Walter person who worked or taught piano here, she assured him, and she declined to take a close look at his badge or make a move to take his card. She nodded at the counter and switched the shaver back on, so Norton left his card beside the little bell and saw himself out. He had expected to see a piano or something. As long as he was near the woods, he decided to take another look around for the patch, but no sooner did he pull his Ford into the parking lot than it began to pour rain. On a hunch, he doubled back to the hospital and went inside. The pale red lady was waiting, whisk broom and dust pan in hand.

"Is the doctor available? The owner?"

She turned away from him, resumed her squatting stance, and filled the dustpan with a quarter of a poodle of fuzz. "He's in surgery 'til noon, but I'll give him your card."

Norton took a look around, as if he had a mind to wait, but the chorus of barking dogs in the chain link kennels out back made him nervous. His interest in the Minnie Mouse tattoo on the lady's freckled back, peeking out between the top of her pants and the bottom of her shirt, was mostly professional. He thanked her and, after grabbing a few of Dr. Bauch's business cards, he headed back out into the rain.

## CHAPTER 52

**AFTER HIS FATHER'S DEPARTURE, RADKIN** pushed the two beds together. He found that the big bed was difficult to make alone, and it was filled with strange dreams. He snuck into Sparklewood and hoisted the season's first buckets of seedlings into the treetops. His water line had not been discovered. He resumed his writing, realizing he had not written a word since hospice had been called in.

Radkin had revised the way that his story would begin with his hero making the bed, either alone or with his wife. Or girlfriend. No, alone. And not the actual manufacturing of the bed itself, because that would require a detour to a factory in, say, Ensenada, with cork tipped hammers tapping and ringing brass tubes and sleeves, and the screams of saws and the whoosh of torches, plus mariachi music on the radio and the tinkle of brass screws in jars. A visit to Peachtree City would also have to be included, where wire, satin, cotton batting, and pallets of Georgia pine would be measured and cut and wrapped and tacked and sewn and swathed and labeled in a long dim mattress warehouse where fans flickered, and looms clattered as shiny women ran sticks across webs of filaments on ratcheting spindles. Not that kind of bed making.

Making the allegorical bed would be his domestic Genesis, and establish the set and setting of the story. First, his hero would stretch a fitted sheet from one corner of the mattress to another, an act of optimism. Or his villain, in desperation, either way. Some primitive version of string theory suggested he would only need to master two points initially, because the sheet would obey a straight line, theoretically. It was the 3rd corner, the formation of the crucial hypotenuse, that was most difficult, and then the fourth corner would be triumphant, the conclusive snuggery.

He still considered whether a couple making the bed before entangling would be less engaging than the bed-making that followed a glorious bed wrecking. He considered practical reasons of motive and credibility. What dainty couple pauses to make a bed before climbing in, anyway? Is it laundry day? How long had they been together? He considered the post-scrimmage bed-making scene as the couple was glazed and flushed. No, forget that. Knowing, without doubt, that his prospective angel was sure to arrive any minute, his expectant hero could make a righteous choreography of the solitary task, especially as he stretched the elastic hem of the fitted sheet to the precarious third and fourth corners. The delicate bedspread would be silk and linen, patterned with crocodilian windowpane, scales of magenta from a bottle of Bordeaux, and Benedictine green, and bands of gold with grain of black oak, brilliant in the dim room. Yes, his bed would be covered with a thin Mandarin flying carpet, made luminous with many washings.

Radkin would furnish his whole story the same way, not with department store beige, but by weaving fractal words together until the stained glass lamp began to glow in the corner of the bedroom and the tortoiseshell kitten, Zorro, yawned and stretched on the windowsill. He decided to begin with the solitary bed-making image, and to end his tale with them making the bed together, on some happy morning ever after. He needed to know the ending before he started, and there was nothing happier, more hopeful, braver, there was no more center-of-the-universe crucible than a man and woman making a bed in the birdsong morning. Let the Italians have their steaming stoves and crowded kitchen tables, let the French smoke at their street side cafes and drink ink from ceramic thimbles. Radkin would make their magic bed, first and last.

Of course, this progression was all hypothetical because Radkin slept in a sleeping bag stretched out on the big bed of perplexing dreams, alone. He managed to hold himself apart from every possible romantic entanglement, mired in ambivalence about the prospect of unacceptable compromise in the course of the mating dance that would lead to the wished-for bed. He had developed an uncanny power to rule out every woman he met, most on first glance, and the rest shortly after the first few chemistry tests had been satisfied.

Radkin was not proud of his fragile capacity to adore. He blamed his monastic life on a traumatic seaside romance during the summer before his senior year of high school. A kindred young lady with synchromesh karma and luminous eyes had entranced him at first glance. They seemed to fit together fast, almost embarrassed by their near-spontaneous combustion. But Radkin was simply unable to unsee the vision that burned his innermost eyeball chakra the very first time she kicked off her shoes, and he saw her hammertoes with toenails painted pink, black and white, like podiatric Good 'N Plenty. Love was complicated. He could never love a woman with such mutant toes. He hid inside his book, where it was safe.

SECTION XI


43 GALLONS OF WHISKEY


"You see, the wire telegraph is a kind of
very, very long cat. You pull his tail in New York
and his head is meowing in Los Angeles…
and radio operates exactly the same way:
you send signals here, they receive them there.
The only difference is there is no cat."
— Albert Einstein

## CHAPTER 53

**ON FRIDAY NIGHTS FROM FIVE** to seven o'clock, the bar and restaurant at Taco-Rita filled up with a cross-section of customers who had at least one important interest in common: an appreciation of being overserved with cheap tequila, the kind that tastes like soap. Along with the men in denim, the migrant apple pickers, the dusty-booted yard men, the sunburned surveyors and tractor mechanics, and the men in plaid flannel who spilled out of pickup trucks in clouds of cigarette smoke and éspañol, there were men in blue suits, shirts with name tags, in scrubs, white button-down shirts, pastel golf shirts, V-necks and swinging medallions, and real and fake gold Rolexes to clank down on the bars and tabletops, in case any señoritas might need to know the correct time.

Some of these señoritas were named Maria and Esmeralda and Felina and Carmen, and also Dominique and Flora and Rosa, and they were mostly animated, petite and angular, with piles of dark curls, dressed in bright patterns of hibiscus and olive and lotus and camellia and magnolia. There was also a contingent of clucking Anglo-Saxon ladies in small after-work groups, in Bible-study-approved blouses and skirts and sensible flats or low heeled shoes. This scrum provided Weatherly with cover, as the happy hour grew louder and happier and more crowded. She held her glass of red wine in front of her face, as she peered through the big fish tank and piñatas and spider plants and hanging lamps and Tecate signs that served as atmosphere. In this polyglot ruckus, an unusual setting for the normally cloistered Weatherly, bits of competing conversations whirled about her in a vertiginous 360° fugue. She pretended to be casual and relaxed, nursing her wine at the bar and scanning the restaurant, while avoiding the sort of eye contact that might invite transactional small talk from the watchful professional small-talking men, who grimaced and grew braver with each swallow of tequila.

Just as a shiny-faced chiropractor with a snoot-full approached and gestured to the empty seat beside her with an arched eyebrow, Weatherly heard a raised voice behind a nearby ficus tree, a familiar voice that had recently bellowed "Federal Agent, Federal Agent!" at her and her dog. This time, however, Agent Norton was litigating his entitlement to a free margarita with the waiter. The waiter was small and bronze and faintly Aztec, and his name tag said 'Santiago.' Dozens of fuzzy balls hung down from the rim of his sombrero on braided strings, and they jiggled as he leaned closer to listen to Norton's animated explanation of his predicament. Weatherly edged around the ficus as the waiter tried to hand a blank punch card to Norton and repeated the mantra "aquí" over and over, from inside a constellation of orbiting balls of red fluff. Norton was waving away the punch card, and just as he drew an immense and frustrated breath to expand his power of persuasion, Weatherly pounced.

"I believe you are a federal agent?"

Norton turned to face her, as she sat down at his table. Seeing his chance, Santiago escaped, hurrying to put in an order for the margarita that Norton had been jabbering about.

"May I speak with you a minute?"

Norton's eyes turned to slits, and he straightened up in his chair so that he towered over her. He looked around the room quickly, making note of the baleful stare of the chiropractor, who was cracking his knuckles at the bar.

She went on. "I am aware that you are a federal agent, and I am prepared to offer some sensitive information to you in your official capacity."

Norton's eyes were practically closed now, as he had inflated himself fully into what he hoped was a suitably eminent posture. Weatherly seized the initiative.

"Is this your Taco-Rita card?" She opened her hand and displayed the precious ticket which would  entitle him to an absolutely free margarita, with just one box to go. It was stained with mud.

At this, Norton deflated his federal chest half way, and slumped forward.
 "What is this all about?  What do you think you're doing with that card?"

Weatherly eased herself into a whispery confession, during which Norton was hypnotized by the punch card she tapped on the table for emphasis. Behind the ficus, Dr. Popright drained his drink, and strained to hear as he repeated his knuckle-cracking ritual, a systematic articular release of his metacarpophalangeal joints, producing tiny pops as he collapsed cavitation bubbles in his synovial fluid.

"It is my intention to offer a confidential tip to you about a matter under federal investigation, but only if you can expressly guarantee that my anonymity will be completely protected."

Keeping his eyes trained on the nine unmistakable sombrero-shaped punches in his card, Norton asked in a husky baritone. "Is this about that criminal Hungarian weight-lifter?"

Weatherly closed her hands over the card and Norton looked up. "Is my identity secured?"

Norton sputtered. "I don't even know who you are or why you have my card, but I'm not on the job right now, and happy hour only lasts another 20 minutes." Just then Santiago bent over the table to present Norton's margarita with a bullfighting flourish, his tilt-a-whirl hat in full jiggly splendor.

Weatherly handed the punch card to the waiter and quietly instructed him to bring the gentleman his free margarita, muchas gracias. Santiago squinted at the card and took it as he nodded, and the fuzzy balls bounced before he returned to the bar.

Norton sat back. He was now fully deflated. There was something familiar about this lady. "What is this all about?"

Weatherly baited the hook. "I have some material information about your investigation in Sparklewood, and I will give it to you once you assure me of my protected status as an anonymous source."

Weatherly enunciated carefully, as she recited the precise United States Code section under which she would be entitled to recover treble damages and attorney fees if the government failed to protect her identity. She also pointed out that his career would likely be at an end, since she knew from public records that he had destroyed governmental property on his last assignment. Through the ficus tree, Dr. Popright's semi-clinical exam detected her slightly stooped posture, and he made a mental note to explain how he could provide discounted treatment of her cervical kyphosis, in the event the big fellow wasn't her type.

Now Norton hid his face behind his glass, as the waiter placed a fresh drink and a fresh punch card on the table. Norton nodded at the waiter, and then sipped his margarita and struck a pensive pose, in order to give himself time to think. His training had been spotty on this whistleblower deal, and the bossy lady seemed to have done some research.

"Well, you don't have your facts exactly right," he condescended in a low tone intended to re-establish his gravitas. He tucked his new punch card into his wallet and removed a business card to give her. "You see, I was held responsible for the malfunction of those defective brakes, but it worked out so that, after most of the damage was repaired,

I got to keep the car. In fact, I drove it here." Stalling for time and eager to show off his surprisingly workmanlike Rustoleum rattlecan  paint job, he pulled back the floral Otami curtain in front of the window beside their table, and invited Weatherly to behold the glory of his Ford. Which, unfortunately, was once again en fuego. On fire.

Agent Norton sprang into action, knocking both his margaritas and Weatherly's glass of wine onto the floor as he jumped up. He grabbed two full pitchers of margaritas from the end of the bar, and elbowed his way through the front door, to hurry across the parking lot and dump them on the flames. Due to Taco-Rita's generous ABV, the alcohol served as lighter fluid and the flames exploded skyward, causing Norton to drop both pitchers at his feet. His effort to flee the resulting shower of fire and glass shards turned into a frantic hokey pokey dance, but there was only minor cosmetic damage to his steel-toed shoes. Norton glanced towards  the bar window to see if this anonymous tipster woman was watching him, but he only saw Santiago, who was busy licking his pencil and adding the cost of the two pitchers to his bill. Chiropractor Popright was watching from the front door, holding a fresh drink.

Norton surveyed the parking lot for a hose or something, as the flames climbed. He did a double take when he heard someone jeering at him from a pickup truck that was waiting to pull into traffic. Blavatsky was jubilant, flashing a middle finger with a "W" at its base, the upside down "M" from his "PUMP IRON" tattoo.

Enraged, Norton raced back into Taco-Rita and, once again, turned loose his highly trained instincts to respond to the emergency. First, he knocked all the bowls of mints and matches and toothpicks off the front counter. Then, employing the same power lifting techniques he had learned from Blavatsky. With his knees bent, legs apart, back straight, and after a bracing breath, out then in, Norton lifted the large aquarium off its pedestal by the cash register. Sensing a second chance with the lady, Popright held the door open as Norton shouldered through the entrance and staggered towards his four door gas grill. The extension cord that ran the pumps and lights popped out of the electric outlet in the wall and trailed behind him, and the fish darted from side to side as the water sloshed back and forth with each step that Norton took.

Pyromaniacs and other scientists would have advised Norton that a few of the Mexican blankets that were folded and stacked for sale by the cash register may have been a superior choice for smothering this sort of fire, but Norton learned this lesson for himself. He received second degree burns on his hands and face as an enormous cloud of steam engulfed him when the aquarium contents met the flames. By the time the fire truck got there, Norton's Ford was a crackling biohazard, with a spiraling plume of flames and toxic smoke ascending and a pool of melting rubber surrounding each flat tire. Tiny boiled tropical fish festooned a whimpering Norton, as medics applied silvadene cream and gauze bandages to his wounds. When he was arrested, for some reason he decided not to pull out his badge and announce his Federal Agent status, or identify Blavatsky as the real criminal.

Seated in the patrol car, as his Ford was sprayed full of foam, Norton remembered that his gym bag, containing the rest of his supply of monkey hormones diverted from the Blavatsky case, was in the trunk of his car. Vandalism and disorderly conduct were minor charges, but the tipster lady had been right. His second vehicle fire and possession of these liquefied monkey bits, if discovered, would probably mark the end of his drug enforcement career. Unless… He took a deep breath to calm the frothing, squirming coil of his mind so he could be strategic. And there it was. His confidential source, whoever she was, had just given him a lifeline. The tip, whatever it was, could be his redemption. He would need to talk to a lawyer, some smart well-connected guy.

## CHAPTER 54

**LEONARD DREYFUS HAD REPRESENTED A** wide variety of accused criminals, some of whom were, as seen in movies and on TV, malicious, intoxicated, greedy, addicted, short tempered, scheming, vengeful, and/or desperately poor. However, Dreyfus had found, sadly, that in real life most defendants were simply a boring combination of stupid and unlucky. This Norton fellow was a prime example. He was sure to be fired by the DEA, having been in trouble before, and now having been charged with vandalism and possession of endangered animal parts. Their interview took an unforeseen turn, however, as Norton began to explain his predicament, while he rubbed his bandaged hands together to ease the itch of his burns.

His jar of adrenal soup had been salvaged from the car by the firemen, and confiscated by the police as evidence, so he was sleepier and duller than usual, and his bail bondsman had required him to empty most of his bank account, so he was desperate. "I like being an agent, and I need to try to keep this quiet, and keep my job. I'm assigned to take down a drug perp right now, and I just received a tip that may be my key to a good bust."

Dreyfus scribbled notes, and without looking up, invited him to explain by circling his pen in the air.

"We've got intel that there's a field of pot growing in Sparklewood, very high grade stuff. And it's been hard to find. But right as that asshole set my car on fire, I was about to get a hot tip from an informant."

Leonard laid down his pen, and leaned back in his seat. His mustache flickered in the thoughtful exhale that followed, as he considered the implications for Ratzlaff. "Sparklewood, you say?"

Norton saw that his disclosure had sharpened Dreyfus's attention so he went on quickly. "Some out-of-town doctor is trying to build a nursing home out there, and I think he might have something to do with the pot. Do you think that I might keep my job if I can get a tip that leads to a conviction?"

Now Leonard Dreyfus was fully engaged. He could interview Norton later about this supposed tip and this Hungarian weightlifter that Norton blamed for the fire. A chance to kneecap Ratzlaff was irresistible. "Let's go over the contract, and the terms of my retainer. If I get started on this right away, we might be able to shut down the prosecution, and protect your job, too." Norton rubbed his gauze mittens together again, and rocked his chair closer to the table to read the paperwork that would explain how much more money

Blavatsky was going to cost him. Dreyfus changed his tone here, slowing down to be sure that his new client was following his favorite history lesson. "Back in the old frontier days, there was no 911, and there were no police forces in those towns, so people hired gunfighters to settle their differences…"

## CHAPTER 55

**WEATHERLY WAS SUSPICIOUS, BUT SHE** remained clinical as she put Mr. Dreyfus on hold, and buzzed Mr. Ratzlaff. Dreyfus had occasionally called her new boss before, usually to ventilate his durable resentment about Ratzlaff having lured his best secretary away with more money and god knows what other incentives, dental and profit sharing. From her desk, she could hear only Ratzlaff's monosyllabic greeting, followed by utter silence. Silence was not how Ratzlaff did business, generally. Whether it was by having the loudest voice, the last cutting word, or the most menacing posture, Ratzlaff treated almost every interaction with another lawyer as a challenge to his superior power. As his silence persisted, Weatherly glanced at the light on her phone several times, to be sure their connection was still intact. Eventually, she heard Ratzlaff deliver a growling sign-off, and after his extension light went dark, she flinched three times at three loud bangs. Ratzlaff's phone was slammed down first, and then his door was flung open and slammed shut, and then Ratzlaff slammed the door to Freeman's office so hard behind him that a dish of paperclips on Weatherly's desk jumped up and landed with a jingle.

Even the receptionist up front could hear Ratzlaff's ensuing tirade, punctuated by the sound of books swept off Freeman's desk onto the floor, and a stream of invective, dire threats of malpractice, of termination, of disaster for the firm and for the client. Stripped of the considerable obscene content, the whole office heard Mr. Ratzlaff inform Mr. Dearborn that Mr. Dreyfus had learned from Federal Agent Norton that Dr. Zuckerman's property was being investigated by the DEA for some sort of drug activity, of which Mr. Dearborn had evidently not seen fit to apprise Mr. Ratzlaff, for some ridiculous preposterous idiotic reason. And by the way, was Dr. Zuckerman aware of this little complication, and either motherfucking way, what the motherfucking fuck?

Freeman's reply was faint, a murmur of pale remonstrance. "I'll handle it." Ratzlaff paused awhile, breathing heavily, before nodding his head. "You're fucking right, you'll handle it. When you figure out how, you just let me know. Get Zuckerman in here first thing tomorrow."

Whenever he was in the office, Ratzlaff's 1962 Silver Cloud Rolls Royce was parked out front, his monument to himself. The Rolls was an immaculate symbol of ostentatious vulgarity, or wealth, either way, with a cabin of tanned, chromed bull hide, and walnut burl. No one entered his office without passing his tax-deductible trophy, which was leased and written off as a business expense since it had a license plate that said "DIFORCELAW." Almost every Wednesday, Ratzlaff used this car to pick up a referring lawyer for lunch, saving all the receipts in a pile on Weatherly's desk, as recommended by his accountant. However, as the Silver Cloud exited the parking lot this time, it did so indecorously, squealing on two wheels, and the V8 exhaust buffeted the conference room window with a shower of mulch blown clear out of the landscaping out front. As this spectacle receded, Dearborn mustered  his remaining dignity and opened his office door, the same door that Ratzlaff had slammed on his way in and on his way out. Without looking Weatherly directly in the eye, Dearborn asked her to please pull together the Zuckerman file and schedule a conference for the next morning with the doctor, but not before 11 a.m., so he would have time to review the file first. Without another word, he quickly walked past the staring staff and drove away in his old Honda. He knew better than to consult with Dreyfus. He knew that he would need to level with Zuckerman, but that would require him to make a recommendation, one that would protect the client, and mollify Ratzlaff, that miserable dwarf. Freeman drove to Sparklewood Forest to do some thinking.

## CHAPTER 56

**WEATHERLY HAD A SOFT HEART,** but she knew better than to volunteer anything resembling legal advice to a client. She had learned the hard way, back at the Dreyfus firm, where she had made the mistake of recommending her acupuncturist to a woman that Mr. Dreyfus was defending in a car crash case. Mrs. Mancini was a kindly grandmother who had rammed her vintage Buick LeSabre into the back of a station wagon full of Cub Scouts at a red light. Her insurance company had hired Dreyfus to try to limit the damages. One day, as she limped out of a meeting with Dreyfus, Mrs. Mancini paused to lean on Weatherly's desk, where she winced and clapped a hand on her low back.

"Oh, Mrs. Mancini, are you all right?"

Mrs. Mancini took a deep breath and explained how, ever since the accident, she got a little jolt of nerve pain down her leg whenever she sat too long. Also, whenever she stood up too long. Really, she admitted, she hurt all the time. Little did Weatherly know how her recommendation of Qi Ping, licensed herbalist and acupuncturist, would end her tenure at the firm.

Dreyfus had long derived a steady supply of hourly income from The Golden Peanut Insurance Company, as he defended a stream of inattentive, drunk, distracted or half-blind drivers, and other varieties of negligent insureds. Initially, he had enticed Golden Peanut with a combination of attractive qualities. His hair was silver, his hourly rate was discounted, and his combination of lofty oration and aggressive defense tactics served to facilitate favorable settlements for the company's insureds. In keeping with his "never charge by the bullet" philosophy, in cases where he had been especially effective, he had learned to multiply every hour on his time sheet tally by two, to make up for his reduced rate.

The Mancini case was the end of his Golden Peanut work. At trial, there was a little snafu. The injured Scouts had all hired different lawyers, and because Mancini had limited liability coverage, there seemed to be no way to craft a global settlement which would be to the mutual satisfaction of all the claimants and their counsel, all of whom huffed and puffed and threatened to blow the modest Mancini house down. As Dreyfus prepared to cross examine the first plaintiff to get to trial, Weatherly was seated right behind counsel table. She was responsible for keeping the file organized, and handing Dreyfus the right papers, each outline, medical record, clipped packet of case law, witness folder and exhibit, precisely when they were needed.

"Young man, is it your testimony today that you still have pain in your neck, even now, almost a year after this unfortunate incident?"

The chubby plaintiff nodded his head vigorously, up and down, with no hint of impairment. Dreyfus looked at the jury with a wink, before he smiled and bobbed his own head with matching vigor as he asked the court reporter to let the record show that the plaintiff had nodded "yes."

The plaintiff was a cheerful boy named Maypo Barlow. At pre-trial, Judge Pinkerton had conducted a brief hearing regarding the advisability of letting a thirteen-year-old claimant testify at trial. An earnest specimen of a trustworthy scout, Maypo had demonstrated a firm grasp on the difference between truth and wishful thinking, the perils of guessing while under oath, and the importance of listening carefully to each question without interrupting. He had not yet, however, grasped the challenge of transcribing a nod of the head.

Judge Pinkerton had ruled that the witness would be permitted to testify, and also that he would be allowed to appear in Court wearing his Scout uniform, complete with neckerchief, his wolf rank badge and a string of arrow-shaped merit badges and silvery service stars on his shirt. Maypo's lawyer was a stocky meatball named Joe Pozzi, whose smiling face graced many bus stop benches, taxi cabs, and train station platforms in and around Adelphi. "Call Joe to win dough!" was his marketing hook, and he wore not one, but two pinky rings, big as lugnuts. At the pre-trial, in his shiniest sharkskin suit, unburdened by a single sheet of paper or cite to case law, Pozzi had presented his arguments like he expected to lose, speaking in a shrill and recriminatory tone, waving his arms about like a man falling backwards through a trapdoor. Pozzi argued that police officers and doctors and nurses frequently testified in uniform, so a Cub Scout should enjoy the same privilege. Dreyfus had shrugged and declined to argue the issue, sure that the tender young witness could be gently and easily impeached regardless of his khaki clothing.

"It's my understanding that, since this accident, you have received more than $10,000 worth of treatment from an outfit called 'Lotus Therapy.' Is that true?"

Maypo nodded again, and when prompted by the Judge, he leaned into the microphone and delivered an earnest "yes." After he flinched at the volume of his amplified voice, he whispered "yes, sir." He looked at the Judge for reassurance, but Pinkerton was busy rocking in his big chair and dreaming of his upcoming audit. A blown-up picture of Mrs. Mancini's car was on an easel beside the jury box, so Dreyfus could show how little front-end damage had resulted from the crash, but Pinkerton was more interested in the original avocado green paint job on her Buick, which was the exact same color as his Hotpoint stove at home.

"And is it true that, during most of your therapy sessions, your therapist at Lotus would place little needles in your arms and back and neck, little acupuncture needles as thin as hairs?" Dreyfus spit out the word "therapist" like it tasted bad, to convey that acupuncture was distasteful quackery, not actual medicine.

Maypo repeated his "yes, sir" without any flinching this time. Dreyfus was pleased to note, once again, the vigor of the plaintiff's head bobbing, free of any grimace or restriction, and he looked at the jury as he mimicked Barlow by nodding his own head repeatedly in an exaggerated manner. Dreyfus accepted a piece of paper from Weatherly at this point, and waved it about as he asked his next question.

"You received $10,000 or so worth of treatment from therapist Ping at Lotus, including something called 'moxibustion' which is a treatment with special needles with," he paused here for effect, "little balls of mugwort, a Chinese herb, stuck onto the end of the needles and lit on fire while the needles were in your neck and back? Isn't that true?"

Maypo looked at his lawyer for help, but Pozzi was busy checking his watch and tightening his lug nuts, and made no attempt to object.

Maypo nodded, and after he was prompted by Judge Pinkerton again, he answered. "I'm not sure about the moxibus or the mug wart part, but some smoky stuff was used on my, on some of my needles, yes, sir. I tried not to look."

Dreyfus stepped away from the lectern and moved closer to the jury box. Juror number two, a ferret-faced woman, was stooped over and scribbling furiously on her notepad, but Dreyfus couldn't read it. He waited for her to finish, and then he waved the medical bill around again and continued.

"And are you surprised, Mr. Barlow, that even after $10,037 worth of needles and smoking mugwort, or whatever it was, you still claim to have some pain in your neck?"

Barlow scrunched up his face, and looked over at his lawyer, who was busy smoothing his tie, a flowery good luck charm that his first wife had bought him in Atlantic City. Barlow then looked up at Judge Pinkerton, who was rubbing his eyes. Barlow looked back at Dreyfus and asked, "What do you mean?"

Dreyfus rephrased his question, even though somewhere in the recesses of his vestigial cross-examination brain, a professor named Irving Younger furiously waved a red flag of danger. "What makes you think this was legitimate and effective medical treatment, this $10,037 worth of acupuncture or moxibustion, or whatever therapist Ping gave you at Lotus?"

At first, Joe Pozzi began to climb to his feet, but then he tilted his head, and resettled in his chair instead, with a frown like he had a bit of indigestion.

Barlow understood now. "Well, sir, every time I went to see my doctor or therapist or whatever she is, there were lots of people waiting in line for her treatments, even that lady right there, the friendly lady that works with you. I saw her in there the first time I went, talking to her, the defendant lady that ran into us, Mrs. Mancini. When I first saw them together in the waiting room, Mrs. Mancini was saying how bad she was hurting, and she was crying a little bit. I knew this needle treatment must be for real."

Judge Pinkerton winced and stopped rocking in his chair. He sadly excused the jury for lunch early. Both Dreyfus and Pozzi braced for a scolding, but before either lawyer could speak, Judge Pinkerton requested the motions for mistrial that he knew they were both obligated to make, and that he was obligated to grant. When Dreyfus turned around to collect his file, Weatherly was gone, and Pozzi and Barlow were both staring at the floor, whispering to each other like they both had indigestion now.

Dreyfus was fired by Golden Peanut that night, by telephone. Some regional claims administrator from Des Moines called him at home, and grumbled about how the limited coverage was, in this case, a big enough problem without any false starts.  The next day, Dreyfus forced Weatherly to admit that she had given Ping's name to Mrs. Mancini, not realizing how the ensuing prejudice might infect Barlow's testimony, simultaneously creating sympathy for Mancini and bolstering Ping's legitimacy in a double-edged snafu. Dreyfus gave Weatherly a stern lecture, stern enough to make her fear for her job. But the truth was that she had been his best secretary by far, despite this incident, and his threat about how he would have to think about whether to find another assistant was just for show. The bill that he had sent to the Golden Peanut Insurance Company for his trial prep time in <u>Barlow vs. Mancini</u> was returned unopened, marked "return to sender."

To Dreyfus' profound surprise and disappointment, Weatherly gave her two weeks' notice a few weeks later, in hushed penitential tones. She explained that she had taken a job at another firm. Dreyfus was speechless, and he was too proud to ask her to stay. He was also too proud to ask where she would be working, or why she had seen fit to seek out another job without talking to him. When he later learned she was working for Ratzlaff, his disappointment was multiplied. That bastard.

# CHAPTER 57

**DEARBORN WANDERED THE TRAILS AT** Sparklewood, wondering how he would explain all this to Zuckerman, and how and why that awkward DEA guy had gotten in touch with Dreyfus. He had left his tie and his jacket in the car, and was seriously reconsidering his career choices. Now, of course, every green patch of ferns and sassafras and poison ivy looked like pot, or whatever it was known as, cannabis.

Ratzlaff had a prominent vein in the middle of his tall forehead that bulged when he was mad, and as his cadenza of "motherfuckings" had washed over his young associate, the masseter muscles in Ratzlaff's jaw had also stood out like straining ropes. Between the vein in his forehead, his clenched jaw, and his bulbous eyes, Ratzlaff had resembled a malevolent Popeye. As Freeman thought about that terrible moment, sandy bits of one of his lower front teeth crumbled and cracked. He had been grinding his teeth for months. He spat out the grit as he walked in circles around the area where this supposed patch had appeared on Agent Norton's map, but there was nothing that looked like drugs. On his way out, Freeman noticed that someone had spray painted a red circle with a diagonal slash over the notice of the final hearing that had been posted beside the parking lot. He went home and tried to sleep.

Freeman woke up at 3 a.m. with a pounding headache and more grit in his mouth. When he was still awake at 4 a.m., he just got dressed and drove to the office. It was eerie in the dark, and when he flicked on the light in his office, the Sparklewood file was on his desk along with his calendar, which showed that Weatherly had scheduled a conference with Zuckerman for 11 a.m.

Some papers were  clipped on top of the file, and they were marked with a series of stick-on flags on which Weatherly had written notes. On top of the pile was a recent memo to the file recounting Weatherly's discussion with Zuckerman in the reception area, describing his mother's miraculous improvement, the restoration of her appetite and acuity, and mentioning Weatherly's recommendation that Zuckerman's misgivings about the project should be discussed with the firm. On the memo, Weatherly had written "Client wants to reassess. Rescind under paragraph 13?"

Beneath this memo, opened to paragraph 13, was the file copy of the Purchase and Sale Agreement that Zuckerman and Bauch had signed. Weatherly's note read "Property is unsuitable due to possible forfeiture/marijuana investigation?" She had highlighted the exact weasel words that Freeman had crossed out in the rough draft. This DEA thing was grounds for rescission by Zuckerman? Freeman felt a twinge, and then the spreading flush of shame and gratitude.

Next in the stack were copies of two Federal Court opinions. U.S. vs. 43 Gallons of Whiskey was marked with Weatherly's note reading "Shepherdized. Land containing still and moonshine was subject to seizure". US vs. John B. Good Real Property was the second case, in which forfeiture of Mr. Good's property to the federal government was affirmed, after an illegal marijuana patch was found there.

Freeman's jaw hung open like the bucket shovel that either would, or would not, excavate Sparklewood Forest for Zuckerman's nursing home project. His headache began to lift. The first rosy fingers of daybreak began to wiggle faintly out his window, and chase the ghosts from his office. He rinsed more grit out of his mouth.

Freeman set about outlining his conference with Zuckerman, accounting for the rude reality of Norton's investigation, the prospect of establishing unsuitability due to potential forfeiture, and the option of rescission. He barely paused in his preparations, researching case law upholding rescission of purchase and sale agreements for similar reasons of unsuitability, right up until the moment Zuckerman's Cadillac pulled into the lot.

Freeman skipped his normal smiling and handshaking performance, and Zuckerman sat and took off his glasses and rubbed his eyes as Freeman closed the door to the conference room. When Freeman asked how his mother was doing, Zuckerman just rubbed his eyes some more, and when Freeman asked about the changes described in Weatherly's memo, the doctor's shoulders began to shake.

At this point, Freeman slid a box of tissues across the table and began to methodically explain the situation at Sparklewood, both the risks and the new opportunity. He confessed that he had dismissed the DEA agent's inquiry as comical, the result of some glitch in the thermal imaging. He apologized that he had not seen fit to mention this development, and that he had hoped not to alarm Zuckerman. At first, he couldn't tell if Ratzlaff had gone behind his back to tell Zuckerman already, but it became apparent that these legal words were unexpected and exotic relief for his client, who blew his nose as he marveled at the mention of rescission, forfeiture, unsuitable for the intended purpose, null and void, refund. Even the threat of a Federal investigation seemed to have no chilling effect on Zuckerman. Freeman kept his summary short, and he was ready to make his recommendation, but only after he explicitly confirmed that Zuckerman was not implicated in this growing operation in any way.

It was at this moment that the cruel hand of fate cut the deck. Ratzlaff's Rolls Royce rolled into his spot outside the window. Seconds later, he entered the room wearing his darkest charcoal suit and reddest silk tie, along with a cloud of the lavish French cologne that he usually reserved for his meetings with women considering divorce from affluent husbands. Ratzlaff muttered something about having been stuck in a meeting and clapped Zuckerman on the shoulder as he lowered himself into the seat beside him. Zuckerman just put his glasses back on and kept his gaze fixed on his virtuous young lawyer. Freeman forged ahead after capping his pen and placing it on his notes, resolving to avoid eye contact with his employer.

"Dr. Zuckerman, our ability to pursue rescission depends on two things. First, can you assure me that you are entirely innocent of any awareness or involvement, direct or indirect, with this alleged growing operation? We're dealing with the Federal Drug Enforcement Agency here, and though the agent involved has been, um, a bit of a bungler, the feds are always eager to make a bust."

Ratzlaff put both hands on the table, and pulled his chair closer at the sound of the alarming word 'rescission.' Among the expensive notes of clove and ylang-ylang and ambergris that emanated from him, a sudden metallic prickle, the precursor to sweat, began to rise on his forehead. Based on the prospect of enhanced billings in this case due to potential wetlands complications and the slaying of Federal drug dragons, along with the inevitable construction management churning he had perfected, Ratzlaff had been pricing a bigger boat.

Of course, Zuckerman had never watered a plant, or grown a single rose or tomato, and he unburdened himself in a rush of relief as he polished his glasses again on the hem of his shirt. "I had a Venus fly trap in college, and it lasted a week before it shriveled up and turned brown. Look, I guess your secretary told you, there's been a big change for us. My mother has put on a dozen pounds, she is laughing at my jokes, and she wants to learn to cook fancy food. She's got me playing the piano every day, and we're discussing an extended trip to Vienna, where I can study with a composer named Fromokiev, famous gypsy guy, and she can intern at an old school restaurant. I'm serious. There's been a big change."

Ratzlaff sat back now, shrinking and reddening, and plotting sulfurous torments for young Dearborn and Weatherly. Here, Zuckerman put his glasses back on, and studied his hands before looking up. He knew better than to mention Radkin and his medicine.

"I'll admit it. I should have diagnosed her problem years ago, it was so obvious. She was severely depressed since my father died, and she had simply stopped eating. Parkinson's Disease got him, and it was slow and especially cruel for her. No, I am not involved in growing any marijuana on the property."

Freeman waited a few seconds before he forged ahead, ignoring Ratzlaff's laser beam stare. "The second thing that needs to happen is not in my direct control, but if the DEA finds some illegal activity on this parcel, we probably can rescind the deal and get your deposit back. Dr. Bauch will have to pay fees if he litigates and loses."

Zuckerman nodded. "She's not ready for a nursing home and I don't want to be in the middle of some investigation. Let's shut it down." Freeman wrote Zuckerman's words down, and closed his file with a snap. Their eyes met, and for the first time in months, Freeman smiled, and Zuckerman pounced. "I still see virtue when you smile!"

Freeman opened the door for the client and followed him out, leaving Ratzlaff mute in his seat, wringing his little hands and wrinkling his face. Zuckerman did not look back to witness this dissolving villain, whose imitation of the melting Wicked Witch of the West featured a sad cloud of cologne, and a red tie that resembled the silky tongue of a mutant Satan. Zuckerman thanked Weatherly on the way out, but only with a surreptitious nod. Freeman handed Weatherly the file and walked directly to his car, hoping to find Dreyfus knocking grapes off his tuna salad at the usual place. As Weatherly glanced through Freeman's notes, she avoided Ratzlaff's accusatory gaze when he emerged from the conference room and realized that Dearborn was gone.

Weatherly knew how to pay attention. Dreyfus had taught her well. She had considered the proximity of the spot where Gibson had been rooting around before his "spell," and the place that Freeman and Zuckerman had noticed a trickle of water. She had noticed that the Federal Agent was looking in the same spot, and she was aware that the animal hospital was located just over the ridge. These coincidences had all pointed to the red-haired stranger who had hypnotized her at The Molecule, who had knelt down over her comatose dog, and who had played Chinese music at The Rumble Seat. At night, walking her dog through Sparklewood Forest, she had heard the same angular banjo sounds through the treetops. Weatherly had "Walter's" phone number on the card he had given her, and she used it that evening, reaching his voicemail. She was brief, ominous, and specific. On Sunday morning, before daylight, a telltale red ribbon was flapping in the breeze behind The Molecule, and Weatherly knew her message had been received. She made another call, this time to Dreyfus, and waited for karma to run its course.

SECTION XII


FEMINA EX MACHINA


"The ghost of electricity
Howls in the bones of her face."

— Bob Dylan

## CHAPTER 58

**EVERY OTHER FRIDAY FOR OVER** a year, Radkin and the Melachrinos had hosted the open mic night at The Rumble Seat, when they weren't out working on the road for Mr. Pilferton. Radkin's ability to blend his band with each musical guest had improved over time. He studied the aura of each guest, their toe tapping and their breathing for clues, and he learned to adjust his own patterns to suit the texture and meter of their offerings. Radkin had gone so far as to study the mechanism that permitted chameleons to change colors and camouflage themselves, but he was handicapped by the fact that his skin was not layered with a lattice of nanocrystals that could be subliminally thermoregulated to shift wavelengths of light absorption. No amount of psychic projection permitted him to budge his skin color from the pale and freckled complexion with which he had been born. That is, until his final open mic session.

As he settled into his new life, Radkin gradually made certain concessions to modern consumer technology. In particular, he had discovered the usefulness of the first primitive cell phones. Once he had saved more than a few dozen coffee cans of silver and gold coins, he paid cash for a Saturn 4, a new and powerful device. During breaks on the bandstand at The Rumble Seat, Radkin would plug his phone into the house PA and stream a playlist he had compiled from his favorite childhood radio hits, the songs that had played on his mother's car radio when he and Wyatt had rattled around in the back of her Ford Fairlane station wagon, robin's egg blue with fake wooden panels. He and Dixie had both noticed how liquor sales were enhanced when the audience was bathed in the sort of nostalgic crystal blue radiophonic persuasion that comforted and emboldened barroom strangers in their ancient mating rituals.

As his station wagon radio playlist was being broadcast over the PA system on this final Friday night, Radkin was talking through the upcoming set with his next musical guests by the dumpster out back. As The Great Slam-Boni was in the process of explaining how, during his cello solo finale, he would need slight compression and reverb, along with high pass filtering at 80Hz, Radkin heard a loud series of amplified answering machine beeps. As he ran inside, he heard a woman's calm voice boom from the P.A. speakers. "Strip all but one of the plants and leave them all on the ground, leave the hose, and leave town before Sunday morning. Stake a ribbon at the edge of the river by The Molecule when you're done. No questions. Delete this message."

By the time Radkin reached the stage to mute his phone, the playlist had resumed and his blood had run cold. Like a chameleon sensing trouble, Radkin turned bright solid red. No one in The Rumble Seat showed any sign of having recognized or understood this strange interruption except Dixie, who stared out from behind the bar, fixing Radkin with a scorching glare. Radkin gave her the same shrug that Jester had taught him.

Radkin trusted certain aspects of the Universe, and he accepted the mysterious message on his phone without any second-guessing after he listened to it several times. The voice was calm, and seemed familiar. He cut the last set short and stashed his musical gear in the basement of the mill. He spent the wee hours of the night in the treetops, wearing gloves and an infrared headlight, trimming and bagging buds, and then dropping each stripped plant through the dense canopy to the forest floor. His harvest was crude but considerable, and he filled his backpack to capacity. As instructed, he dropped one intact plant, the smallest one, to the ground without trimming the buds, as much as it conflicted with his Puritan sense of thrift. He wiped off the rest of his equipment and left it concealed in place in the treetops, the Greenwells and extra rope and tools all packed in buckets inside the camo hammock, all the while reassuring himself that his anonymous guardian angel was clearly privy to some intelligence that justified this emergency retreat. Before he left, he arranged all the plants in formation a little way from the trail in the thick bushes, next to the buried water barrel and hose. Well before dawn on Sunday, he locked up the house and closed the barn. Then he returned to The Molecule, sealed the last harvest in several layers of foil coffee bean bags and concealed them in the back of Jester's deep freeze. He left Jester a note that read, "Forget me awhile. Check the freezer. Watch out." As he left, he hammered a stake topped with a bit of red ribbon into the gravel at the edge of the creek. He headed east on his motorbike, just before Jester arrived to open the kitchen.

## CHAPTER 59

**DREYFUS CHECKED HIS ANSWERING MACHINE** messages himself, early every morning like clockwork, and he took notes on a message pad booklet with carbon copies beneath each page. Here's what he wrote that Monday: "DEA proof is waiting at the hot spot. Protect my identity as discussed with your client. US v John B. Good Real Property. US v 43 Gallons of Whiskey. Erase this message. No questions. Hurry." He played the message a few times before he called Norton to his office.

Since Norton's misadventure at Taco-Rita, he had been placed on administrative leave from the DEA, pending investigation of the cause of the latest fire in his assigned vehicle. Norton had also been charged with vandalism for his destruction of Taco-Rita's surprisingly expensive fish tank full of surprisingly expensive tropical fish. The local DA was dithering about bringing charges for trafficking in illegally harvested wildlife parts, because the fire had boiled the monkey bits into a soup with questionable evidentiary value.

Norton squinted as Dreyfus explained the tip that he had received, and how this new information could possibly be used to salvage his job and avoid prosecution, if it panned out. Norton could not provide a detailed description of the informant, what with the tequila and the excitement, but he did recall that she had very clear gray eyes. Dreyfus was impassive as he took notes. After getting Norton's consent, and instructing him a dozen different ways to stay silent, utterly silent, Dreyfus placed a call to Deputy Milgram to propose a global and mutually beneficial solution to the Agency's problems with Agent Norton.

Dreyfus made his pitch forcefully, and demanded a reply within hours, giving Milgram time to consult with his staff counsel and get authority to strike the deal. He told Milgram that Norton had received a confidential tip about the growing operation. If Norton was able to assist the agency in getting a conviction in this Sparklewood investigation, Dreyfus proposed that his client would receive a *nolle prosequi* clearing him in every aspect of the Taco-Rita events, and he would be reinstated as a DEA agent in good standing, with a raise, a promotion and back pay. And another car. Dreyfus knew a senior guy at the U.S. Attorney's office, and he suggested to Milgram that they would certainly be interested in acquiring the Sparklewood Forest parcel through forfeiture, if it was determined to be the site of a criminal activity. Dreyfus cited the case law.

Milgram sounded weary when he called back to work out the details. However, he had one reservation, a condition to which Dreyfus readily agreed as Norton hung his head. The Agency would, under no circumstances, pay for the bar tab or the fish tank. Deputy Edgar Milgram added that he was scandalized to learn that his agent had consumed more than two entire pitchers of margaritas at one sitting. Dreyfus raised his fist in warning when Norton opened his mouth to correct this misunderstanding, and Norton closed his mouth again, just as the Zebra Shovelnose catfish, the Blue-Eyed Plecos and the juvenile Discus fish had gulped when Norton had wrenched their aquarium from its stand. As an afterthought, Milgram mentioned that he had received a message from Ratzlaff's associate, Dearborn, but hadn't returned the call yet. Dreyfus had no comment except to confirm that, as long as the source was going to be protected, they had a deal, and that Norton would be waiting for Milgram at the location in question at 9 a.m. sharp, the next morning.

## CHAPTER 60

**NORTON WAS JUBILANT, DESPITE THE** fact that they only found a half dozen scraggly potted plants. Dreyfus had declined to accompany Norton to Sparklewood, explaining that there was some threat of an appearance of impropriety. Milgram had brought along another agent to process the evidence, an experienced forensic chemist named Melissa Cargill. Agent Cargill was quiet and efficient, and Milgram watched with trepidation as she performed a field test on the untrimmed plant, still laden with heavy buds. After swirling some test tubes around, she nodded and quietly announced that these bushes were, in fact, illegal cannabis. Norton fixed his gaze on Milgram, who remained impassive. Cargill photographed the plants and the position of the hose and the buried drum of water. Norton insisted on helping bag and tag one of the plants, even though he needed help filling out the evidence log because his hands were still bandaged. Norton was not asked to explain how he had missed the plants before, so close to the edge of the trail.

By the time the agents had loaded their vans to leave, Radkin was in Maine, almost 200 miles away, swinging in a hammock. He had chosen a sheltered spot beside the Chimney Pond trail, beneath Mount Katahdin, near the northerly terminus of the Appalachian Trail. His small knapsack held a water filter, a Nalgene, a rain suit, a fleece, extra socks, some nuts, a few fresh pens and a fresh notebook, a small transistor radio and a roll of gold and silver coins. His deactivated phone had been mailed to L'Estacion des Tortugas, in care of Green Gene, with no return address. His motorbike had been carefully concealed, wrapped in garbage bags and covered in pine boughs in a rocky declivity between two fallen trees, with a full tank of conditioned gas, no VIN and no license plate.

Public disclosure of the bust was delayed until after Cargill traced the hose back to the Sparklewood Veterinary Hospital kennel. After the DEA issued a press release, the Daily Blast put out a gaudy cover story that could be found in every checkout aisle of every supermarket in the land. Dreyfus made sure that there was no mention of Dr. Zuckerman in the article, which featured a color picture of Dr. Bauch and his wife at some glitzy gala, raising drinks. The headline blared "Monkey Business Bust!" The story described the marijuana farm on Bauch's property, his stockpile of ivermectin and ketamine, his wife's prodigious spending, and the discovery of his supply of orangutan adrenal glands, imported from Malaysia in bags labeled 'palm nuts.' These nuggets of "Pongo Pygmaeus" were, of course, of special interest to Norton.

After the second car fire, Norton had begun (without authorization) collecting garbage from the dumpster behind the storefront gym that Blavatsky had rented, where he trained a variety of Eastern European nightclub bouncers, body-builders, hoods, boxers, and other referrals from a shiny-faced local chiropractor who worked at Lotus Therapy. After Norton found what appeared to be orangutan adrenal gland residue in discarded packaging that had been sent by

Bauch to Blavatsky, he began harvesting both Bauch and Popright's trash, too. It was a free country, he figured. His notes said the <u>Greenwood</u> case confirmed there was "no expectation of privacy" when bad guys threw out incriminating evidence. He began  bagging and tagging discarded medical grade plastic IV bags and mailers with a return address of the Sparklewood Veterinary Hospital. Norton was not surprised to learn that the mugwort had also been imported by Dr. Bauch, and resold to Popright's clinic. The residue, to Norton's utter delight and the relief of Milgram, was tested by Agent Cargill and she found it to be positive for mugwort and simian adrenal tissue. Paperwork from the trash also revealed that Bauch had tripled the price before selling mugwort to Lotus Therapy and Popright, labeled as "artemisia vulgaris." The ambitious Bauch had also sold the monkey glands to Popright, at a jacked up price, and Popright had tripled the price again before reselling it to Blavatsky. The chain of custody was secure after the same latent strain of virus, simian varicella virus, was isolated from all the monkey bits scavenged from each of their dumpsters.

Norton considered whether it was a coincidence that Chiropractor Popright had been advertising on the same benches, buses and taxis as Joe Pozzi.  Popright also advertised on billboards promising to cure erectile dysfunction with low back manipulation, in conjunction with an herbal tea infused with Malaysian mugwort. When the manipulation and tea regimen had run its course and his patients were still unable to perform, Popright would refer the most gullible and desperate patients to Blavatsky for "strong injections."

Dr. Bauch was in no position to defend himself from the DEA's prosecution, as the evidence mounted. His future ex-wife had thoroughly accessorized herself in a final binge of outings to Lord & Taylor and Saks Fifth Avenue, as accurately reported by the Daily Blast. Of course, she had hired Ratzlaff to file for divorce. Bauch's purchase-and-sale agreement with Zuckerman was rescinded after Bauch was advised by his lawyer, the estimable Joe Pozzi, that he could avoid liability for Zuckerman's attorney fees by refunding the up-front deposit to Zuckerman from the escrow account. Pozzi's advice was based on the textbook claim of fraudulent misrepresentation and unsuitability for the property's intended purpose that Freeman had alleged in a letter so long and so dense with case law citations that Pozzi could not read the whole thing in a single sitting. Freeman had signed this letter, the last bit of work he performed for the Ratzlaff firm, the same day he resigned.

Eventually, both Blavatsky and Popright pled guilty to trafficking in illegal animal parts and mislabeled herbal supplements, and the terms of their pleas required them to cooperate by testifying against Bauch. The federal prosecutor offered Bauch a deal, agreeing to recommend 4-6 months of incarceration in a clean new low-security facility. In return, Bauch would be required to consent to outright forfeiture of the Sparklewood property, due to his use of the land for the cultivation, transportation, and/or distribution of illegal narcotics. Dr. Bauch had no choice, as Pozzi saw it, despite his strenuous denials and unsupported suspicions about his phantom night watchman. Bauch had never paid the guy a penny, didn't know his real name or have any direct proof of any wrongdoing, and no fingerprints or DNA had been detected on the hospital grounds or on the buried hose and water drum that linked the hospital to the plants. Walter Fellows had left no trace, and Pozzi's team of investigators, beefy former cops in golf shirts and glasses with bright yellow tinted ballistic lenses, could not generate any leads. Bauch took the deal, and surrendered the property to the Feds.

The forfeiture of Sparklewood Forest was briefly delayed by a possible defect in the description of the southwestern corner of the property, an irregularity in what the lawyers called 'metes and bounds.' Some surveyor had specified "a large oak tree" as the marker of that spot, but one of Pozzi's Boy Scout clients told him that the tree was an ash. Joe Pozzi saw a chance to extend his lucrative representation of Dr. Bauch by threatening to contest the forfeiture due to the inadequacy of the description in the deed relative to the location of the alleged drug farm, but Bauch was flat broke by then. After the prosecutor hired an arborist who wrote up a tutorial, complete with contrasting pictures of these trees, their leaves and bark, Bauch promptly fired Pozzi. In an abundance of caution, the Federal Judge paged through the arborist's report with mild amusement, and after noting the absence of anyone contesting the forfeiture, she entered judgment transferring the Sparklewood tract to the United States, forthwith. Even though Agent Cargill had done all the key investigative testing, Dreyfus forced Milgram to give Norton credit for the bust, and per their deal, his promised reinstatement, and a promotion and raise, along with back pay and a reconditioned Ford Mustang that had been seized from a meth dealer in Providence. The thing burned oil, but it hauled ass and the exhaust had a growl that you could hear for a mile.

## CHAPTER 61

**SPARKLEWOOD NATIONAL PARK WAS SCHEDULED** to open, with some modest regional fanfare, two years after Norton's big bust. There was a poorly attended ceremony with a table of local maple syrup, IPA's and cheese, and a reggae band represented by Spanky Pilferton's agency. On the day that the deadline for submission of park ranger applications was set to expire, a spindly hiker walked into the office at the National Park Service office in Woodstock, Vermont. The newly appointed Northeastern Regional Superintendent of Park Management, Mr. Freeman Dearborn, and his administrative assistant, Ms. Grace Weatherly, watched this ruddy gentleman collect an application packet and find his way to a table by the window. He wore a pair of vintage Limmer hiking boots in the Tyrolean style, so buttery and burnished that they may as well have been passed down from Daniel Boone to John Audubon to John Muir to Walt Whitman to Edward Abbey. The applicant carried a waxed canvas rucksack and a walking stick, and he was accompanied by a dog, a mutt, that also wore a small pack. As his dog laid at his feet, he threw his hat on the table, unzipped an outside pocket on his pack and extracted a fountain pen and a small bag of dried peaches.

He looked over the paperwork, and paused at intervals to chew one peach at a time and look around the office. When he was finished filling in the forms, he delivered the packet to Ms. Weatherly at her desk. As he handed it to her, he asked if he might be able to meet the person responsible for the hiring decision. A tiny spark jumped from his hand to hers, probably static from friction between the new carpet and the thick soles of his boots. Weatherly looked at the top page and her pupils dilated. The application had been filled out with a black fountain pen, and the penmanship was unmistakable, a familiar stylized geometric architectural print. She stood and retreated to Dearborn's office. As the applicant waited he noticed a pencil sketch lying on her desk, a drawing of a tea cup, rendered with three dimensional precision. A rangy red dog was sprawled asleep, under Weatherly's desk. He could hear a baseball game on a radio in the back office, a lo-fi murmur of fans in distant bleachers. A minute later, Weatherly emerged and beckoned the man into Dearborn's office. There was a triptych on the wall, three more views of a tea cup in parallax perspective. A few fragrant logs were criss-crossed in a small brick fireplace. Behind his desk, Dearborn scribbled some notes in the margins of the application as the interview progressed. It quickly became apparent to Dearborn that this candidate was familiar with the Sparklewood tract. after the applicant asked about the plan for management of the bikers, the fate of the nursing home project, and the status of the animal hospital that once stood on the property.

The rest of the applicants had been soft and pale men with academic and bureaucratic credentials, heavy on administrative and fundraising skills and other desk-bound experience. This guy was an outdoorsman, fit and sunburned. He claimed to have a background in conservation as a volunteer for protection of endangered turtles in the Caribbean and extensive hands-on experience in forestry and agriculture. He said that he had just completed a hike from one end of the Appalachian Trail in Maine to Springer Mountain in Georgia. And back.

The candidate explained how his extended hike had been a chance to get his youthful wandering done, and finish writing his first real story. One thing led to another, and the interview stretched into something different after a while, a comfortable meeting of new friends. Radkin offered Freeman a dried peach, which was accepted. Radkin asked about the framed check on the wall, and Freeman was glad to explain his theory of pitching, based on deception. As Freeman spoke, Radkin took liberties with his radio, rolling the tuner knob back and forth a few times until the signal cleared up.

Dearborn concluded that this candidate was ready to settle down and, compared with the other applicants, his experience established his suitability by an overwhelming order of magnitude. When asked about his name, Radkin waved him off. "It's my legal name. Long story." Dearborn offered him the job, subject to some paperwork, after reciting the salary, benefits, and responsibilities. Radkin accepted, subject to nothing at all. As they shook hands and walked back to the reception area, Radkin's dog roused and padded over towards Weatherly's desk and snuffled at Gibson before lying down next to her.

"When can I start?" he asked, as he pulled a notebook from his pack. He smiled over at Weatherly, and turned back to Dearborn. "Also, do you know a patient editor?"

Thank you for reading *A Beginner's Guide to Electricity*.

billectric

P. S. Russell was published in his high school and college literary magazines, then spent 39 years practicing law. He is a musician and has reviewed music online under the name of Hambone Sparklewell. This is his first novel.

9 798218 585587